READING HER

Praise for Amanda Radley

Under Her Influence

"Light, sweet, and remarkably chaste, this sapphic love story will make as enjoyable a vacation pick as it is an armchair getaway."—*Publishers Weekly*

"My heart is just…filled with love and warmth! Finally, I have found an author who does not rely on sex to make a book interesting!! I'm probably going to go on an Amanda Radley read-a-thon."—*Periwinkle Pens*

"*Under Her Influence* by Amanda Radley is a sweet love story and leaves the reader feeling happy and contented. And that's exactly what I want from a romance these days. Ms Radley keeps angst to a minimum and lets her readers enjoy the blossoming of love between her characters."—*Kitty Kat's Book Review Blog*

Detour to Love

"If you're on the lookout for well-written sapphic romance with stellar characters, wonderful pairings, and outstanding plots, I wholeheartedly recommend any of Amanda's books!!"—*EloiseReads*

Flight SQA016

"I'm so glad I picked this book up because I think I've found my new favourite series!…The love brewing between these two is beautifully written and I was onboard from the beginning. I had some laugh out loud moments because this is British rom-com at its best. The secondary characters really added to the novel and the rollercoaster ride that is this book. The writing is tight and pace is perfect."—*Les Rêveur*

Lost at Sea

"A.E. Radley knows how to write great characters. And it's not just the main characters she puts so much effort into. I loved them, but I was astounded at how well drawn the minor characters were…The writing was beautiful—descriptive, real and very funny at times." —*Lesbian Review*

"This book was pure excitement. The character development was probably my favourite overall aspect of the book…A.E. Radley really knows how to keep her readers engaged, and she writes age-gap romance books beautifully. In fact, she probably writes some of my favourite age-gap romance tropes to date. A very intriguing book that I really enjoyed. More Captain West, please!"—*Les Rêveur*

"Absolutely amazing, easy to read, perfect romance with mystery and drama story. There were so many wonderful elements that gave twists and turns to this adventure on the sea. I absolutely loved this story and can't rave about it enough."—*LesbiReviewed*

Going Up

"I can always count on this superb author when it comes to creating unforgettable and endearing characters that I can totally relate to and fall in love with. A.E. Radley has given me beautiful descriptions of Parbrook and the quirky individuals who work at Addington's." —*Lesbian Review*

"It was an A.E. Radley story, so naturally, I loved it! Selina is A.E. Radley's iciest Ice Queen yet! She was so cold and closed off, but as the story progresses and we get a good understanding of her, you realise that just as with any other Ice Queen—she can be thawed. I loved how they interacted, with a wit and banter that only A.E. Radley can really deliver for characters like these."—*LesbiReviewed*

"This story is a refreshing light in the lesfic world. Or should I say in the romance lesfic world? Why do you ask me? Well, while there is a lot of crushy feeling between wlw characters and all, but, honestly that's the sub-plot and I've adored that fact. *Going Up* is a lesson in life."-—*Kam's Queerfic Pantry*

"The author takes an improbable twosome and writes such a splendid romance that you actually think it is possible…this is a great romance and a lovely read."—*Best Lesfic Reviews*

Mergers and Acquisitions

"This book is fun, witty, and adorable. I had no idea which way this book was going to take me, and I loved it. Each character is interesting and loveable in their own right. You don't want to miss this one—heck, if you have read any of A.E. Radley's books you know it's quality stuff."—*Romantic Reader Blog*

"Radley writes with a deceptively simple style, meaning the narrative flows naturally and quickly, yet takes readers effortlessly over rocky terrain. The pacing is unrushed and unforced, yet always leaves readers wanting to rush ahead to see what happens next."—*Lesbian Review*

The Startling Inaccuracy of the First Impression

"We absolutely loved the way the relationship between the two ladies developed. There is nothing hurried about the relationship that develops perfectly organically. This is a lovely, easy to read romance."—*Best Lesfic Reviews*

Huntress

"The writing style was fun and enjoyable. The story really gathered steam to the point of me shirking responsibilities to finish it. The humor in the story was very well done."—*Lesbian Review*

"A.E. Radley always writes fantastic books. *Huntress* is a little different than most of her books, but just as wonderful. The humor was fantastic, the story was absolutely adorable, and the writing was superb. This is truly one of those books where the characters really stick with you long after the book has ended. I wish I'd read it sooner. 5 Stars." —*Les Rêveur*

Bring Holly Home

"*Bring Holly Home* is a fantastic novel and probably one of my favourite books by A.E. Radley…Such a brilliant story and one I know I will read time and time again. This book has two ingredients that I love in novels, Ice Queens melting and age-gap romance. It's definitely a slow burn but one I'd gladly enjoy rereading again."—*Les Rêveur*

Keep Holly Close

"It was great to go back into the world of the Remember Me series. The first book in the series, *Bring Holly Home*, is one of my favourite A.E. Radley books. I love Holly and Victoria; they tick all the boxes for me when it comes to my favourite tropes. Plus, Victoria's kids are adorable, especially little Alexia. She melts my heart."—*Les Rêveur*

"So much drama…loved it!!! I already loved Holly and Victoria from the first book in the series, *Bring Holly Home*, so it was brilliant to be back with them. Victoria hasn't changed and I adore her as much as before. She was utterly brilliant at every moment of this follow-up story and she even managed to surprise me from time to time. The Remember Me series is so beautiful and one of my all time favourites. 5 of 5 stars."—*LesbiReviewed*

Climbing the Ladder

"What a great introduction to what will undoubtedly be another fantastic series from A.E. Radley. After I finished it I just kept thinking that this book is amazing and it's just the start…enough said!"—*Les Rêveur*

"Radley has a talent for giving us memorable characters to love, women you wish you knew, and locations you wish you could experience firsthand."—*Late Night Lesbian Reads*

Second Chances

"This is an absolute delight to read. Likeable characters, well-written, easy flow and sweet romance. Definitely recommended."—*Best Lesfic Reviews*

"I always know when I get a new A.E. Radley book I'm in for a treat. They make me feel so good after reading them that most of the time I'm just plain sad that they have finished…The chemistry between Alice and Hannah is lovely and sweet…All in all, *Second Chances* has landed on my favourites shelf. Honestly, this book is worth every second of your time. 5 Stars."—*Les Rêveur*

The Road Ahead

"I really enjoyed this age-gap, opposites attract road trip romance. This is a romance where the characters actually acknowledge their differences and joy of joy, listen to each other. I love it when a book makes me feel all the feels and root for both women to find their HEA. Hilarious one minute, heart-tugging the next. A pleasure to read."
—*Late Night Lesbian Reads*

Fitting In

"Writing convincing love stories with non-typical characters is tricky. Radley more than measures up to the challenge with this truly heart-warming romance."—*Best Lesfic Reviews*

By the Author

Romances

Mergers & Acquisitions

Climbing the Ladder

A Swedish Christmas Fairy Tale

Second Chances

Going Up

Lost at Sea

The Startling Inaccuracy of the First Impression

Fitting In

Detour to Love

Under Her Influence

Protecting the Lady

Humbug

Reading Her

The Flight Series

Flight SQA016

Grounded

Journey's End

The Remember Me Series

Bring Holly Home

Keep Holly Close

The Around the World Series

The Road Ahead

The Big Uneasy

Mystery Novels

Huntress

Death Before Dessert

Visit us at www.boldstrokesbooks.com

READING HER

by
Amanda Radley

2022

READING HER

ISBN 13: 978-1-63679-075-6

THIS TRADE PAPERBACK ORIGINAL IS PUBLISHED BY
BOLD STROKES BOOKS, INC.
P.O. BOX 249
VALLEY FALLS, NY 12185

FIRST EDITION: FEBRUARY 2022

CREDITS
EDITOR: RUTH STERNGLANTZ
PRODUCTION DESIGN: STACIA SEAMAN
COVER DESIGN BY TAMMY SEIDICK

For the readers.

CHAPTER ONE

L auren Evans pulled a disposable cup from the dispenser on the side of the water cooler. She filled it up and then drank the deliciously cool liquid while surveying the gym. It was good to be back. The bass-heavy music, the sound of weights machines clinking, the bright lights, and even the smell, somewhere between sweat and industrial cleaning fluids—she'd missed it all.

Most people would have enjoyed a week off work, but Lauren loved her work so much that being away from the gym for a prolonged period was like torture. It was her job and her social life.

"Early for your shift, I see."

Lauren downed the rest of her water and turned to smile at her boss. "Jim Wilkinson," she exclaimed, "it's been forever."

He shook his head at her foolishness. "You know, some people enjoy the time off work and hate coming back, not the other way around."

"I did offer to give you my week off," Lauren reminded him. "You know, as I didn't really want it."

"It doesn't work like that," Jim told her, not for the first time and probably not for the last, either. "You have days to take—you gotta take them. Paperwork."

"Paperwork," Lauren muttered.

Lauren had worked at the gym for six years and only taken a handful of days off. Jim hadn't noticed until the previous month when he told her that she'd need to take a week off immediately.

She'd dragged her feet as long as she could, but eventually he'd threatened to lock her out of the building.

"Do anything nice with your time off?" Jim asked. He folded his arms and surveyed the gym floor. The converted industrial unit was large and impressive in scale. Initially, the gym had only occupied a quarter of the building, but through hard work and local support, they had quickly taken over the entire unit.

While many gym owners enjoyed small buildings or places in the middle of town, both she and Jim knew they had struck gold, opening in an industrial building. High ceilings were perfect for large fans, lighting rigs, and the speaker system. Large windows overlooked the car park and other industrial units. They had room for the typical large range of cardio machines and weights stations as well as rooms for classes. They'd even had a new hot yoga studio built when the trend really started to take off.

It was mid-afternoon, and only a handful of members were using the facilities. It was the quiet time before the office workers signed off for the day and arrived en masse for workout sessions and classes.

"I painted the fence," Lauren said. "Fixed a door that didn't want to close properly. Re-did the sealant around the bath."

Jim slowly turned to look at her. "I said, did you do anything *nice*?"

"It's nice to have fresh sealant," Lauren pointed out.

"You were meant to take the week to relax. You remember relaxing? Watch some television or go to a bar and meet someone. That kind of thing."

"Sorry, the week off didn't come with an instruction manual," Lauren said. "Most of the time I was bored and wishing I was here. You know, because I actually enjoy my job."

"Can't work all the time," Jim said.

"I think you can if you like what you do." Lauren's life revolved around work. She knew that many people would consider that to be a bad thing, but she didn't see it that way at all. Her colleagues were her friends. She enjoyed exercise, and being in a gym all day was great.

Her clients were one of the best things about her job. While she was primarily the assistant manager and took on all kinds of managerial tasks, she was also a personal fitness trainer. There was something deeply fulfilling about taking someone on a journey of fitness and helping them to reach their goals.

"Great, then maybe you can take Sam's spin class tomorrow?" Jim asked.

Lauren laughed. "I said I enjoy *my* job, not Sam's job."

Jim looked at her for a few seconds, and Lauren sighed. "Fine. But don't put me on hot yoga again. Seriously, I think it actually melted some brain cells the last time. It's not normal."

Jim patted her shoulder. "I wouldn't do that to the members. No one needs that stink."

He hurried away, and Lauren glared after him. It was all playful banter, but she discreetly sniffed her underarm just in case. As she suspected, she was fresh as a daisy.

A guy walked away from the weights machines, throwing his bag over his shoulder and swigging from a sports bottle. Lauren headed that way and reset the machines to a more reasonable load. It was common that members—often men—would leave the machines set to such a high resistance that other users thought the machines were broken. More than once she'd had to rescue a lightweight older person from dangling after they'd made an attempt to pull a resistance weight down to ground level.

While in the weights area she did a quick clean-up and made sure everything was in order. During her check she noticed a boy struggling to make much headway with the leg curl machine.

He looked no older than fourteen, which wasn't all that unusual. Gyms were becoming popular and seen as a cool place to hang out, though Jim had recently pushed the prices a little higher to encourage the teenage rabble back to the council-run leisure centre in town. Lauren hadn't been upset to see the back of the younger members. They often liked to hang out in packs and chat while monopolising machines and leaving a mess wherever they went.

Like most gyms in the area, they had a rule that under-sixteens could join as long as they had their guardian's permission and had completed the induction. For a while there had been a lot of very bored-looking parents and guardians in the gym in order to officially say they had completed the induction and were happy to have their teenager treat the gym as a semi-formal day-care unit.

Lauren didn't recognise the boy so assumed he'd joined during her week off. She pretended to adjust a machine as she watched him struggle to even perform one rep. His clothes were top quality, new trainers completely devoid of dirt and top-of-the-line shorts and T-shirt that looked like they had barely been worn. His premium clothing didn't hide the fact that his technique was awful.

She walked over to him. "Hey, how's it going? You must be new. I'm Lauren—I'm deputy manager here, so if you need anything, just let me know."

The boy stopped his struggling and took a frustrated breath. "I'm Hugo. I joined last week."

"Ah, I was off last week. Welcome, who did your induction?"

Hugo frowned. "I don't remember his name, sorry. Actually, I was nervous, and I've forgotten most of it."

Lauren nodded. It was very common for people to forget the hour-long race around the gym to get acquainted with all the machines, staff, rooms, rules, and classes. The induction was a legal requirement, but she'd yet to meet anyone who managed to remember even half of what they were told.

"That's not a problem." She leaned against a nearby machine. "What are your fitness goals, Hugo?"

"To get buff," Hugo said with a serious expression.

Lauren smothered a smile. It was a typical teenage boy thing to say, and she was absolutely sure that he had no idea whatsoever what getting buff would entail. Lauren looked him over. He was a little chubby and had no muscle definition to speak of.

"I'll put the work in," Hugo said. "I'm here every day."

Lauren had met plenty of people who started off attending every day. Often the novelty wore off, and they fell into a pattern of every other day or even once a week. Around half of new members dropped away entirely to return in the first week of January and do the same thing all over again.

Of course, she wasn't about to burst Hugo's bubble. There was every chance that he had the determination needed to attend the gym every day. For all she knew, he'd be a future athlete.

Lauren's job was to give people the tools and the training they needed to reach their goals. It didn't matter what she thought of those goals or the likelihood of the person's ability to reach them. The motivation of an individual wasn't something that could be judged by others—she knew that only too well.

"Training every day is a great start," she said. She walked over and adjusted the weight to something more reasonable. She pointed to the label stuck to the machine. "Read the instructions on every machine. Don't worry, it's super easy. It's all pictures. Start at the lowest resistance you can. It's about how many you can do, not how much you can lift. Don't overdo it."

She took hold of his knee and locked it into position. "You want to push with these muscles." She pointed to the label and the graphic of the muscles engaged by the machine. She grabbed his hands and put them on the handlebar.

Hugo looked at the graphic with interest. He wiggled his legs a little to get them into place, tested the resistance of the machine, and then performed his first real leg curl. His face beamed with excitement.

"Cool!"

"Isn't it?" Lauren agreed. "Remember, don't overdo it. Keep the resistance or the weight low to start with. You can build up later. That's how you get buff."

"Thanks, Lauren," he said, now happily performing a series of curls.

"No problem, that's what I'm here for."

She watched him do a couple more reps to satisfy herself that he wasn't about to injure himself. The hum of conversation had started building, and she turned to see the spin class was starting to arrive.

"Gotta go and cycle for my life," Lauren said. "Catch you later."

Hugo nodded a goodbye. He was too out of breath to attempt actual words. Lauren suspected that he would do too much no matter what she advised him. Nearly everyone did.

She wondered who had inducted the boy. Inductions often led to personal training, which was the bread and butter of most of their trainers' salaries. Members often joined and attended an induction and did their own thing for a couple of weeks before realising they needed a proper plan and someone to crack the whip. Most times they signed with the person who had introduced them to the gym, which was why the inductions were fairly distributed among the team. Hugo might be the kind of kid who needed a little more assistance to reach his fitness dream of getting buff, but Lauren didn't want to tread on any toes. The opportunity should first go to the person who did the induction.

She crossed the gym floor and entered the office. Jim sat at his desk with piles of paperwork and member folders strewn across his desk.

"Two new people want to join the spin class, and I have someone who wants fitness training. They asked for you personally," Jim said.

"Who?" Lauren asked.

"Mike Henshall. The guy who wants to do the multiple marathons for charity."

Lauren nodded. Mike was fit and could run, but he needed the full package of dietary and technique advice. He'd almost hospitalised himself the previous year by attempting two marathons in three days.

"Oh yeah, Mike's going to need some intensive help if he wants to reach that goal," Lauren said.

"He told me. Thirty marathons in sixty days, was it?"

Lauren nodded. "Can be done."

"Yeah, but can Mike Henshall do it?" Jim asked.

"Never underestimate someone," Lauren reminded her cynical boss.

"Yeah, yeah." Jim opened up the schedule book and pulled out a few forms. He looked at her apologetically.

Lauren sucked in a deep breath. "Jim, I don't have time for paperwork now. I have this class to do."

"We'll catch up after," Jim said. "We'll do it together. No fuss." Lauren appreciated Jim's understanding when it came to her issues with paperwork and the amount of time it took her to psyche herself up to try to complete any.

"Put it in my schedule," Lauren said. She grabbed a sports bottle from the rack and headed out of the office. She didn't know why a gym needed so much paperwork anyway. Everything seemed to be forms, folders, accounts, and logs. All she wanted to do was train others. It surely didn't need to be that hard.

Jim was constantly surrounded by paperwork, like a child in a ball pit. He seemed to always be able to put his hand to whatever he needed, but just the sight of it all gave Lauren palpitations.

Thankfully, she'd be able to sweat out her anxiety in the spin room.

CHAPTER TWO

"Thirty seconds," Lauren said. "Come on! You can do it."

"Dying…" Hugo panted.

"Die in twenty-five seconds and you'll have hit a personal best, come on. Dig deep."

Hugo grunted but maintained his pace on the rowing machine. Lauren stood next to him with her stopwatch in hand and an eye on the readout from the machine.

Hugo had been coming into the gym every weekday for the past two weeks, and Lauren was impressed with his perseverance. He worked hard, struggled greatly, but returned every day at the same time and put more effort in.

At first, she gave him only a little guidance, simple things, like advising him to split his time between cardio and weight training. Like most teenage boys, he favoured the weights areas as a way to suddenly become a muscled Adonis. She'd explained that he'd need to work on cardio machines like the cross trainer, treadmill, and rowing machine to reach his goals.

After a little while, Lauren had come up with a loose training plan for him. While he wasn't one of her personal fitness clients, she had taken a shine to him and respected his work ethic. He also came in at a time of day when the gym was fairly quiet, and so it was easy to hang out with Hugo.

He'd confessed fairly early on that he was bullied at school, and Lauren could see why. He was well-spoken, a little overweight, wore glasses, and had slightly ginger hair. If someone asked an artist to draw a picture of a kid most likely to be bullied, it would look like Hugo.

She wished she could give him useful advice on the bullying front, but she'd never managed to conquer the problem while she was in school, so she didn't know what the answer was. Her solution had been to stop attending classes altogether, something which had caused her a lot of trouble and was still having an effect on her life today.

"Time," she called.

Hugo hooked the handles back onto the machine and collapsed in a heap on the floor.

"Good job," Lauren said. "That's so much better than last week. Your fitness is improving fast—you should be proud."

"I'm still fat," Hugo muttered.

"You're insulated," Lauren admitted. "But losing weight takes time. Getting your stamina up will help with that." She picked up his sports bottle and handed it to him. He took it and took a long swig of water. "How's things at school?"

He shrugged.

"That bad?"

He nodded.

Lauren didn't know what to say to that. He hadn't given her any details, and so she didn't feel she knew what advice to give him. Not that much advice was useful when it came to the matter of bullying. Speaking to teachers was rarely the right thing to do. Teenagers couldn't be reasoned with, and fighting was never the answer. Especially when you were as uncoordinated as Hugo.

"When I'm buff, I'll show them," Hugo said.

"No, you won't," Lauren told him firmly. "If you're planning to fight someone, then I'm going to have to ask you to leave my gym. I'm not helping you so you can go and beat up some kid."

Hugo paled at that. "Why are you helping me?"

"Because you're dedicated. You want to train hard, and you put a lot of effort in. I want you to reach those goals we talked about last week. To lose weight, to build stamina, to change your lifestyle.

I want you to be fit and healthy." Lauren pushed away from the machine and started to walk away. "But if you're doing all this to take a swing at some kid, then you're on your own."

"I'm not!" Hugo called after her.

Lauren stopped and turned to face him. "Really?"

"I mean…I want to be able to defend myself," Hugo confessed, "or be able to run away further than ten metres without feeling like my lungs might explode. It's not my fault they pick on me. I should be able to defend myself. I can't right now."

Lauren looked him up and down and debated what the truth was. Hugo had more than once commented that when he was fit, he would enact some kind of revenge. But then he'd also said that he just wanted to look less bullyable. It was impossible to know the truth.

What she did know was that Hugo seemed to be a sweet boy who was scared of his schoolmates. That knowledge took Lauren right back to her own time at school, and it was enough for her to nod her head.

"Okay. Go and cool down in the weights area. You've done really well today—you should be proud."

Hugo beamed. "You'll help me with the pull-up bar tomorrow?"

Lauren chuckled. "I'll try, but I'm telling you—the pull-up bar makes mincemeat of people. I've seen grown men cry because they can't lift themselves no matter how hard they try."

"Can you use it?"

Lauren rolled up her short sleeve to the top of her shoulder and flexed her arm. "What do you think?"

Hugo looked at her muscle and grinned. "I wanna look like you. But like a boy."

Lauren rolled her sleeve back down. "Then you have to work hard every day. Like I keep telling you. Honestly, there's no magic to it. Just hard work. Lots of it. Gotta go—same time tomorrow?"

Hugo nodded. "Thanks, Lauren."

She ruffled his hair as she passed him. She picked up a few empty disposable cups from around the water cooler and threw them into the recycle bin. She took a look at the bottle and realised it was nearly out.

"Hey, Lauren, are you going to be running HIIT again soon?"

Lauren turned to see Kim looking at her reflection in one of the large mirrors. Kim was the epitome of vain. She ran her own business and had time to be in the gym multiple hours a day. In fact, she often conducted her business in the gym via loud telephone calls. She worked out solely to look good, often ignoring all advice about diet and safety. Energy drinks and protein bars kept her going for days on end when she wanted to lose a pound or two. Lauren had tried to gently explain how potentially dangerous that was, but Kim was also a know-all and refused to listen to common sense. She was happier to be distributing advice rather than listening to any.

Kim had been a member for years. Jim often joked that the woman had one day stood still long enough for him to build a gym around her. She was an outspoken advocate of the gym and brought many friends and work colleagues to classes and sessions.

"I think it will be in a couple of weeks," Lauren said, removing the old water bottle. "The schedule will be online, I think."

Kim turned to the side and eyed her reflection critically, squinting at her reflection and moving individual strands of hair. "It wasn't this morning." She moved another strand of hair and smiled at the result.

"I'll nudge Jim. He does the computer stuff, you know me."

Kim chuckled. "Yep. I honestly don't know how someone your age can be so anti-technology. Honestly, you need a smartwatch. You'd love it. I need to show you my new one soon. Technology is getting better and better, and now I'm able to track so much more."

Lauren had zero interest in fitness trackers but knew that Kim was obsessed with them. She had the designer clothes, the latest trackers, drank the gimmick shakes. Not that there was anything wrong with all that. It was just that Kim was more than a little showy. More style than substance, Lauren thought.

"Sounds great." Lauren put the empty bottle in the recycling rack, picked up a new one, and swiftly positioned it on top of the cooler.

"Have you seen the new Sweaty Betty gym vest made from recycled plastic?" Kim asked.

"Nope." Lauren bought her workout clothes from the supermarket or the large sporting goods chain that the gym shared a retail park with. She didn't need to spend fifty pounds on some leggings when she could spend fifteen pounds on something that did the same job.

"They are to die for," Kim said.

"I'll check them out," Lauren said politely. "Nice top, by the way."

"Thanks, I got it yesterday. Already trashed it with a heavy workout session, but you have to, don't you?" Kim laughed.

Lauren was about to reply when something caught her eye. Her heart rate spiked.

"Excuse me a minute," she said, jogging towards the exit.

Through the windows she could see that Hugo had been stopped by a woman in the car park, and he didn't look too happy about it. When he'd turned to leave, she'd reached out and grabbed his rucksack to hold him in place.

Lauren burst through the fire escape and sprinted across the car park. A Mercedes was parked up haphazardly with the engine on and the driver's door open.

"I don't want to go with you," Hugo shouted.

"Get in the car," the woman demanded. She started to drag Hugo backwards by his backpack.

Lauren approached the woman from behind and secured her in a loose back chokehold. She wanted to hold the woman immobile but not hurt her. "Get inside the gym, Hugo."

"Get off me at once!" the woman cried out. She let go of Hugo's bag and gripped ineffectively at Lauren's arms.

Lauren had heard about kids being abducted in broad daylight but never thought she'd see such a thing in her little part of England. She was relieved she happened to be in the right place at the right time.

"You're coming with me," Lauren declared. "I'm going to call the police."

"Please do," the woman replied angrily, "and you can explain to me why my son has been attending your establishment without my knowledge under a stolen credit card."

CHAPTER THREE

Allegra felt the strong arms release her. She took a step forward and spun around to look at the woman who had attempted to incapacitate her in the middle of a public car park. She was young, incredibly fit, and looked extremely confused.

"I'd like to know why you have allowed a minor to join your gym," Allegra asked, using the confusion to her full advantage.

The woman blinked and looked at Hugo. "She's not kidnapping you?"

Hugo shook his head, looking rightfully ashamed. "This is my mum. Mum, this is Lauren."

Allegra raised her eyebrow. Clearly Hugo had been attending the establishment for longer than she'd suspected if he knew the staff by name.

She'd only caught the extra line on her credit card the previous evening. A quick look online and she'd found out that the reference number was for a local gym. She reasoned that the only possible time Hugo would have to attend a gym without her knowledge was after school. When he was supposed to be in after-school clubs. Allegra knew he sometimes blew them off to hang out with friends but was now discovering that she had very little idea what her son got up to between the end of school and when she got home for dinner.

"He's a member..." Lauren said, still deeply puzzled if her creased forehead was anything to go by. "He has a PIN."

"A PIN?"

Lauren pointed to the building. "To get in the door. All members have a PIN. It's the only way you can get in. If he is inside, he's a member."

Allegra sighed. "Then you must investigate making your systems more robust. He stole my credit card. Do you let just any child in to…to…lift weights and what have you?"

"No, of course not. He had to have an induction." Lauren looked at Allegra. "He had to have an induction with *you* present."

Allegra laughed. She looked at the building and sighed. The large sign proudly proclaimed the company name to be *Jims Gym*.

"Do you really think I'd be seen dead in a place like that? You're missing an apostrophe." Allegra looked at Hugo. "Do you want to explain yourself?"

Hugo ducked his head. "I wanted to join a gym, but I knew you wouldn't let me. I signed up online, and they sent me the PIN to get in. When someone asked me if I'd had the induction, I just said I had, and they left me alone."

Allegra folded her arms and looked smugly at Lauren. "Seems to me that your induction process leaves a lot to be desired."

Lauren folded her arms in response. "Seems to me that your credit card security leaves a lot to be desired." She looked to Hugo. "Sorry, I'm going to have to ban you."

"What?" Hugo cried.

"You need your mum's permission to join, and you joined on a credit card that you didn't own. I can't allow you to stay a member—sorry, buddy. I'll refund your membership, and we'll say nothing more about it. Everything else is for you two to discuss." Lauren unfolded her arms and looked at Allegra. "I'm sorry for the confusion and for the, um, grabbing. I thought you were snatching him."

"I appreciate you looking out for him," Allegra admitted. While she'd not enjoyed the sensation of someone holding her against her will, it was nice to know that Hugo was safe and protected even when Allegra had no earthly idea of where he was or what he was doing.

Lauren nodded and made her way back towards the gym building.

"Right, let's go home," Allegra said.

Hugo's cheeks were bright red and his eyes blazed with fury. "I can't believe you," he shouted. "You ruin everything."

"Get in the car. We're going home," Allegra instructed.

"No. I'm walking. I don't want to be in a car with you." Hugo spun around and stalked away from her.

Allegra watched him go. She knew she couldn't very well wrestle him into the car against his will. He was fourteen, and his growth spurt had been as much outward as it had upward. Gone were the days when she could just scoop him up mid-tantrum and toss him into his car seat.

She got into the car and closed the door, watching her son stomp his way across the car park. They didn't argue often. On the whole Hugo was a very well-behaved child. Allegra had heard horror stories about teenage boys, but Hugo had thankfully not careered off the tracks like so many did.

She looked at the gym and tried to fathom why on earth he had felt compelled to join. He'd never been interested in exercise in his life. The few times she'd asked him if he'd like to join her for a walk, he had laughed heartily and returned to his games console.

Sighing, she clicked her seat belt into place. It seemed they'd be having a conversation about it that evening when Hugo had cooled down.

She slipped the car into gear and took one last look at the building.

"Jims Gym," she muttered under her breath. "What a name."

CHAPTER FOUR

Lauren marched into Jim's office. She was angry at having been embarrassed and told off by a complete stranger. Worse, she deserved it. Someone had let Hugo in without an induction. Somehow she'd been personal-training a credit card thief for the last two weeks.

"Who gave the kid his induction?" Lauren asked.

"Which kid?" Jim didn't look up from his paperwork.

"Hugo—ginger kid, comes in every afternoon."

Jim looked up and shrugged. "It wasn't me. I think it might have been Rose? Not sure."

"No one did," Lauren explained. "He's been here two weeks without having the induction. He stole his mum's credit card, signed up, and just waltzed in. His snotty mum just gave me a verbal spanking about it."

Jim grimaced. "Christ. Is she going to make a complaint?"

Lauren picked up the stress ball from the desk and gave it a squeeze. "No idea. She's pretty upset. She's just found out her kid has been spending his afternoons here rather than, I dunno, Latin class or wherever she expected him to be."

Jim leaned back in his chair and laced his fingers behind his neck. "I suppose we're going to have to do some spot checks on younger members. We can't have a load of kids skipping the induction or being here when no one knows they're here."

Lauren flopped into the guest chair, tossed the stress ball in the air, and caught it again. "Yep. We probably need to tighten up the sign-up process, too."

"But without making it too difficult for new members to join," Jim added. "This is going to be a headache. One of the reasons we have the system we have now is because it's nice and easy to sign up and get your PIN. Easy to be a member. Immediate access, nice and easy. It's what people want."

"True," Lauren agreed. "But it's being misused."

"Was the mum angry?"

"She wasn't doing cartwheels," Lauren said.

She tossed the stress ball up in the air again. She felt annoyed at herself that she'd gone out and restrained the woman. It had no doubt added to the anger Hugo's mum was feeling. If she'd just kept her cool for a couple more minutes, then she would have seen that it wasn't the most brazen attempt at a child abduction in history but just a normal parent having it out with a teenager.

She felt bad for Hugo. The kid was in big trouble, that much was clear. And now he was banned from the gym, too. He'd shown such promise and determination.

The phone on the desk rang and Jim answered it. "Jim speaking." His face immediately softened. "Hey, love. How are you? How is Bea?"

Lauren put the stress ball back on the desk and indicated that she'd be outside in the main part of the gym. Jim's daughter, Shelly, rang frequently with updates on Jim's granddaughter, who had been born with a heart condition and was now one very sick five-year-old.

Jim had a heart of gold and helped everyone he encountered. Without him, Lauren didn't know where she'd be. Nowhere good, that was for sure. Lauren didn't know how he managed to stay so chipper and upbeat considering how ill little Bea was. She was sure she wouldn't be able to find that kind of strength. He'd once told her that the Lord only gave what a person was able to handle, which only made Lauren all the more impressed by Jim's ability to cope with difficulty.

Lauren returned to work, knowing that they'd need to have

another conversation about inductions at a later time. The moment she left the office, Kim approached her.

"What was that all about in the car park? Who was that hot piece of ass you had your arms around?"

Lauren ground her teeth at the disrespectful language. There was a time she might have said such a thing herself, but she'd matured and was constantly surprised to find other people hadn't. Yes, Hugo's mother was undeniably attractive, but that wasn't the point. That didn't define her. But people like Kim didn't seem to think like that. So many of the members of the gym were obsessed with looks and more interested in rating people's looks out of ten rather than getting to know anyone.

"Nothing much, just a case of someone coming to the gym without their mother's permission," Lauren said, trying to make it sound like less of a big deal than it was. The last thing she wanted was gossiping Kim to spread the news. Hopefully, downplaying the whole incident would make it boring enough so Kim would move on.

"Never have kids," Kim advised.

"Getting a girlfriend would be a start," Lauren said. She picked up the cleaning wipes and headed over to the treadmills to start giving them a quick clean.

Unfortunately, Kim followed her. "Do you want some dating advice?"

Kim excelled at handing out advice. To Kim, there was nothing she didn't know about. Supposedly a consultant by trade, it was literally her job to dish out her knowledge. Lauren had yet to hear Kim give her any good advice, though, so she wondered how Kim managed to stay in business.

"I do okay," Lauren said. "Besides, it's not like I want anything serious. Don't want to get tied down."

Lauren wiped down the first machine and hoped that Kim would catch on that she was busy and didn't want her dating advice. With luck, she would quickly return to her preening in front of one of the many mirrors.

Kim laughed. "Babe, you're over thirty. Perhaps you should think about settling down before the looks go."

Lauren did her best not to react. Kim was over forty and did everything she could to dress and act like she was in her twenties. Lauren reminded herself that Kim wasn't being rude because she honestly thought she was being helpful. As hard as it was to believe sometimes, Kim's heart was in the right place, even if her mouth wasn't.

"I think I have a couple of years left in me yet," Lauren said.

Thankfully, Kim's phone rang. She looked at the screen and rolled her eyes.

"Sorry, it's a client. I have to take this."

"Sure, no problem," Lauren said, grateful for the reprieve.

Kim answered the call and walked away. After a few moments Lauren realised she was still cleaning the first machine in the row, which was now almost slippery with cleaning fluid. She'd become distracted by thoughts she tried to keep at bay. The truth was that she knew she would never settle down. As much as the thought used to hurt her, she'd finally started to grow comfortable with the fact. Settling down would mean telling someone else everything about her, even her deepest, darkest secrets, and that was something she just couldn't do.

Lauren had known for years now that finding The One would be impossible. She'd long ago accepted that she would grow old alone.

CHAPTER FIVE

Allegra sat on the floor of Hugo's bedroom with her back to the closed en suite bathroom door. As she'd driven and he had been on foot, she ended up arriving home thirty minutes before Hugo and had expected to have a conversation with him when he got in. Instead, he'd gone to his bedroom and then locked himself in his bathroom.

An hour had passed, and Allegra had asked, threatened, and then pleaded for him to come out. Stubbornness ran in the family even if they weren't blood relations. She supposed she'd made him as wilful as he was, which maybe said a lot about her.

Eventually, she decided to sit outside and wait for him to be ready to talk. She looked around his bedroom as she waited. It was an odd blend between the childhood room she knew so well and somewhere she didn't particularly recognise.

Hugo was growing up. At fourteen, he was acting more and more like an adult every day. The problem was that Allegra struggled to know when to treat him like an adult and when to treat him like the adolescent he was. On the occasions where she did decide that she knew what was best for him, it didn't endear her to her son one bit. The silent treatment was something she was becoming sadly familiar with.

Not for the first time, she cursed that the adoption papers hadn't come with a manual. She wasn't at all prepared for the fact that her little boy was walking to and from school by himself and had done for some time. He never needed her support with his homework, and he knew far more than she did about technology and the internet.

Yet he was still a child, and she was still his mother.

"Hugo?" She tried again.

It was only the occasional sound that told her that he was in there.

No reply was forthcoming, and she let out a sigh and rested the back of her head on the door. If her colleagues could see her now, they would be shocked. Allegra Whittaker, highly sought-after barrister who was paid to speak for a living, was easily being bested by a child. And it wasn't as if today was the first time.

While Allegra frequently stood up in court and presented her case with no issues whatsoever, speaking with her son was becoming increasingly difficult. As time went on, it seemed to get worse. She wondered if that was simply the mother and son relationship when living with a teenage boy, or if she was simply too old to connect with him nowadays. Fifty-three wasn't ancient to her eyes, but she imagined it was to Hugo. Not that he'd ever been cheeky enough to say such a thing.

"I'm weak," Hugo whispered.

Allegra's heart soared at hearing him speak. She frowned. "What do you mean, darling?"

"I'm fat, but I'm weak," Hugo said.

"Darling, you're not fat. It's puppy fat—all teenagers get it. You'll grow out of it."

She heard the door unlock and got to her feet. The door opened, and Hugo stood in the doorway with tears in his eyes.

"The other boys aren't fat. Just me. They are bullying me. I wanted to go to the gym to lose weight and to know I could defend myself if I had to."

Allegra reeled from that information and pulled him into a hug. "Darling, I had no idea. Why didn't you tell me?"

She felt him shrug. Deep down she knew exactly why he hadn't said anything. She worked long hours, and when they did see each other these days, they didn't get much time to really talk.

Being bullied was not a five-minute by the way that came up

before leaving for school in the morning. It was a conversation that took time and trust to get into the meat of was happening, time they rarely had together, and trust that she wondered if she was losing.

"I liked the gym," he whispered through sniffles. "I was getting good at it. I lost some weight."

"You're perfect the way you are," she whispered into his hair.

"No, I'm not," he muttered. "I'm not happy the way I am. I can't be perfect if I'm sad."

Allegra felt her heart break at that statement. She held him tighter and promised herself that she would try to turn the tide on the distance that was growing between them. She needed to get home at a reasonable time and make more quality time available for them.

Most of all, she needed to fix what she had most recently broken.

CHAPTER SIX

Allegra drummed her fingers on the top of the steering wheel and watched Hugo walking through the school gates. It had been weeks—maybe months—since she'd last dropped him off at school. He'd been happy to walk, and she'd been happy for the extra time in the office.

Now she was wondering if that had been a mistake. They'd somehow drifted apart, and the ten-minute drive to school wasn't much, but it was quiet time where they could talk without distraction.

She looked at the other children, some of whom she knew and some she didn't. That didn't stop her from judging the ones most likely to be bullies. Anyone with an untidy school uniform, unbrushed hair, and dragging their feet immediately went on her list of suspects.

Hugo wouldn't tell her a thing. The previous evening she'd showered him with attention, ice cream, and the opportunity to watch any movies he wished. She knew the ice cream wouldn't help with his perceived weight issue, but at that time her only goal had been to cheer him up.

She'd tried a couple of times to get some information on who the bully was, but Hugo shut her down very quickly. In the end, he made it clear that if she got involved in any way whatsoever, he would never, ever talk to her again. She was used to hyperbole from her son, but his stern expression had told her that he was deadly serious.

Allegra wanted to remind him that she dealt with bullies of the criminal variety as well as justice every single day. She liked to think that she was somewhat of an expert in the matter. But it was clear that her assistance was not welcome, and she had to respect that.

Dropping him off at school was her way of reassuring herself that he was okay. It was the only way she could keep a watchful eye over him as long as possible until he disappeared through the gates and into the building.

She pulled away and carefully drove down the narrow street packed on either side with children on their way to school. She had another important errand to run before she attended court that morning. A potentially embarrassing one.

Hugo had made it very clear that he enjoyed going to the gym, that it had made him feel better—physically, emotionally, and mentally. As upset as she was by his deceit and theft, she knew he'd only taken such drastic action because he felt there was no other choice.

A few minutes later she drove into the car park of Jims Gym and wished that Hugo had chosen somewhere with acceptable grammar. She got out of the car and approached the entrance and frowned. There were four curved glass entrances, which all appeared to only be accessible via a keypad. She looked around, but there was no normal door nor a way to contact those inside.

"This is ridiculous," she mumbled.

She took a step back. The gym was open, and through the large windows she could see a number of people exercising but had no idea how she could get inside. She wasn't about to tap on the window. The glass entrances seemed to be small pods that would allow access following the correct code being entered. Without a code she appeared to be stuck.

"Morning!"

Allegra turned to see a Lycra-clad woman in her forties approaching. She had a cocky grin that put Allegra on alert.

"You look lost. Didn't I see you here yesterday afternoon?"

"Quite possibly," Allegra agreed. "I'd like to speak to the manager, but I have no idea how to get in."

The woman took a sip from her sports bottle and allowed her eyes to slowly drag themselves up and down Allegra's body. Allegra didn't react. She'd worked in law long enough to know that the best way to defuse a situation was to remain calm and quiet.

"You need a code," she said when she had finished both drinking and staring. "Allow me."

She gestured to one of the doorways and tapped a code onto the keypad. She gestured for Allegra to step inside as the door opened.

"Thank you," Allegra said. The woman was obviously a player, but she was also being helpful. They waited in the tiny glass tube as one door closed and another opened. She stepped into the entrance foyer and found herself blinking at the interesting smell of sweat and cleaning chemicals.

Allegra had never been in a gym. The last time she'd gotten close was as a schoolgirl, completing the legally required minimum in her local high school gymnasium once a week where she did all she could to avoid actually doing anything taxing. It was a far cry from the loud, bustling place she was in now.

The woman entered through another door. "There we go, nice and easy. The office is just over there. Lauren's probably in by now."

The name rang a bell, and Allegra recalled the young woman from the day before. She'd been hoping to avoid her, but that seemed unlikely now. She thanked the woman again and marched towards the office as she was keen to get away from the prying eyes that she knew still lingered. Why some people felt it was permissible to stare at someone's body in such an obvious manner baffled her.

The office door was open, and she stepped straight in. She stopped dead at the sight of someone dangling from the ceiling. Some kind of bar hung from a couple of metal brackets, and Lauren was easily performing what Allegra assumed were called pull-ups on the bar. She knew she should make her presence known, but for some reason she stood there in stunned silence, watching.

Lauren had her back to the door. She wore tiny shorts and a crop top that left little to the imagination and displayed Lauren's extremely impressive physique. Every time Lauren pulled herself up, Allegra found herself in the front row for an impressive show, courtesy of the back muscles that glistened underneath a small film of sweat.

Allegra had never been impressed by bulging muscles and the ability to lift heavy objects, but for some reason she was struck into silence as she watched Lauren easily lift her entire body up and down. She knew Lauren must have weighed a reasonable amount because she was tall and well-built. But the way Lauren lifted herself suggested an ease that implied she weighed no more than a feather. It was hard not to be impressed.

Lauren dropped herself to the floor and picked up a towel from a nearby table. She wiped at her forehead. She wrapped it around the back of her neck and turned around.

Allegra tried to look as though she had just arrived and hadn't been watching the workout. She was quite sure she failed miserably.

"Oh, hi," Lauren said. "Look, I'm really sorry about Hugo coming here. I really had no idea that he didn't have your permission. Obviously, if I'd known, then I never would have let him in here. I cancelled his membership like I said I would."

"Can it be reinstated?" Allegra asked.

Lauren frowned. "Um, sure?"

"I may have been a little hasty," Allegra admitted. "Obviously I'm not ecstatic about the lying—or the theft of my credit card—but his goals were good even if his actions were not."

Allegra averted her eyes as a trickle of sweat ran down Lauren's neck and made its way down her chest. For a tiny drop of liquid, it was incredibly distracting.

"I can reactivate him," Lauren said. "What made you change your mind? We haven't invested in that apostrophe yet."

Allegra swallowed nervously at the memory of the judgement she'd hurled at Lauren and the business less than a day ago. She forced herself to meet Lauren's gaze.

"He explained to me how much he enjoys coming here, and it surely wouldn't do him any harm to get fit," Allegra said. "He also mentioned that he was having trouble at school."

"With the bullies," Lauren added with a nod. "He mentioned."

Allegra felt a flare of jealousy bubble up inside her that Hugo had confided in a complete stranger but not his own mother. She reasoned that was probably because the stranger had been there for him while she was busy working.

"Well, we can definitely get him set up again. But we'll have to do this right this time." Lauren wiped her face with the end of the towel that hung around her neck. "Or people's mothers get upset in our car park."

Allegra rolled her eyes.

"I'll need to get him booked in for the induction. And you'll need to attend as well," Lauren continued.

Allegra bristled at the idea of having to come back and waste even more time in a place she had no interest in being. "Is that really necessary? Surely there's something I can sign now as a waiver?"

Lauren shook her head. "Nope. We were once told that our induction process leaves a lot to be desired, so we're very strict these days. You'll need to be there for it and watch the whole induction process. Then you'll need to sign a form to say that you were happy with what we told Hugo and that you also understand it."

Allegra sighed. She guessed she deserved that one. "Fine."

"Great. When should I book you both in?"

Allegra didn't know. She'd not told Hugo of her plan to get him back to the gym simply because she didn't know if she'd burned her bridges the day before. The only thing that would make her more unpopular than she already was would be to promise his return to the gym just to find that the gym refused because of her own behaviour.

"I can do this afternoon," Lauren offered. "Hugo usually turns up around three thirty. Obviously, we can do later if you're working."

Allegra wasn't due in court that day, so she could be flexible with her schedule.

"Three thirty is fine," she said. She'd text Hugo later and let him know her decision and the good news. She only hoped that would go some way towards mending fences. It was already clear to her that she had a way further to go.

"Great, I'll see you both then." Lauren smiled. "If you'll excuse me, I need to shower before I start work."

"Oh, I'm sorry. I didn't realise you hadn't started your shift," Allegra said.

"Not officially, but I'm always here. I work out before and after my shift."

"That's very dedicated of you."

"Not really. I just enjoy my job. I'm Lauren, by the way."

"I remember. Allegra." She held out her hand.

Lauren looked at the outstretched hand and smirked a little before shaking it. "Allegra and Hugo, should have guessed."

"What's that supposed to mean?" Allegra asked.

"I look forward to that induction this afternoon." Lauren changed the subject and walked out of the office. Allegra stumbled a little to catch up with her quick strides.

"Do I need to bring anything?" Allegra asked.

"Just Hugo," Lauren said. "Unless you're signing up, too?"

Allegra shook her head. "No, thank you. I'm fine."

Lauren stopped by the door to the ladies' changing rooms. "It's because we don't have an apostrophe, isn't it?"

"Yes, that's it." Allegra couldn't help but smile.

"Damn. I'll tell my boss we need to get one. I'll find a grammar store online." Lauren opened the door and entered the changing rooms. "See you later."

Allegra watched the door close and let out a small sigh. It had gone better than she expected. Lauren appeared to have a smart mouth and attitude, so Allegra imagined that she wasn't quite finished with teasing Allegra for her behaviour just yet. She had a feeling that there would be more jokes levelled at her throughout the induction process. While that ordinarily would have irked her, there was something about Lauren's manner that soothed the words. The twinkle in her eye and the lopsided grin were the things that first sprang to Allegra's mind.

She shook the thought from her mind and took her phone out of her bag to text Hugo the good news.

CHAPTER SEVEN

L auren checked her watch and looked out into the car park again. She tried to tell herself that she wasn't eagerly awaiting Hugo and Allegra's arrival but knew it was pointless trying to fool herself.

Of course she did have an appointment for an induction, and so it was natural to want to be prepared. But this was more than that. The memory of Allegra's eyes on her body that morning had stayed with Lauren throughout the day. It had been obvious that Allegra didn't want to look but had found it hard not to, and that made Lauren feel very pleased with herself.

Lauren knew she was in good shape, and she worked very hard to have a body that she was proud of. When someone complimented her, or their eyes spent a little too long looking over her physique, she appreciated the attention. When it was someone sophisticated like Allegra, she appreciated it all the more.

She imagined that Allegra wasn't ordinarily the kind of person to stare at a stranger's body in that way. The fact that she hadn't been able to tear her eyes away meant there was a chance that she might be interested in Lauren. Which was good news because Lauren was certainly interested in Allegra. There was something about an attractive older woman that Lauren appreciated. And when said woman was condescending and needed bringing down to earth with a bump, Lauren enjoyed that, too.

Lauren was looking forward to Hugo's induction because

it would give her the chance to test her theory that Allegra was interested. She intended to show off a little and see what reaction she received in return.

But now they were running late, and Lauren was clock-watching. She hated the thought that the tables had turned already. She needed to be cool and in control, not eager. She was always in the driver's seat in relationships. She usually initiated them, often intensified them, and always ended them. She had no interest in anything serious, but Lauren's kind of woman wasn't the sort that would make the first move or engage in one-night stands.

The power dynamic was part of what attracted her to older women. Someone like Allegra was used to being in charge, and so to be wrapped around the finger of someone like Lauren was often a surprise to them. It meant that Lauren was in control, and she enjoyed the feeling. Often her partners enjoyed relinquishing control for a while, too, once they got used to the idea. Both Lauren and whichever woman she was dating were happy until the whole thing ran its course.

A familiar Mercedes pulled up in the parking lot, and Lauren took the opportunity to pretend she was adjusting the weights at one of the weights stations, rather than eagerly waiting.

Unfortunately, that took her nearer to Kim.

Lately Kim was spending more time than ever at the gym. Something to do with having gained a couple of pounds recently and wanting to get her arms back into shape. Lauren suspected it was more to do with something that had happened at work, judging by the number of calls Kim was taking.

She reminded herself that a busy gym was a great advertisement, and she wasn't going to complain about the company. She just wished that Kim would get the hint that she had no desire for Kim to be her life coach.

"Ah, she's back," Kim said.

Lauren looked up casually and watched the mother and son leaving the car. "Oh yeah, Hugo's having an induction."

"Well, that answers what she does for a living," Kim commented.

Lauren looked at Allegra and frowned. She couldn't understand what Kim had seen that she was missing. "What do you mean?"

"She's a barrister," Kim said.

Lauren looked from Kim to Allegra. "How do you know?"

"The shirt. She's missing the wig and the swoopy black gown, but the shirt's a giveaway. You see them on television all the time, mincing around a courtroom talking about the Right Honourable gentleman this and My Lord that."

Lauren hadn't noticed the shirt. Her eyes were too focused on the knee-length skirt, tights, and high heels. When she managed to drag her gaze higher, she noticed that the crisp white shirt below the black jacket had a high collar and two pieces of material pointing down in an upside-down V.

Lauren wasn't entirely sure what a barrister did, except she knew it had something to do with the law, and they made a whole lot of money.

Kim grabbed her bag and slung it over her shoulder. "I have a date to get ready for, good luck. Don't break any rules—she'll clap you in irons."

Lauren laughed politely. In the back of her mind she thought it would most definitely be the other way around. Allegra was all talk, but Lauren could see through her. She'd met women in positions of authority before, and in her experience they often wanted to let go of it in bed, not assert it.

They approached Lauren, and Allegra held up a hand. "I'm sorry we're late, entirely my fault."

"Happens entirely all the time," Hugo added.

Allegra blushed but didn't reply, which suggested to Lauren that Hugo was accurate.

"No problem, you're both here now." Lauren folded her arms and looked down at Hugo. "This induction isn't skippable. It's important, not just because we want to show you how to use the machines and introduce you to the gym, but because it's a requirement of our insurance. You'll give it your full attention, okay?"

Hugo nodded sharply.

Lauren was still a little miffed that Hugo had lied to her, but that didn't overshadow the huge soft spot she'd developed for him. But he didn't need to know that. If he thought she was cross with him, there was more chance that he'd focus fully.

Lauren launched into her welcome speech about the gym. Hugo knew it all already, but she was determined to double down and make him hear it. Sometimes she skipped over the odd segment or two that she didn't think was relevant for the inductee, but she'd already decided that Hugo's punishment would be to hear all of it. And some of it she'd repeat just because she could.

She walked around the large space and pointed things out to the pair. She occasionally stopped and looked at Hugo to ensure he was still listening and paying attention. When she did so, he nodded sharply again to prove he was following along. Allegra followed them and looked baffled and completely out of place in her suit and heels.

They started in the weights area, and Lauren methodically went from one piece of equipment to the next. She explained what each machine did and talked about the safety requirements before demonstrating by using the machine herself. After, she instructed Hugo to perform a couple of reps on each machine, so she could be satisfied that he knew how to use them.

She could feel Allegra's gaze on her as she showed each movement and machine to Hugo. Now and then, Lauren took the opportunity to point to exactly which muscle groups a machine was working by flexing her own muscles and pointing them out.

A quick glance in Allegra's direction proved to Lauren that her attempts were having the desired effect. Allegra's cheeks were red, her pupils dilated, and she seemed to be struggling to know where to look.

Lauren enjoyed flustering her. There was something pleasing about taking her down a peg or two from her judgemental attitude the previous day. However, she wasn't about to spend all her time playing games with Allegra. Lauren was there to do a job, and it wasn't fair to use Hugo as a pawn simply to mess with his mother.

She fully focused her attention on Hugo and had him repeat the safety information back to her. He easily repeated everything and proved that he was as keen and eager as he had been before.

"What about classes?" Hugo asked when they finished with the induction. "Am I allowed to join them?"

"You are, with your mum's permission. I'll let you know which ones you'll find the most helpful. But remember that classes run at certain times of day that might not fit in with your schedule. A lot of them are for office workers." Lauren watched Hugo's face scrunch up as he considered if that would work out for him or not.

"How would you feel if I offered you one-to-one tuition with me?" Lauren asked. She figured that she was practically doing that for Hugo before, so there was no real reason to stop now. She liked the kid, and he was a lot easier to work with than her regular private fitness clients.

Hugo's eyes lit up. "You'd do that?"

"Sure, why not? You work hard, and you do as I say. You'll be one of my easier clients." A penny dropped in her brain and she quickly added, "If your mum is okay with that?"

Lauren wanted to kick herself for just offering the service to Hugo on a whim. She didn't know if that was something Allegra would want or not. She looked over to Allegra with an apologetic look on her face.

Hugo looked pleadingly at Allegra.

Allegra nodded quickly. "That sounds very kind of you. What's your fee?"

"I'll train him for free," Lauren said. "He comes at quiet hours, and he does what he's told. It's hardly work."

"Does he now? That's new," Allegra quipped. She looked down at Hugo with a warm smile.

Hugo rolled his eyes and turned his attention back to the cross-training machine they were standing beside. He got on and set up a program.

"Can't hear you," he said over the noise of the machine starting up.

"It's okay, I'll wait. We can discuss it any time," Allegra shot back.

Lauren smiled at the mother–son banter she was witnessing. It was another side to Allegra that she hadn't seen yet, and she enjoyed it.

"Consider the one-to-one training an apology for our poor induction process at the start. And our lack of apostrophe, of course." Lauren had no idea why they needed one, but she'd heard people complain about it before, and it seemed to make Allegra smile any time she joked about it.

"That's very kind of you," Allegra said, chuckling at the joke.

"I want to lose two kilos a week," Hugo announced.

"A third of a stone?" Lauren easily converted new measurements into old for Allegra's benefit.

Allegra looked horrified. "To what end? How stick-thin do you wish to be?"

Before they started getting into a full-on debate about body weight, Lauren approached Hugo. "It doesn't quite work like that. Besides, muscle weighs more than fat, so we don't think about this as weight loss, more body toning. But I don't want you to worry about that side of things. We're not going to be doing weigh-ins with you. You're a teenager, and your body is changing too much for us to monitor things like that. We'll be focusing on stamina and reps, nothing more. Okay?"

Lauren knew Hugo was desperate to lose weight but wanted to get him to understand that fitness and weight were not linked in the way he thought.

"Okay." Hugo nodded half-heartedly, already getting out of breath on the cross-trainer.

Lauren leaned across the panel and pressed the stop button. "That's enough for today—you've done more than you think. We'll start afresh tomorrow, so come ready to work."

Hugo beamed and nodded. "I will!"

"Go and cool down," she instructed. "I'll see you same time tomorrow."

Hugo jogged away to the quiet area dedicated to warm-ups, cool-downs, and Kim's preening. Allegra raised a surprised eyebrow at his enthusiasm. "I've not seen him run for anything for years."

"It's the tone of voice," Lauren said. "I can get anyone to do anything."

It was deliberately suggestive, and Allegra swallowed before speaking again. "I appreciate your offer of free tuition, but I understand it's time you would usually charge for, and I'm happy to pay. I don't want you to be out of pocket."

Lauren shook her head. "It's fine—I'm happy to do it. He has a lot of motivation, and I want to harness that and help him out."

"Still, I should compensate you for your time," Allegra insisted.

"No need," Lauren maintained.

They stared at one another defiantly for a few moments before Allegra eventually nodded her agreement. "Very well. Thank you, and obviously if that changes, then let me know. I think I might pop in now and then, just to check that he is behaving himself."

Lauren tried to smother the smile that thought brought to her face. "You're more than welcome, any time."

Allegra looked like she wanted to say something else, and Lauren waited patiently. She was interested to see where this new connection they'd developed would end up next. It wasn't the time to push things along. She could see that the wheels in Allegra's brain were still turning, and she was processing the feelings that were being stirred up. Lauren didn't need to do anything. If she was right, then Allegra would soon be back.

In the end Allegra didn't say anything. Instead, she indicated with a tilt of her head that she would be joining Hugo.

Lauren smiled and nodded. "Any time," she added softly.

CHAPTER EIGHT

Allegra shook her head and placed her glasses down on the desk in her home office. She'd been staring at the same piece of paper for the last ten minutes but had yet to take any of the details in.

She was exhausted and distracted. A new case with enough history to send most people into a long sleep had found its way to her. The previous barrister had been fired by the client, and Allegra was playing catch-up. She needed to learn everything about the case before going to court in a few days' time.

It wasn't unusual, but it also wasn't Allegra's common practice. She liked to spend time getting to know her case and client and not be rushed into catching up with details that the other side already had.

It meant long hours and bringing extra work home, which she had only recently decided that she would try to limit. Now she was already breaking that promise she'd made herself. It was only a week into her attempt to be home more, and while it had started out well enough, she was now back to bringing case notes home with her.

Thankfully, Hugo was preoccupied with his new exercise plan. He'd been back at the gym for just over a week, and Allegra was pleasantly surprised by the change in his mood, like night and day, from being sullen to practically bouncing around the house with excited energy. If Allegra had even an inkling that joining the gym would have affected him so positively, then she would have suggested it some time ago.

Not a day went by when Hugo didn't talk to her about his progress. Every morning, evening, and mealtime was peppered with how many somethings he could now lift and for how long he could now run, row, or some other form of movement that Allegra knew little about.

Of course she smiled and nodded and did her best to show an interest. She had little idea about the world of exercise, but Hugo seemed to be enjoying it immensely, and that brought her pleasure. And top of the list of things Hugo wanted to tell her all about was Lauren. Everything Lauren said, did, thought, or suggested was spoken about at length.

Apparently, Lauren was great in every way. It was very clear that Hugo had an idol.

Allegra could understand fully why her son had taken a shine to his trainer. She'd been on Allegra's mind too but for completely different reasons. While Hugo had enthused about Lauren's ability to seemingly do any sport or physical activity and marvelled at how cool she was, Allegra's mind drifted elsewhere.

While her son talked about Lauren's words of wisdom, Allegra fantasised about cheeky grins and perfect skin atop rippling muscles.

"Stop it," she muttered to herself.

For some reason her mind had taken to providing her with memories of Lauren's toned body performing push-ups at the most inopportune moments. It wasn't like her to drool over someone's body, but there was something about Lauren that seemed to blast past her usual defences and place itself right in the forefront of her thoughts.

The sexy body was distracting, but the quick wit and the brazen nature didn't help either. She'd tried pushing thoughts of Lauren away, but that had been completely impossible. Any moment when Allegra lost her focus on work was the opportunity for her scheming brain to present her with more memories of Lauren. Flexing muscles and beautiful brown eyes consumed her thoughts.

She sat back in her chair and sighed. She was doing it again. She had no idea when she had become the kind of person who reduced a woman down to nothing more than an attractive body, but apparently that was what she was now.

While she did think about Lauren's sharp intelligence and playful nature, she always ended up daydreaming about Lauren's impressive physique.

"Been alone for too long," she mumbled. "Forgotten what a body looks like."

She frowned as she wondered how long it had been since she'd had any kind of intimate company or even been on a date. After a few moments she realised that needing to think about it for any amount of time meant that it had been far too long.

The doorbell rang, and she looked at her watch. It was eight in the evening, which definitely meant it wasn't anyone for Hugo. She went to the front door, looked through the spyhole, and smiled at seeing Roberta standing there. She checked her reflection in the hallway mirror quickly before opening the door.

"Good evening." Allegra couldn't help but smile. She was very happy to see her friend and colleague, especially when she was struggling to focus on work anyway.

Roberta hugged a stack of papers to her chest. "Hi, I'm sorry to drop by so late, but I thought you might like the notes for the Drayton case."

Allegra looked at the large amount of paperwork and let out a small sigh. Just once she'd love one of her cases to be able to be summed up in under fifty sheets of paper.

She took the stack from Roberta. "Thank you, I'd forgotten about these. Would you like to come in?"

"Love to."

Allegra led the way into the kitchen and placed the paperwork on the counter. She'd known straight away that Roberta would want to come in. There was no real reason for her to come by of an evening and drop off any work. They were the same pay grade, and it certainly wasn't in Roberta's job description to be ferrying around paperwork of an evening. Coming over was obviously a subtle way for Roberta to say she wanted to talk. And Allegra was very happy for the distraction—it wasn't as if she was in the right frame of mind to get much work done anyway.

"Wine?" Allegra offered.

Roberta nodded appreciatively and took a seat at the kitchen table. Allegra grabbed a bottle from the rack and pulled a corkscrew out of the cutlery drawer.

"How's David?" Allegra asked. She suspected that she already knew the answer, judging by the weary look on her friend's face.

"Exhausting," Roberta said. "He's refusing to talk about divorce, still."

"He can't ignore your wishes," Allegra reminded her.

"He wants to talk. To see if we can fix things." Roberta let out a long sigh. "But things are beyond that—I've moved on. *Emotionally* moved on, you know what I mean?"

Allegra nodded. She poured two glasses of wine. "Have you told him that?"

"He won't listen. He thinks some time will heal everything."

Allegra passed Roberta a glass of wine and then sat down opposite her.

"I just don't know how to get through to him," Roberta said. "He seems to think this is a small blip and something we can overcome. But it's years and years of drifting apart, and now we're at a point where—and I feel terrible saying this—I just don't want to fix things. I don't want to invest more time and effort in a relationship that has failed and I don't think can be recovered."

"You need to tell him that," Allegra said. "I know it's not easy, but he needs to hear it."

"I try. But he just wants to wait and talk when things have calmed down—his words. He thinks I'm upset and will feel differently when I've thought things through."

Allegra could feel the frustration rolling off Roberta in waves. She'd been unhappy in her twenty-two-year marriage for the last five years. It had come to a head the previous summer, and Roberta was ready to move on. Sadly, her husband was not.

"It sounds to me like he's trying to hold you hostage," Allegra observed, "refusing to talk until he thinks you'll say what he wants to hear. Wearing you down. Have you considered moving on to the next step without him?"

Roberta put her wine glass down and nodded. "I think I'm going to have to. But I hate it. I know he's hurting, but this just prolongs the hurt for everyone."

"You have to think about yourself. It's not selfish to do so," Allegra reminded her.

Roberta nodded. "You're right. In fact, look at you—you got it all right. Free to do as you please. No being tied down, just freedom."

Allegra chuckled. "Do I need to remind you that there's a teenage boy upstairs?"

Roberta smiled. "That boy is an angel."

"He has his moments," Allegra admitted. While their relationship had become a little more strained lately, she knew she was luckier than most. On the whole he was thoughtful, kind, and loving. He was struggling with the journey to becoming an adult, but who hadn't? "But I'm still a single mother. It would be nice to just once have someone else here to remind him to tidy his room. Or to say no, so it's not always me doing it."

Roberta took a sip of wine and looked at Allegra thoughtfully. "You know, I can't remember the last time you went on a date. And I know you tell me everything. So am I being forgetful, or has it been a very long time since you've seen anyone?"

Allegra played with the stem of her wine glass and sighed. "It's been a very long time. It's hard sometimes with work, and I have Hugo to think about, and…you know, it's not easy."

"How long?" Roberta asked.

Allegra felt a blush touch her cheeks. "Well, let's just say that she was the one who taught Hugo to ride a bike."

Roberta's eyebrow rose. "Either Hugo suffered an inner ear imbalance right up until his teenage years, or you haven't been on a date for—"

Allegra held up her hand. "Let's not. It's been a long time. Let's not put an actual date on it and give it the reality of a fixed number.

I'm not sure I can handle the thought. Besides, we're talking about you, not me."

"You need to get out there!" Roberta declared, seemingly very happy to change the subject. "You look great, you're successful—you'll find someone great in no time. You just need to get out there and let people know you're looking. How do women find women to date? Is there an app?"

Allegra shook her head quickly. "No, no. We're not joining any dating websites or swiping on any apps. *No.*"

"You have to be proactive," Roberta told her. "You can't wait around for some woman to show up and sweep you off your feet. That's how you end up not dating for years. As if I need to tell you that."

Allegra bit her lip as Lauren popped into her mind. "There is... maybe...someone."

Roberta grinned like the cat that got the cream. "Oh, look at you. Keeping secrets from me."

"There's nothing to tell yet. You know I said that Hugo joined the gym? There's a fitness trainer there. I'm pretty certain she was flirting with me and..." Allegra shifted in her seat. She was already embarrassed to admit to herself that she was so preoccupied with Lauren. Now she was about to say it out loud and give it life. "I can't stop thinking about her."

It was out there, and Allegra knew that the past week of keeping a lid on her feelings was now over. She couldn't lie to herself any more. Whether or not anything would ever come of it, she was smitten with Lauren.

Roberta made a noise a teenage girl would make when told similar news, and Allegra flopped over her dining room table with utter embarrassment.

"So, who is she?" Roberta pressed. "A fitness trainer, eh? Is she..."

"She's built like a goddess," Allegra confessed from her tabletop refuge. "She has muscles I didn't know existed, and I *hate* that I notice that."

Roberta laughed heartily. "So you noticed and appreciated a nice body. What's wrong with that?"

"It's not very respectful," Allegra said. She sat up. "Reducing her to nothing more than a body. It's not very nice, is it."

"What's she like?" Roberta asked.

"She's cocky." Allegra chuckled. "Smart mouth, answer for everything. She's quick-witted, and some might consider her funny. Hugo loves her. Apparently, she's great at everything she does. She's the deputy manager of a gym with a grammatically incorrect name, but I'm trying to forget about the crime against apostrophes. She seems to be very good with people."

"So not just a body."

Allegra let out a long breath. "I suppose not. But it's the first thing I noticed about her, and it's also the thing I constantly seem to be focused on when I think about her."

"She's a fitness trainer—presumably she wants people to notice that she's in shape." Roberta sat forward with excitement gleaming in her eyes. "How did you leave it with her?"

Allegra laughed. "I didn't. I just…left."

"But she flirted with you?"

"I think so." Allegra wasn't sure any more. She'd spent so much time overthinking everything so much that she wasn't entirely sure she'd met Lauren at all. It could all have been a dream as far as she knew.

"Then get back in there, and do something about it," Roberta challenged.

Allegra winced at the idea. "How? And should I? I mean, what about Hugo?"

"You're right." Roberta took a sip of wine and nodded sagely. "You're absolutely right. You should wait until he's married before you even think about dating someone again. I mean, you've only put your life on hold for a decade, what's another decade? Remind me, how old will you be then?"

Allegra swallowed at the thought of trying to find a date when she was in her sixties. She'd struggled in her forties. She just wasn't the confident sort who could easily ask people out on dates. The idea sent a shiver up her spine. She'd almost rather be single than go through the horror of having to ask someone on a date. But now time was marching on, and she was getting older. She'd never believed in sell-by dates until she'd started wondering if she was approaching hers.

"It's not marriage," Roberta pointed out. "It's a date. Food, some fun, maybe a kiss. Maybe more. You said yourself that she's funny. Who doesn't like to be around someone funny?"

"She thinks she is," Allegra agreed.

"Then talk to her. Honestly, don't wait, Allie," Roberta pleaded. "We're both wasting away for different reasons."

Allegra knew she was right. She'd convinced herself that fantasising over Lauren from afar was all she could do, but in truth she could go back to the gym and scope out the situation. She was fairly sure that Lauren had been flirting with her, so what was to stop her from checking the water and seeing if her instincts were right? She could always retreat if she felt that she'd misread the situation and Lauren wasn't interested after all and was simply being playful.

A drink and maybe some dinner could be nice. Talking to people she didn't either live or work with would be a refreshing relief. She just needed to push her fears away and think of it as what it was, a casual enquiry. Nothing more, nothing less.

"You're thinking about it, aren't you?" Roberta asked with a gleam in her eye.

Allegra sipped her wine. "We're supposed to be talking about you, remember?"

Roberta rolled her eyes. "Fine, fine. I did want to run an idea by you…"

CHAPTER NINE

Lauren felt a swell of pride. Hugo was running on the treadmill beside her and keeping a decent pace while not panting for breath as they carried on a conversation. His stamina was improving at a staggering rate. Two weeks ago, Hugo would not have been able to say more than two words while exercising, and now they were running side by side and chatting comfortably.

"But the PlayStation is so much better than the Xbox," Hugo explained. "Especially the newest version."

"Cool," Lauren said. Not being a video game fan, she had little to add. But it was getting Hugo talking, and that was helping him build stamina and remember his breathing patterns. "Do you play video games with kids at school?"

"A couple," Hugo said. "Most aren't into games. That's one of the reasons they don't like me. That, and I'm fat."

"If you were skinny and didn't play games, I think they'd still bully you," Lauren said. "Bullies are bullies. It's not like they're massively offended by something about you. They just find something to fixate on and use it as a crutch."

"That doesn't make me feel any better," Hugo said.

"That's not part of my job description—I'm here for fitness," Lauren joked.

"Thanks," Hugo said, then sighed.

"But seriously, I'm sorry the kids are being little shi—terrors. I wish I had some advice for you, but all I can tell you is that it does get better."

"Everyone says that, but I don't see how."

Lauren understood how Hugo could feel that way. She'd been the same at his age. The possibility of a life without the bullies taunting her had seemed impossible. She'd often wondered how life would have been if she could go back and tell herself that it would all be okay. During high school she could never imagine being an adult with a home and a job and not having to worry about the kids who made her life a living nightmare. She knew it would be an equally uphill struggle to try to convince Hugo.

"You just need to ignore them and do your own thing," Lauren said. "Keep your head down, do your schoolwork, succeed. The bullies in my school were the same as yours, all talk and no substance. They ended up going nowhere."

Hugo's head snapped up, and he looked at her, slack-jawed. "*You* were bullied?"

Lauren laughed. "Well, yeah. Most people are at some point, Hugo."

"Mum wasn't."

"Well, if your mum had gone to my school, then I can guarantee you that she would have been bullied," Lauren said. "But she probably went to some posh school where everyone was just like her and wanted to get to Oxford so they could run the world or whatever."

"She went to Cambridge, not Oxford," Hugo corrected.

Lauren rolled her eyes. Of course Allegra Whittaker would be a Cambridge graduate. Knowing that she'd been to the prestigious university just made Lauren want to bring Allegra down to her level even more.

Lauren knew she had a problem with authority figures. But it wasn't like she spent her time being a criminal. She just enjoyed cajoling certain attractive women out of their comfort zones. The joy of seeing someone in a Ted Baker suit slumped in a worn-out booth of a sticky pub after doing too many shots sent a thrill through her. She dreaded to think what a therapist might say about that.

"As I say, your mum didn't go to a normal school like you and me." Lauren raised the incline on her treadmill. If she was going to spend time on the machine, then she reasoned she might as well get some benefit out of it by straining herself.

"Why were you bullied?" Hugo asked.

"Because kids are sh—" Lauren laughed to herself. "Shockingly rude sometimes."

"You can say kids are shits—I'm fourteen, not six." Hugo raised the incline on his machine to match Lauren.

"Fine, kids are shits." Lauren shrugged.

"But why would they bully you?" Hugo pressed.

Lauren didn't particularly want to remember those times. She'd spent most of her adult life trying to forget about her school experience. Laughing it off was a strategy that only half worked when the wounds were so deep. But if sharing at least a small part of her experience would make Hugo feel happier and convince him that things would get better, then she owed it to him to share.

"I was a skinny little kid," Lauren admitted.

"You?" Hugo couldn't sound more shocked if he tried.

Lauren chuckled. "I worked hard to look like this. I was skin and bone when I was your age. I had to bulk up, eat right, train hard. But when I was at school, I was always the new kid. And super skinny."

"Did your parents move around a lot?"

"I don't know my parents. I was a foster kid, got bounced around a bit. In and out of different schools."

Silence dragged on, and Lauren looked up and realised that he was looking at her with a lost expression. It was clear he didn't know what to say. Hugo was mature in many ways, but sometimes Lauren realised he was still a kid. His gaze held pity and questions, but before he got a chance to say anything else, Lauren noticed a new arrival to the gym.

"Your mum's here."

Hugo turned in surprise and waved. Allegra waved back shyly and crossed the gym towards them. She wore a skirt suit and high-collared white shirt as she had done the previous time. Lauren realised in that moment that the strait-laced attire, not showing an inch of skin, was turning her on. She itched to unbutton the blouse and see the long neck that it obviously hid.

"Hello, darling, I thought I'd pick you up as I'm home early today," Allegra said. "No hurry, though. Do finish up whatever it is you're doing."

Lauren looked at the clock on the wall and realised they were coming near the end of their scheduled time anyway. "I think we're done, don't you, Hugo?"

Hugo slammed the stop button on the machine and took a few steps until it came to a stop. His head fell forward, and he sucked in a few much-needed deep breaths.

Okay, so they still needed to work on stamina. "Go to the weights area and cool down, and then take a shower," Lauren said.

Hugo hopped off the treadmill and headed towards the weights mats to do his end-of-workout stretches. Of all her clients, Hugo was the only one who took the after stretching seriously, and Lauren was certain that was why he was able to push so hard every day without injury. If she could bottle the energy and discipline he had, she would be the most sought-after trainer in the country.

She turned off her treadmill. Allegra was looking at her and smiling.

"What?" Lauren asked.

"You'll have to tell me how you make him so compliant," Allegra said. "I asked him this morning to make his own sandwich for lunch, and you'd have thought I'd asked him to pay back rent for the last fourteen years."

"A sandwich? You monster." Lauren grinned.

"I know, I'm a truly awful mother. I don't know how he puts up with me." Allegra smiled back.

Lauren had a suspicion that this wasn't a casual chat. Allegra stood with more confidence than the last time they'd spoken. She was making more self-assured eye contact, and there was just something about her manner that made Lauren think that Allegra was there for a reason. She decided she'd happily play along until Allegra came out with the real purpose for her unexpected appearance.

"He told me it was for the food and the PlayStation," Lauren said. "That aside, I don't think he really needs you."

"True. I think you've taken his place as favourite lately. There's rarely a day that goes by when he doesn't talk about you," Allegra said.

Lauren stood tall and jutted her chin in the air. "I am pretty great," she joked. It was nice to hear that Hugo seemed to like her as much as she liked him. Training him had become a part of the day she looked forward to. Hugo did as he was told, worked hard, and was easy to talk to. She wasn't allowed to have favourites, but it was hard not to when Hugo was so different to her other clients.

"Thank you for the private tuition," Allegra said. "I take it you still refuse payment for it?"

She flashed Allegra her *What do you think?* look.

"I thought as much. You seem stubborn," Allegra said with a smirk. "How about dinner? Could I offer you a meal at mine?"

Lauren schooled her expression, not wishing to seem too keen. Inside she felt the familiar rush of adrenaline race through her. She'd been right that Allegra's wandering gaze had meant interest and maybe even attraction. Her instincts had been right that Allegra hadn't just been dropping in to give Hugo a ride home. She'd clearly come by specifically to see Lauren and ask her over for a meal.

"Sounds great," Lauren said.

While she didn't want Allegra to know how excited she was about the invite, she wasn't going to make the mistake of playing hard to get, either. She suspected that Allegra would easily be put off and give up if Lauren pretended that she wasn't interested.

"Wonderful." Allegra swallowed. It seemed as if her courage was teetering on the edge already. "When is good for you?"

"Tomorrow?" Lauren suggested. She didn't want to give Allegra the chance to take back the invitation as it seemed her bravery might start wearing off.

"Sure. Great." Allegra nodded sharply. "Um. Any dietary requirements I should be aware of?"

Lauren closely monitored every bite of food that entered her body. She didn't diet, but she knew what she was eating and what her body needed in order to maintain her fitness goals. But she'd happily ignore those rules for an evening with Allegra. She could adapt her workout to burn through whatever Allegra fed her.

"None. I'm easy."

She watched Allegra swallow again and decided she must be something of a sadist to enjoy torturing her so much.

"What's the address?"

Allegra took her handbag from her shoulder and started to look through the contents. "I'll write it down for you."

"It's okay, I'll remember it," Lauren said.

Allegra looked at her with a raised eyebrow. "If you're sure?"

Lauren nodded. "I have a good memory. Especially where food's concerned."

Allegra smiled. "Number eighteen, The Gables, it's—"

"Up by the old factory site on the new estate, I know it." Lauren knew the houses well. She'd grumbled with her friends when the expensive development had been green lit by the council. They'd wondered who on earth would be able to afford such houses but were proved wrong when they'd all been snapped up in no time at all. She'd complained of gentrification and being priced out of the area, and now Lauren was invited to dinner there.

"Dial number eighteen at the main gate when you arrive, and I'll buzz you in. There are visitor spaces to park in just on the other side of the gates—you'll see them," Allegra said.

"I don't drive," Lauren said. "I'll cycle or I'll run."

"Run?" Allegra blinked.

Allegra's reaction wasn't uncommon, and Lauren was used to people looking at her as if she'd said she'd arrive by an alien spacecraft.

"Yeah." Lauren jogged in place. "Like this. Do you remember running?"

Allegra chuckled. "I'm aware of it. Would you like me to come and pick you up? I don't mind."

"It's a ten-minute run, if that," Lauren said.

"I don't think I've ever heard of anyone running to a dinner date," Allegra mused.

"Now you have. I'm glad to be the first, and I can also guarantee I won't get stuck in traffic."

Lauren loved to run. It was a quick and free way to exercise. She happily ran to and from the supermarket, the post office, and work. Now and then she cycled if she had things to carry or somewhere to be in a hurry. But if given the choice, she would run everywhere.

She was aware that people often thought it was because she couldn't afford a car or a bus journey, or just that she was mad. Lauren didn't mind being considered strange as she knew she'd have the last laugh when she was older and just as fit as she'd always been, and they struggled to catch their breath after a short flight of stairs.

"Shall we say six?" Allegra said.

"Sounds good. Should I bring anything?"

"Just your body…I mean, yourself. Just bring yourself. Obviously."

A blush touched Allegra's cheeks, and Lauren bit her lip to prevent a joke slipping out. It was obvious Allegra was finding this a little difficult, and Lauren didn't want to push her too far and have the invitation snatched away before she got the chance to try her luck.

Lauren was rarely wrong when it came to the dating game. Allegra's gaze had been glued to Lauren's body the previous times they met, and now Allegra was struggling to make eye contact. Allegra was trying her best to keep the attraction in check.

Which only made Lauren even more determined to push her a little further during dinner.

CHAPTER TEN

Allegra looked up upon hearing the knock on her home office door. Hugo was already walking into the room with a protein bar in hand. Not long after starting the gym, he'd made the decision to change up his diet, and Allegra was fully supportive of the idea. Hugo's sweet tooth was renowned, and over the past few years snacking had become a problem.

It was rare to see Hugo without a snack of some description, and when Allegra had commented on it in the past he'd naturally become terribly upset. Now he was all about protein bars, which were conveniently covered in chocolate. Allegra had looked them up and was surprised to see that they were considered healthy. She didn't have a full understanding of what Hugo's new diet meant, but apparently muscles needed protein and so protein they received.

"Why did you invite Lauren for dinner?" Hugo asked. He sat on the sofa and looked at her expectantly.

"Because it's a nice thing to do." Allegra removed her glasses and put the lid on her fountain pen. She'd been making an effort to make more time for him. Continuing to work while he spoke to her was rude, and yet she'd done it for years. Now she was trying to turn that corner and give him her full attention.

"Why did you invite Lauren for dinner?" he asked again. He took a giant bite of the protein bar and chewed noisily while awaiting an answer.

Allegra cocked her head to one side. She wondered where

he was headed with his line of questioning. "Because she's kindly helping you for free, and as I said, it's a nice thing to do."

He continued to eat and shook his head. "Nope. People have done nice things for me before, and you've not invited them for dinner."

Allegra sat back in her chair and regarded her son through narrowed eyes. He was getting too astute. As a legal professional, she'd always attempted to guide Hugo towards finding the truth no matter what obstacles stood in his path. The world was so full of fake news and competing theories that it was important to peel all of that away and uncover the facts.

Now he was using that very skill set against her, and she wondered if maybe a little fake news would have been good for him now and then.

"I'll confess," Allegra admitted, "that I may be a little fond of Lauren and want to get to know her better."

She looked closely at him while trying to discern what he thought of that. Unfortunately, Hugo had a poker face, and Allegra sometimes found it difficult to read him, especially when her nerves were on edge and she was worried about what he might think about a matter anyway. Hugo's opinion mattered now more than ever. If he didn't want her to see Lauren, then she wouldn't. It was as simple as that.

He nodded. "Good. Lauren's cool."

She felt relief flood through her but attempted to hide it.

"So you frequently tell me." Allegra picked up her pen and twisted the lid around and around nervously. "It's okay with you that I invited her over?"

"Yeah, of course."

"And that I'm…" Allegra gestured with her hand rather than go through the embarrassment of having to say anything specific or embarrassing.

"Sure." Hugo shrugged. "I'll go to Tom's."

Allegra's legs shook despite her seated position. "No, no, you'll be here."

"Why?"

"Because it's dinner, the three of us. As a thank-you to Lauren for her training services. There's not much point in inviting her over to thank her if you're planning to go out. It's as much for you as for me."

Hugo frowned. "But you just said that you're…What did you say? Fond of her?"

"Maybe a little fond," Allegra corrected.

"Right. That. So I shouldn't be here. If it's a date."

"It's not a date," Allegra squeaked. She reached for her water glass and took a big sip. "It's a thank-you."

Hugo looked at her as if she was insane. "Is this some weird dating thing I don't understand? Like, we're pretending it's not a date. But it obviously is a date, right?"

"It isn't a date," Allegra emphasised. "The dinner isn't a date. There might be dates that follow, but this isn't one. This is a thank-you dinner. I'm not sure what you're not understanding."

Hugo threw up his free hand. "Okay, okay. Calm down, it's not a date. I get it."

Allegra looked down at her desk and concentrated on getting her breathing and heart rate back to normal. Of course she wanted it to be a date, but she had no idea how Lauren felt about that. The thought of reading the situation incorrectly and Lauren backing away and grimacing at the thought of dating an old woman was more than she could stand.

A thank-you dinner was safe. There were agreed parameters and no potential questions about what to wear or whether or not there might be a kiss at the end of the night.

She had been positive Lauren had flirted with her, but as time drifted on and the dinner drew closer, she began to wonder and worry that she had misread the entire situation. Maybe Lauren was just spirited and had no interest in her at all.

Hugo was a safety blanket, the thing that connected them and the supposed reason for the dinner. Allegra needed him there. He'd gladly fill any awkward silence and would be the bridge they needed if all went wrong.

"She likes you," Hugo said.

Allegra snapped her head up to look at him. "She does?"

He nodded. "She talks about you, asks about you now and then. She wouldn't if she didn't like you."

A desperate urge to know everything surged through her, but she pushed it deep down. The last thing she needed was her inner barrister to cross-examine her own son. She'd also prefer not to advise Hugo exactly how nervous and possibly excited she was. She adored him but knew he'd tease her endlessly with such precious information.

"Well, hopefully we'll all have a nice meal together tomorrow." Allegra gestured to her piles of work. "I'm sorry, darling, but I need to read up on this case. Do you need anything else?"

Hugo shook his head. "Nah. I'll be playing my game."

"Good luck with the invasion." She put her glasses on and pulled a file closer.

"We completed the invasion. Now we just need to hold the town," he informed her.

"Marvellous."

She had little clue about his games other than they were all warlike situations. They'd had long discussions about the realities of war, and she'd sat him down twice to watch documentaries about life in war zones. Being a single mother was difficult. She didn't want to smother him in protective BubbleWrap, but she also didn't want to give him more freedom than he would know what to do with.

She wished so desperately that he'd come with a manual. If she had a question on the law, she simply consulted her library and an answer could be found. Sometimes those answers were difficult, but guidance was always available. Raising a son, especially as a woman who had never known her own father and had no male role models or family members in her life, was hard.

Allegra couldn't deny that knowing that Lauren and Hugo got on well was a huge hurdle already overcome. She didn't like to play what-if but could feel her resolve breaking as she pictured what that life might look like. The three of them seemed to fit together somehow. Lauren could easily fill the gap that Allegra tried to pretend didn't exist.

She shook her head and reminded herself not to get ahead of the situation. They hadn't even gone on a single date yet, and she was already thinking of the future. She needed to remind herself to take things slowly and enjoy the adventure. That's what Roberta would tell her to do. That was the sensible thing to do.

She sighed.

She just hoped she was able to do it.

CHAPTER ELEVEN

Allegra rushed into her office and removed her gown. She hung it up on the coat stand by her desk and then removed her court wig and placed it on the holder. For all the media depictions of barristers and solicitors rushing around courthouses, the court was usually quite a sedate place. There was never a need to hurry, and everything took its time. Which was why Allegra was now late.

Her clerk, Jake, entered the office with an armful of folders. "I didn't think we were ever going to get a ruling."

Allegra grabbed items from her desk and practically threw them into her bag. "The Honourable Mr. Justice Smythe has never been known for his brevity."

"I thought someone was going to have to go up there and poke him with a stick," Jake said as he placed some files in her in tray and some in the filing cabinets.

"I would have done it if he'd insisted on reading through the docket one more time," Allegra confessed. "It was clear he was going to refer it up the ladder. I don't see why he couldn't have done it this morning."

"Rumour has it that he only arrived at court after lunch," Jake said.

"Well, then it's a very good thing that we don't listen to rumours," Allegra replied.

Of course Allegra did listen to rumours. Any nugget of

information on a judge could be potentially helpful in the future. But if the general public had any idea that the wheel of justice could occasionally be turned by knowing when to book an afternoon session due to the judge's dislike of an early morning, then anarchy would surely ensue.

She glanced at the clock. "I have to get going. Can you return Lucy Morgan's call and tell her I'll get back to her first thing in the morning? Can you also email me the new notes for the Highgrave case?" She grabbed her coat and felt for the pockets. "And where are my keys?"

Jake pointed to the edge of her desk where her keys sat in plain sight.

She grabbed them. "Oh, and clear my appointments for three o'clock next Monday. I'll need to show my face at the service of commemoration for Justice Stewart's wife."

She picked up her bag and gave her desk one more look-over before heading towards the door. A thought struck, and she paused. "Ask if we can move Friday's hearing to court three. I want to throw Barry off his game by putting him in the small court. Less room for him to march about looking important and gesturing like a conductor."

"Sure. I'll get all that done. Do you have a hot date tonight or something?" Jake laughed.

Allegra glared at him, and the laughter abruptly stopped. "Look for a new expert on forensics for next week. Alan won't want to be cross-examined by Beatrice again, not after last time."

Jake nodded sharply. "On it. Um, have a nice evening."

She looked over the office once more before turning and rushing to the exit. It wasn't how she had hoped her afternoon before the dinner with Lauren would go. Gasbag Smythe had put to rest any plans she had of a quiet afternoon preparing herself.

Not that there should be that much preparation needed, she reminded herself. It was just a thank-you dinner.

❖

Allegra noticed the meal delivery service van pulling up outside the house just as she arrived home. Hugo stood in the doorway having clearly just buzzed them through the gates. He looked at her pointedly before making a song and dance of looking at his wristwatch and then shaking his head in mock disappointment.

"Little comedian," she muttered to herself. She pulled her bag across the passenger seat and exited the car.

Hugo took the delivery box from the driver and thanked him. Allegra barely got to the door before the driver was back in the van and hurrying to his next delivery.

"Late for dinner again," Hugo said. "I don't know what I'm going to tell the kids."

Allegra didn't reply and simply took the box from his hands. "Thank you for taking the delivery and not making a big deal about the fact that I'm late, darling."

"What are we having?" Hugo asked.

She walked into the kitchen, and he closed the front door behind them.

"Chicken, wholegrain pasta, and salad," Allegra said.

She put the boxes down on the counter and plucked the delivery card from the envelope in the top one. She turned on the oven and read through the instructions before placing two of the boxes in the oven at the low temperature listed to keep them warm until they ate.

When she stood back up, Hugo was staring at her.

"What?" she asked.

"That sounds…healthy."

"I hope it is." Allegra removed her coat and placed it on the coat rack in the hallway.

"Why are we eating healthy food?" Hugo asked, following her like a panicked puppy.

"Because I can't imagine that Lauren eats very much lasagne. I ordered something that I think she'll be able to eat, and you'll simply have to suck it up. Besides if you want to be all muscled and impressive, then you'll be eating that kind of food before long anyway. Might as well start now."

Hugo let out a small sigh but stopped arguing remarkably

quickly, which Allegra was very grateful for as she simply didn't have the time for a debate on the matter. She looked at her reflection in the hallway mirror. Tired eyes and flat hair greeted her. She ran her hands through her hair to try to bring it back to life. There was nothing to be done about the tired eyes now.

The intercom rang, and Allegra jumped. A glance at her watch told her that Lauren was right on time. She'd expected her to be late. Something to do with the devil-may-care attitude, she supposed.

"Should I get it?" Hugo asked.

"Please, I just want to freshen up." She was already halfway up the stairs and wondered if she was running away. She hurried across the landing while cursing under her breath that The Honourable Mr. Justice Smythe and his long, slow sentences had ever decided to take up a career in the law.

She burst into her bedroom and instantly forgot every item of clothing she owned. For some reason she'd been under the illusion that she had plenty of time, but suddenly she had less than a minute. That most definitely wasn't enough time to think about what to wear—never mind locate it and put it on.

She could hear Hugo opening the door downstairs and knew her time was running out. What she didn't know was how Lauren could reduce her to an indecisive wreck without even being there.

She removed her suit jacket, collarette, and shirt in quick succession and threw them onto the bed. She opened the wardrobe and picked out an off-the-shoulder cashmere sweater. It was a go-to wardrobe piece that she knew looked good on her and worked in a casual or formal setting. She kicked off her heels and fumbled for the fastening of her skirt.

Mumbled voices downstairs told her that Lauren had arrived, and Hugo was making small talk. The thought that he was about to blurt out something embarrassing spurred her on to hurry up and join them as quickly as possible.

She kicked off her skirt and removed her tights. She reached for a pair of black jeans and hesitated. Too casual? They were black—would they be too dressy?

She had no idea what Lauren would be wearing. For all she

knew it could be a pair of shorts and one of the tight Lycra T-shirts that crept into her dreams.

"Anything's better than your underwear," she muttered to herself. She jumped into the jeans and pulled them on as quickly as possible. She grabbed a pair of simple black socks, put them on, and rushed towards the door.

It had been years since she'd worried about what to wear, and the feeling was foreign and yet warming all at once. A break from the normal was sometimes just what was needed. Allegra couldn't recall a day when she had felt butterflies in her stomach like she could now. She felt a smile tugging at the corner of her mouth. For all of her nerves, she was excited, too.

She paused at the top of the stairs and took in a deep lungful of air before making her way downstairs.

The sound of Hugo's giggles got louder and louder as she approached the kitchen. She stopped dead upon entering the room. Lauren was on the floor performing a push-up with Hugo sitting on her back.

"I'm telling you, I can do this all night," Lauren said, not sounding even remotely winded.

Hugo stood up. "Fine, you win."

"Win what?" Allegra asked.

Hugo spun around with a wide grin on his face. "Lauren said she could do ten push-ups with me on her back. I said she couldn't. Now I've got to do three miles on the treadmill tomorrow."

Hugo was practically glowing with exhilaration, and Allegra couldn't recall the last time he was so animated. Probably when she replaced his games console with the latest model.

Lauren stood up and wiped her hands on her light khaki trousers. She was smiling almost bashfully. "Hi."

"Hi," Allegra replied.

Lauren wore a collared work T-shirt with her company logo on her chest. Allegra briefly wondered if Lauren wore the T-shirt because it was smarter than her usual work outfit or if it was because of the awful grammar travesty that was the company name. With the trousers and clean white trainers, Allegra had to admit Lauren looked good even when fully clothed.

"Thank you for coming," Allegra said.

"Thank you for inviting me," Lauren replied politely.

"Food!" Hugo announced loudly, breaking the awkwardness in just the way Allegra had hoped that he would.

"I hope you didn't go to much trouble," Lauren said. "Hugo mentioned you just got home from work a few moments ago."

"We order in most nights," Hugo said.

Allegra suddenly regretted his presence. "A home-cooked meals delivery service," she explained. "For a while we ordered takeaway whenever I worked late, which wasn't a long-term solution. A friend from work recommended a service that makes a range of home-cooked meals better than I could make myself."

"All of this is a scam," Hugo said as he gestured around the large, modern kitchen. "The kitchen is basically for getting drinks and heating things."

Allegra wanted to deny it, but it was true. She wasn't the domestic sort, and there was no point in pretending that she was. "I don't have time to cook," she admitted, feeling a bit defensive.

"Hey, you don't have to explain to me. If you want to get someone else to cook your meals, go ahead. I'm sure they appreciate the business." Lauren looked around the room. "Can I help with something?"

For the first time since they had met, Lauren appeared to be a little nervous. Not that Allegra was necessarily surprised. She knew little about Lauren, but she doubted she lived in a house like hers. She was aware how intimidating her home could be to others. One of Hugo's friends had gasped when he first visited before turning to her and proclaiming that they lived in a castle.

It wasn't a castle, nor a mansion. But it was a nice house. It was expensive, probably too large, well-decorated and furnished. Allegra was unapologetic about the fact that her hard-earned career afforded her an extremely comfortable life.

However, that didn't mean that she wasn't fully aware of how uncomfortable it could make others feel. The last thing she wanted to do was give Lauren a reason to feel insecure.

"We'll eat in here," she told Hugo.

She didn't want him to think they were eating in the dining room. While it was a wonderful space for dinner parties and family events, it was absolutely not the right environment for a casual dinner with the three of them. "Maybe you two can lay the table while I plate up."

Hugo gestured for Lauren to follow him to the cutlery drawer.

"I'm doing a sponsored silence for a friend who needs medical treatment. Will you sponsor me?" Hugo asked Lauren.

"Absolutely, will you start right now?"

Allegra chuckled. She had her doubts Hugo would manage the twelve-hour silence he had signed up to do. It seemed that everyone he'd asked to sponsor him had felt the same way.

"I'm doing it at a weekend, so you won't get to appreciate it," Hugo said.

"I bet your mum will be delighted," Lauren said.

"I won't get to appreciate it either. He will be at said friend's house on that day," Allegra replied.

She removed the food from the oven and stood on tiptoe to reach the serving dishes on the top shelf. Lauren appeared beside her in a flash, easily taking the dishes and placing them on the counter.

"So no one will be there to confirm he actually does remain silent?" Lauren asked.

"No, except the person who will benefit from his sponsorship money. Like my kitchen, it's a scam, but a good cause." Allegra pointed to another serving dish on the shelf.

Lauren grinned and reached up to grab it.

"I'll get the form," Hugo said. He was gone in a flash and running up the stairs to his room.

"Nice house," Lauren said. She handed Allegra the dish.

"Thank you."

"Is there a troll bridge to the east wing?"

"Yes, cross his palm with silver, and you'll be fine."

"There's just the two of you who live here, right? Hugo didn't mention a dad and four brothers."

Allegra playfully rolled her eyes at Lauren's teasing. "Just the two of us. Two guest bedrooms, as my sister often comes to visit from India. And my home office is here—that takes up quite a lot of room. Not that I'm justifying the size of my house."

"Of course not." Lauren walked over to the bifold doors that overlooked the garden. She turned back, hand to her chest and a shocked expression on her face. "No tennis court?"

"I don't play." Allegra grinned.

"You should—the skirt would suit you." Lauren winked.

A cloud of butterflies bounced around Allegra's stomach, and she turned away as she felt unsure what to say next. Just as she started to feel comfortable with Lauren's subtle flirting, Lauren seemed to turn the intensity up, and Allegra needed to recalibrate.

Hugo entered the room with his clipboard and held it out for Lauren to take.

"What's that?" Lauren looked at the clipboard but made no move to take it.

"My sponsorship form," Hugo said.

"You want me to sponsor you *and* do your admin?" Lauren asked. "I charge for that. By the word."

Hugo swiftly turned the clipboard around, unclipped the pen, and started to write. "What should I put you down for?"

"What's everyone else put?"

"Mum gave me a hundred pounds, everyone else five or ten."

"Don't you feel sad that your mum is willing to pay a hundred pounds just for you to be quiet for a while?" Lauren joked.

"It's for a good cause," Allegra said. "Besides, as I mentioned, I won't benefit from it."

"Do I talk a lot or something?" Hugo asked.

"Yes," Lauren and Allegra replied both immediately and simultaneously, causing Hugo to narrow his eyes and look between them.

"Put me down for ten pounds," Lauren said. She ruffled his

hair. "And you can talk as much as you like, as long as you can run on the treadmill while you do it."

The gentle banter continued as they ate. Allegra had placed the serving bowls in the middle with a couple of jugs of water. It looked much healthier than what they usually ate, and she wondered if a change might be in order. For all of Hugo's complaints he happily ate a portion of chicken and pasta and even picked at a second helping of pasta. Thankfully, Lauren seemed to enjoy the food.

Allegra tried to look as though she wasn't keeping a close eye on her dinner guest, but she was also keen to check that Lauren was comfortable and had everything that she needed. Being a good hostess had been drilled into Allegra as a child, and now more than ever she really wanted to make sure that Lauren was having a pleasant evening.

Everything seemed to be going well. Hugo was keeping easy conversation flowing, Lauren was enjoying her meal and appeared to have relaxed, and Allegra's pulse rate had finally returned to a normal level.

Things were going just fine, and she was starting to wonder what on earth she'd been so stressed about.

"Right, I'm heading over to Tom's," Hugo announced. He stood up and took his plate over to the dishwasher.

Allegra's blood ran cold. "What?"

"I'm going to Tom's. You said I could." Hugo looked at her with large brown eyes and a confused expression.

She wasn't buying it for one second. This was blackmail, pure and simple. She had two choices—force him to stay and then worry about what might slip out of his mouth next, or let him go and pretend it had been agreed upon some time ago.

"Homework done?" Allegra asked.

"Yep. And I cleaned my room. Well, the clothes are off the floor so Maria doesn't trip over them." Hugo shrugged.

"Maria?" Lauren asked.

"The cleaner," Allegra said.

"Of course." Lauren nodded.

"I'll be back by eight thirty, like you said," Hugo added. He looked at Lauren. "See you tomorrow?"

"You will—I have a bet to cash in." Lauren leaned back in her chair and smiled at him.

Lauren didn't appear to be offended by Hugo's vanishing act, and Allegra couldn't think of a reason to keep him there. She levelled a look at him, hoping to impress upon him that she knew exactly what he was doing and that they'd discuss it at another time.

"Eight thirty," she agreed.

"Cool. Bye Mum, bye Lauren." He grabbed his keys from the bowl on the counter, and a few seconds later the front door closed behind him.

Allegra swallowed, turning to Lauren and hoping to look like she hadn't just been placed in an uncomfortable situation by her son. She wished she could get over her nerves around Lauren. She frequently dealt with criminals, judges, and government officials. And yet her normal confidence had been punctured by a fitness trainer.

"Did you plan that, or did he drop you in it?" Lauren asked casually.

"He dropped me in it." Allegra reached for the bottle of wine that sat on the table. She'd offered some to Lauren before dinner, but she'd declined. Allegra had valiantly attempted to stick to water, but now she needed something stronger. She indicated the bottle towards Lauren.

Lauren picked up her tumbler of water and shook her head. "No, thanks. I'm good."

Allegra took the stopper out of the bottle and poured herself a glass.

"Dinner was delicious," Lauren said.

"Thank you, I'll email the chef."

"Do you really never cook?"

Allegra thought about it for a few moments. "Does pouring breakfast cereal count?"

"No." Lauren chuckled.

"Toast?"

Lauren shook her head.

"Then no. Not for a long time." Allegra sipped her wine. "Does that make me terrible?"

"No. It makes you different to most but definitely not terrible."

"Are you a good cook?" Allegra asked.

Lauren laughed. "Absolutely not. Most of my meals come in a shaker or a bar. My oven broke three years ago, and I haven't fixed it because I found I didn't use it."

Allegra's jaw dropped. "And you're making comments about *me*?"

Lauren bit her lip and smiled. "I don't think I actually made any comments. The difference is that you feel embarrassed about it. I don't."

"I'm not embarrassed."

Lauren tilted her head and regarded Allegra for a moment. "You are. A little. You feel judged, and you don't enjoy that feeling. You're different to other people, and you're not sure you like that. But then you're not willing to change either."

Allegra gripped her wine glass and maintained eye contact with Lauren. She wondered how she had managed to analyse her so perfectly and so quickly. "What makes you say that?"

"You're a single mum and a woman in an impressive career who has bought herself a nice house. You're not a domestic goddess—your words, not mine. Of course you feel people are judging you. I'm going to guess by the way you look at me that you're not straight. Which is another thing to make you different from the average boring person. And if we stick out, then we're judged. Or worried about being judged. Am I right?"

"About me not being straight?"

Lauren bit her lip. "I'm pretty sure I know the answer to that."

"Oh, really? And how do you think I look at you?" Allegra knew it was a dangerous game to play, but Lauren made her want to play it. Just for once she wanted to inflict the same level of nerves on Lauren that Lauren shot through her. Just once she wanted to see a light blush on Lauren's cheeks. Just once she wanted to feel she had the upper hand.

"Like you want me to kiss you," Lauren said.

Allegra immediately wished she hadn't thrown down the gauntlet because now she struggled to know what to say next. She did want Lauren to kiss her—that much was obvious to her. But she was pretty sure that she hadn't stared longingly at Lauren like some lovesick teenager.

Had she?

"Which is completely understandable," Lauren continued. "Because I'm an exceptionally good kisser."

Allegra cupped her own cheek, to cover her smile with the palm of her hand. "Oh, are you?"

"Absolutely. I mean, I don't tell everyone, of course. It's a very sensitive matter. Wouldn't want everyone knowing," Lauren said.

"I'm honoured that you're willing to share such sensitive information with me," Allegra said, playing along.

They were both walking down a path and about to meet in the middle. She knew that there was no stopping now. Allegra didn't want to stop it. Lauren was fun, attractive, and—most importantly—seemed to want to kiss her.

"I'm sensing that you're not convinced," Lauren said. She stood up and held out a hand.

Allegra decided to throw caution to the wind. She placed her hand in Lauren's and allowed herself to be pulled to her feet. "Well, you can't believe everything you hear."

The moment Allegra was standing upright, Lauren didn't hesitate. She leaned in and kissed her. Allegra would have staggered backwards if she hadn't had the presence of mind to reach up and place a steadying hand on Lauren's shoulder.

Is this how you kiss? Should I be doing more? Less? Allegra couldn't remember, and any chance she had of piecing together coherent thought was diminishing as she became lost in the overwhelming sensations. Lauren's lips were warm and soft, and while Allegra logically knew that's what they would feel like, it was a revelation to her. The sensation hit her in a way that she hadn't expected. Goosebumps stood to attention along her arms, and her legs shook gently.

When had she decided she didn't need this in her life? How much time had she wasted?

Lauren eased back and looked down at Allegra with a soft smile.

"You okay?"

Allegra nodded. "It's been a while."

"Let's make up for lost time." Lauren lowered her head again, and this time Allegra was ready to respond with the enthusiasm she knew the moment deserved. The moment she tilted her head up a little more, Lauren slipped her tongue into Allegra's mouth.

Allegra's knees wobbled, and she held tighter on to Lauren. Suddenly Lauren broke the kiss, and in one swift movement lifted Allegra as if she weighed nothing more than a feather and placed her on the kitchen counter.

Before she had time to even form a thought about the sudden relocation, Lauren was in front of her and kissing her again. She distractedly wondered if she'd ever sat on a kitchen worktop before, never mind been lifted so easily onto one.

Focus. You're experiencing one of the best kisses of the decade. Focus.

She lifted her hands and cupped Lauren's face to attempt to hold her in place and gain some kind of footing in what was becoming a very welcome onslaught.

As had become their practice, the moment Allegra matched Lauren's actions, Lauren upped the ante and moved higher still. This time was no different. As soon as Allegra took hold of Lauren's face and returned the kiss with the same fervour, Lauren's hands moved from her waist. One hand cupped the side of Allegra's face and pulled her in closer, and the other was quite suddenly under her sweater, softly grasping at her naked side.

She moaned into Lauren's mouth.

"Still okay?" Lauren asked.

"Yes," Allegra whispered, hating how desperate she sounded. But she was desperate. These feelings had become distant memories, and she was now being reminded how wonderful it was to have someone's kiss and touch.

Lauren's mouth was now on her neck and making its way lower. She turned her head to the side to allow her access. A small voice at the back of her head told her to do something, but she had no idea what. She'd hardly known how to talk to Lauren during dinner, so the protocol for being ravished on her kitchen counter was most definitely not going to come to her.

"I want to see you," Lauren whispered. Her eyes bored into Allegra's, pleading and full of desire.

Allegra nodded despite having no idea what Lauren meant but willing to say yes to anything right then.

Lauren quickly removed the off-the-shoulder sweater. Allegra wasn't entirely sure how she managed to do it with such ease but decided that was another glaring signal that it had been far too long since she'd been with someone.

Before the cool air of the kitchen managed to hit her skin, Lauren's hands and mouth were on her and keeping her warm. Any inhibitions she might have had vanished. There was nothing but Lauren and her nimble fingers making quick work of Allegra's bra and Lauren's warm mouth upon her breasts the second they were released.

She pressed her body closer to Lauren's in the desperate need for connection. She parted her legs further and wasn't disappointed by the speed with which Lauren occupied the newly available space and pressed her body against hers.

"I want you," Lauren whispered.

Allegra found that she didn't care what Lauren did next. She just never wanted the sensations to end. She'd realised a while ago that she was completely unprepared for this wonderful woman, and all she could do was hold on and enjoy the journey.

"Can I?" Lauren asked.

Allegra didn't know what Lauren was asking. All she did know was that each question asked meant Lauren's mouth was no longer on her skin and Lauren's hands had stilled. Which felt completely unacceptable.

"Yes," Allegra said.

Lauren unbuttoned Allegra's jeans and effortlessly moved her into a position that allowed her hand to snake into her jeans and underwear. Allegra gasped at the contact of Lauren's hand between her legs.

Lauren stood firm in front of Allegra, one hand buried in her jeans, the other holding her waist to keep her from writhing too much. Her mouth raced between Allegra's breasts and her neck as if desperate to feast and not knowing where to spend her time.

Hundred-metre sprints lasted longer than Allegra. In an embarrassing display of just how long it had been, she moaned and gasped like an X-rated movie and then climaxed a few seconds later.

Her body refused to cooperate, and she was wilting, slipping from the counter. Lauren chuckled and removed her hand from Allegra's jeans and lifted her into a sitting position. Allegra braced herself on Lauren's shoulders with what little strength she had left.

"Hi," Lauren said, a wide smile on her face.

"I…" Allegra had no idea what she wanted to say. *I've never done that before. I'm sorry. It's been so long. What do we do now? I'm terrible at this.*

"That was fun," Lauren said. "Maybe we can do it again sometime?"

Allegra wondered what they must look like. Lauren, fully clothed and practically holding her up, while Allegra panted for breath, topless and with her jeans open, on the kitchen counter of all places.

She hoped to God that Hugo didn't come home early.

"Hello?" Lauren asked, the grin still on her face. She seemed exceptionally pleased with herself.

"Should I…?" Allegra gestured to Lauren vaguely. "I mean, obviously I want to, I just need a—"

"Next time?" Lauren asked. She placed a kiss on Allegra's forehead. "Or, you know, whenever you're ready."

Allegra wanted to deny any accusation that she wasn't ready but knew it would be laughable. She could hardly hold herself up, and her mind was in such a spin that she wouldn't have been able to recite the months of the year right then.

"I have an early shift tomorrow, so I better get going." Lauren swiftly lowered Allegra to the floor, checking she was stable before letting go.

"Oh, I..." Allegra looked at the dining table and wondered if she should be saying something, offering something, *doing* something. Her hostess manual had never given her the protocol for the after events of being taken on her kitchen counter.

Lauren kissed her again. It was sweet, careful, full of promise and meanings that Allegra couldn't yet place. Or maybe she was just hoping it was because she couldn't imagine this ending just yet. Not already. Not when she'd just rediscovered the joy of companionship and someone else's touch.

"I had fun. I hope we can do it again," Lauren said. "I'll see myself out."

Allegra nodded and watched Lauren leave. She didn't have a lot of choice, considering her legs had decided to stop working properly, and her brain was giving her nothing useful to say.

She had no idea how her thank-you dinner that might hopefully lead to more had turned into sex on the counter. Nor did she have any idea what to say or do next. She'd never had sex on a first date. She'd never had a one-night stand, which she hoped would remain the case. She wanted to see Lauren again. Wanted to feel her lips on hers again, and in other places.

Realising her jeans were still unbuttoned, she pulled them up and fastened them.

"Wow," she whispered to herself. She imagined it would be a few hours before her brain had time to process what had just happened and she'd have any further words to add.

CHAPTER TWELVE

Lauren whistled a cheerful tune as she stacked weights. She was sure nothing could puncture her happy mood. The previous night had been unexpected but wonderful. She hadn't planned to do anything other than enjoy dinner, but Allegra was just too enticing to ignore.

Once Hugo had left—God, how she loved that kid—Lauren had seen an opportunity and decided to take it. Allegra had been an adorable blend of nerves and confidence, pushing forward with flirty comments but hiding her blush when Lauren responded in kind.

As far as Lauren was concerned, there was only one way to fix that kind of situation, and that was to rip the plaster off. She didn't think she could take another week, fortnight, or God forbid a month of nervous back and forth while Allegra wondered whether or not they could possibly be something more.

The tension would have been too great. So she'd taken the initiative and exactly what she wanted. She'd made sure to check in with Allegra frequently and then left her to process the events without the need for awkward conversation.

"Having a good morning?"

Lauren rolled her eyes at the sound of Kim's voice behind her. "How are you doing, Kim?"

Kim took a seat at the chest press and narrowed her eyes. "You're glowing. You're not pregnant, are you?" She laughed and took a long glug from her protein shake.

"Well, it would be a surprise," Lauren joked in return.

Kim continued to stare at her, her eyes like a scanner seeking a barcode.

"What?" Lauren asked, suddenly nervous that Kim would solve the mystery with nothing more than an inquisitive look. "I'm just happy."

"You got some last night, didn't you," Kim said. A vulgar smirk appeared on her face as Lauren felt a blush touch her cheeks. "You did! Good on you. It's because I reminded you those looks will fade, isn't it? I didn't mean to be rude, babe. Just saying."

Lauren quickly finished putting the weights back in order, so she had an excuse to get out of there. She didn't want a laddish chat with Kim, and she certainly didn't want Kim making assumptions about who Lauren had been with. The thought of Allegra thinking she'd been boasting in the gym the next day was enough to make her feel queasy.

"If you want to tag team at Catz this weekend, let me know." Kim dropped her bottle in the holder and adjusted the weight pin on the chest press.

The idea of watching Kim prowl for unsuspecting women made Lauren shiver. The thought of being beside her as she did it actually made Lauren walk away. "Thanks, I'll let you know."

Lauren reminded herself that Kim was a client, a good one. And someone she needed to be pleasant to at all times even if she really didn't want to. She entered the office to grab some cleaning things and noticed Jim on the phone.

"I'll see what I can do, love," he said forlornly. "I'll call you later. Let me know if you hear anything else."

Lauren watched from the corner of her eye as Jim's shaky hand put the phone down.

"What's up?" she asked, knowing that Jim needed a prompt before he opened up. He was a typical man in his sixties who rarely admitted to having feelings, never mind offering to talk about them.

"Bea's taken a bad turn." Jim's voice shook. He stood up and ran a hand through his thinning hair. "I need to...um."

Lauren realised what was happening immediately. She plucked

his coat from the coat stand and picked his keys up from the desk. "You need to go and be with your family, come on."

Jim took the coat but didn't move. "I can't leave you all in the lurch."

"Of course you can," Lauren told him. She took the coat and held it out for him to put on. "You're the boss. You can do what you like. You've left me in charge before, and I've not burned the place to the ground yet." Jim put his arms into the coat sleeves, and Lauren placed his car keys in his hand. "Are you okay to drive? You want me to call someone? I can get Billy out of bed and get him to drive you."

"The accounts are due next month. I've not dealt with the two new members. The post will be here in a minute—I'm expecting the invoice for the new mats in the studio," Jim said.

Lauren took his face in her hands and forced him to focus on her. "Family comes first. I'll manage. You'll be on the phone if I need you, which I won't. Go to your daughter and granddaughter— they *do* need you."

That seemed to sink in, and Jim nodded sharply. "They need me."

Lauren let go of him. "You need me to call Billy?"

"No, I'll be okay."

Lauren regarded him for a few moments to convince herself that was the case. Whatever shock he'd been in seemed to be clearing, and he seemed more like himself with each passing moment.

"Are you sure you'll be okay?" he asked. "I don't know how long I'll be."

"Be as long as you need to be. I'll figure it out," Lauren said, reassuring him.

Jim looked at her for a few seconds. "Call Anna—she'll deal with the paperwork and stuff. As I say, the accounts are due. There's going to be a lot of stuff that you—"

"I'll call Anna," Lauren said. "I can deal with everything else. We're a great team. The two of us nearly make one of you."

A ghost of a smile tugged at the corner of his mouth. It vanished as quick as it had appeared. "The offer still stands, if you want to go back to school. The business will pay."

Lauren bit the inside of her cheek. She really didn't want to have the conversation again, and especially not right now. She already felt terrible that she couldn't cover for her boss when he was pulled away. Having to rely on help from an outside freelancer was demeaning. But it wasn't as if things were going to change. The words wouldn't suddenly make sense. The letters wouldn't stop from bouncing around in front of her eyes. Most of all, the terror of picking up a piece of paper covered in meaningless characters wouldn't simply vanish.

Lauren had accepted the reality that reading was not for her. The heavy shame of realising she'd never be able to do something that came so naturally to most was a weight she sometimes felt she couldn't carry. The only thing that kept her going was the knowledge that almost no one knew her terrible secret.

Jim knew the extent of her lack of skills. Anna seemed to suspect something, but Lauren doubted she knew the full truth. Aside from those two, no one knew. And as far as Lauren was concerned, no one needed to know. It was her secret, and she'd found it not all that difficult to deflect people from discovering the truth. She'd created a whole host of ways to keep her lack of reading ability from people. Sadly, the primary one was not letting people get too close, a fact she thought on as little as possible.

"We'll talk later. Just go." She gently turned him around and shoved him towards the door.

She watched him quickly cross the gym floor and exit the building, keeping a smile plastered on her face in case he turned around. Once he was gone, she walked back into the office and let out a sigh.

Family always came first as far as Lauren was concerned, despite the fact she'd never really had a family of her own. Yes, she'd had foster families, and now she had found family and friends, but that was different. She'd never experienced what it was like to be a part of an actual family. To know they had your back no matter what happened. To be able to rely on someone else and not always have to look after yourself. It was a fantasy for Lauren but a reality for Jim.

His family needed him, and that meant he needed to be with them, and Lauren would move heaven and earth to make that happen. Even if that meant leaving her and Anna to deal with the mountain of paperwork Jim referred to as a desk.

CHAPTER THIRTEEN

Allegra exited the courtroom and marched towards her chambers with a spring in her step. She felt invigorated and ready to take on anything.

"What's next?" she asked over her shoulder to where Jake was struggling to keep up with her pace.

"Erm, I'll need to check the diary. That case was supposed to last the whole day."

Roberta stepped out of her office, paperwork in her hand and glasses perched on her head. She looked up at Allegra and smiled. "Do you have some time for me at some point? It doesn't have to be today."

Allegra paused and looked to Jake with a questioning look. As her clerk, he was in charge of meetings and knew what time she could spare and when.

"She's free now," Jake said. "She just killed it in court two."

Roberta raised an eyebrow. "What happened?"

Allegra remained silent, knowing Jake would do the job of explaining.

"Her summing up was so good that the defendant cried and confessed everything," Jake said. "You should have seen it."

Roberta stared incredulously at Allegra.

"Justice Blake will make a decision on sentencing next week," Allegra explained. "Which saves the taxpayer the cost of two more full court days."

"She broke him," Jake said, shaking his head. "Full-on tears. Anyway, I better get to the office and rearrange your schedule."

He edged past them and hurried away. Roberta continued to look at Allegra, a suspicious edge to her gaze.

"What's going on?" Roberta asked.

Allegra opened her mouth to deny that anything was going on but stopped. Something was very much going on. Something she very much wanted to talk to someone about. She had precious few close friends she could speak to about such things, and Roberta was one of them.

The only problem was that Allegra didn't know if she was ready to have the conversation. To talk about what had happened the previous night might just give life to the worries that she had attempted to spend the last eighteen hours ignoring.

"Allie?" Roberta asked.

Allegra looked around the hallway for a moment before taking Roberta's arm and dragging her into a small supply cupboard. She turned on the light and closed the door.

"The fitness instructor I mentioned? I invited her to dinner," Allegra confessed.

Roberta's eyes widened. "And?"

"And she lifted me onto my kitchen worktop, and we..." Allegra waved her hand in lieu of finishing the sentence.

Roberta barely covered a smile with her hand. "No!"

"Yes!" Allegra paced the tiny space. "It was meant to be nothing more than an innocent dinner. I thought that I'd maybe get a sense of her as a person and possibly see if there was something there. But then Hugo went to his friend's house, without warning me that he was planning on abandoning me. Suddenly she's flirting, and then we're kissing. And before I know it, I'm being lifted—*lifted*—onto the kitchen worktop for some of the, no, the best sex of my life."

"You lucky devil," Roberta said.

"I barely know her," Allegra pointed out, doubts starting to seep in. Now that she was actually verbalising what had happened, she was, as she'd suspected she would be, coming down from her high and beginning to worry. She always worried. It was a key component of her personality that she'd never been able to shake.

"So?"

"Well, I should probably know...something about her. We... you know."

"Did the dirty in your kitchen on the first date?" Roberta asked.

Allegra stopped pacing and looked at her friend. "This is serious."

"Is it?" Roberta leaned against the shelving. "I'm guessing you had fun."

Allegra sighed and nodded. "Yes," she whispered.

"Well, there you go. Maybe it will go somewhere else, and maybe it won't. Live in the moment. You had a great time, and you are allowed to do that, you know. It's not something you need to be worried about—it's something you need to just enjoy. How did you leave it with her?"

"Nothing concrete," Allegra said.

She'd cursed herself for letting Lauren go without clarifying what had happened, what it meant, and what came next. "She said she had fun and hoped we could do it again. But I don't know if she actually meant that."

"Why would she lie?"

Allegra shrugged. "I don't know, perhaps people do? I've never done this before. I've never had sex on a first date. Never in my kitchen. Anyone's kitchen!"

Roberta put a calming hand on her shoulder. "Hey, it's okay. Take some breaths."

Allegra did as advised. She hated that she had become emotional. She'd been so careful to only enjoy the positives and ignore any lingering doubts, and now all those concerns were flooding out.

"You need to talk to her," Roberta said.

"I know," Allegra agreed. "I'm just not entirely sure what to say. Or if I'll be happy with whatever she has to say. We're night and day, Berta. She's a ridiculously attractive fitness instructor who lifted me like she was lifting a bottle of water. I'm…me. You'd need to add her and Hugo together plus some before you reached my own age. And there's Hugo, of course."

"Are you thinking of proposing?" Roberta asked. "Because I think you're getting quite ahead of yourself. She obviously sees something she likes in you to come to dinner and to escalate things. And she said she'd had fun and wanted to see you again. Just take it one step at a time, and stop throwing obstacles in your path."

"I'm not that kind of person," Allegra said. "I like certainty. I like to know what's happening now and what's happening next."

"Which explains why you haven't been in a relationship for years," Roberta pointed out. "And why you're jumping around like a child on a sugar high at the joy of having experienced some intimacy. Allie, you need to talk to her. Just so you know where you are. But don't go in there with every reason why you shouldn't be together and every reason why it won't work. I know you hate the idea, but you just have to let this run its course. The more you try to define it, the less likely there will be anything to define."

Allegra let out a long breath. She knew her friend was right. She'd always had a tendency to want a full roadmap of everything that was going to happen. From a case journey through the court schedule, through to Hugo's school trip to France. Certainty and detail were cornerstones of how she planned her life.

Any potential relationship with Lauren couldn't be smothered with that kind of pressure. She had to learn to embrace whatever it was or run the risk of losing it entirely. Even if it was nothing more than a brief sexual encounter, she would have to happily accept that. Lauren had made her feel things she'd thought were long gone. She'd felt attractive, wanted, sexual, and excited. Hours after, she'd been unable to wipe the smile from her face.

She wanted that feeling to last but knew she had to prepare for it to end. Somehow, the person with a need for absolute control would need to be happy with whatever came next. Even if that meant nothing at all. Or something casual, whatever that actually was. She'd never really understood the term.

"Go talk to her," Roberta said. "But don't expect a schedule of events. Just play it cool."

Allegra laughed. She'd never been accused of being cool in her life.

CHAPTER FOURTEEN

L auren noticed Hugo walk over to the scales and rolled her eyes. The boy was obsessed with weight, specifically his desire to lose some of it. She watched as he stood on the platform, squinted at the readout, and then dejectedly stepped away.

"Lost any weight since you weighed yourself when you arrived?" Lauren asked.

"I've put weight on!" Hugo said.

"That's life, bud." Lauren shrugged. "Your weight varies throughout the day, but as I keep telling you, weight isn't the be-all and end-all. You're doing great—you're stronger than you were when you started, and your stamina is so much better."

"I know," Hugo mumbled miserably.

"Muscle weighs more than fat," Lauren told him for what felt like the hundredth time. "You are losing weight. Trust me, I can see it."

His face lit up. "Really?"

Lauren sighed. She didn't want to reinforce his apparent need to lose weight. She had noticed that his muscle tone had become a little tighter, and some of the weight on his cheeks had definitely melted away. But Lauren wasn't about to tell him so and have him standing beside Kim in front of the mirrors all day.

"What's the hurry?" she asked.

"No hurry." He turned away and picked up his towel from where he'd hung it on a resistance machine.

He was a terrible liar. Lauren knew that he was desperate to lose weight, and every word and action he took backed that up. She hadn't fathomed out the root of his problem yet but suspected it was either the school bullies, or his own issues with the way he looked. Either way, she was working on him, slowly but surely.

"Like I said to you earlier, fitness is for life. You don't just go to the gym and tick it off your to-do list. You should be doing some kind of exercise for the rest of your life. It's a lifestyle."

"Like reading," he said. "The brain is a muscle, too."

"Sure. Anyway, time to go and shower. I'll see you before you leave."

She walked away from the cool-down area and almost straight into Allegra. Lauren couldn't help but smile. She'd been hoping she'd turn up at some point that day but wasn't sure if she might have scared her away.

"Hi, welcome to Jims. Would you like to sign up?" Lauren grinned.

Allegra looked around the building as if seriously considering it. "A lovely offer but I'm not here to sign up."

Lauren folded her arms and leaned against a pillar. "Oh, why are you here?"

She couldn't help but exchange quips with Allegra—it was fast becoming her favourite pastime.

"I'm picking up my son." Allegra grinned in return. "That's all."

"Shame, I thought it might be to see me."

"A nice bonus," Allegra admitted. "How was he? Was everything okay?"

Lauren looked over her shoulder to check Hugo had gone to shower and wasn't hovering around the scales instead. "Good, his stamina is building. I'm going to try some HIIT with him later, might see if I can get him interested in a spin class. He's obsessed with losing weight. Which he has done, even if he can't see it himself. All in all, he's doing well."

Allegra bit her lip. "I meant…did he say anything about last night? About us?"

"Oh, right." Lauren nodded. "Yeah, he asked. I told him I took you on the kitchen counter. Then we did some reps on the knee curl."

Allegra's complexion paled. Lauren kept her face neutral for as long as she could before she finally burst out laughing. Allegra slumped in relief and then hit Lauren on her upper arm. Lauren suspected it was supposed to be a real thump, but it just bounced off her like nothing.

"He didn't say anything, and neither did I."

Allegra smiled and shook her head. "I swear I'm not usually this gullible."

"It's cute," Lauren said.

The sound of Kim entering the gym and having a loud conversation on her mobile phone caused them both to look at the entrance. Kim blatantly looked Allegra up and down as she passed. Lauren couldn't believe how brazen Kim could be and just shook her head.

"That woman looks at me a lot," Allegra said, seemingly unaware of why.

"You're very hot," Lauren informed her.

Allegra blushed and ducked her head, seemingly not believing that to be a factor. Lauren wondered how Allegra could be blind to her own attractiveness. Kim was still on the phone but still admiring Allegra from across the gym.

"Lauren, call for Jim for you," Billy called out from the staffroom.

"I've got to take that in the office," Lauren said. She could see that Kim was eager to get off her call and was possibly planning to make a move on Allegra. The thought of Kim cuddling up to Allegra in order to use her and then spit her out again had Lauren gritting her teeth. "Join me?"

Allegra nodded and followed her towards the office. Lauren felt a little bad for blocking Kim from Allegra—it wasn't as though they were an exclusive item. Allegra could certainly make up her own mind about who she might want to see. In fact, Kim would probably be a better match, being both older and more financially successful than Lauren. But she wasn't about to help hand Allegra over to the wolf like that. She knew how Kim treated women, and if she could stop Allegra from becoming just another conquest, then she would.

In the back of her mind Lauren knew she was doing almost the same thing as Kim. There was no future relationship on the cards between her and Allegra—it would have to end eventually. But Lauren did hope that she'd be able to manage Allegra's delicate emotions better than Kim ever would.

She entered the office and picked up the phone, selecting the line that was flashing. She watched Allegra enter the office and look around with interest. Lauren half listened to the call, but mainly she watched Allegra.

Allegra walked with such grace and seemed almost otherworldly in comparison to the people Lauren saw on a daily basis. As usual, she wore her traditional barrister suit, and now that Lauren knew the riches it covered up, she wanted more than ever to tear it off her. She wondered if Allegra had any idea how alluring the buttoned-up outfit was. Probably not, she guessed.

But Lauren was beginning to realise that her interest wasn't simply sexual. Allegra fascinated her, as she was so different to the people Lauren usually dated. Even if it couldn't last for long, Lauren fully intended to enjoy it while it did.

"Sure, I'll pass on the message," Lauren said, ending her call. She hung up the phone and then called the staffroom. "Hey Billy, that was the Women's Institute. Jot this down, will you? They want to move their yoga classes on Thursday and Friday to five thirty, and then they want the spin studio after that on Thursday for a spin class with Alex. From the fifteenth of next month, they'd like to have the eleven o'clock Pilates moved to Wednesdays. They are changing the number of people for the cardio session on Tuesday from eleven to fourteen, and they have three referrals for full memberships who will want to talk to someone at the Zumba class tomorrow."

She made sure Billy had all the information he needed and then hung up the phone.

"Good memory," Allegra commented.

"Sorry?"

"That you remembered all of that without taking notes."

"Notes are for wimps," Lauren joked.

"As is filing, I'm guessing." Allegra gestured to the stacks of paperwork.

"Jim is away, and I'm running things while he's out. Things get a little hectic. I'll clear it up later." Lauren looked at the desk and realised that in a very short amount of time, she'd created what could be referred to as a health and safety violation. She'd been moving stacks of paper from one place to another as she had no idea what to file where. Thankfully, Anna was due to come in that afternoon. "Most of it is just filing," she added.

Allegra pointed to an envelope which had been haphazardly thrown on the desk. "Well, that one you might want to look at."

Lauren looked at the bold red letters and lifted a shoulder casually. "I'll get to it later." She walked around the desk, planting herself between Allegra and the mountains of paperwork. "More importantly, when can I see you again?"

A blush touched Allegra's cheeks, and she looked away. "Hopefully soon, I am busy but I'm certain I can find some time."

"I hope so." Lauren reached out and touched one of the strips of white material that hung from the front of Allegra's crisp white shirt. "What is this?"

Allegra looked down at her front. "Bands, part of the collarette."

"And that means...?"

"It's part of the uniform," Allegra explained. "Lets people know I'm a barrister, in case they were in any doubt. It's historically significant."

"So, do you wear one of those white curly wigs?"

"I do sometimes. Depending on the court."

"What does that mean?"

"Well, we're not required to wear them in a civil case, or a family case."

Lauren stared at the strip of material for a second and realised what different worlds they came from. Allegra casually mentioned court, criminal cases, and judges as if they were commonplace, but to Lauren those words had extra meaning. She'd never been to court, never had to address a judge, never been accused of a crime. But even the thought of any of those things made her palms clammy.

She reminded herself that it didn't matter. It wasn't as if they were a serious item. They were just having some fun, and it was nothing more serious than that. They'd be ships that passed in the night and never needed to know too much about each other's worlds. In fact, it was probably good for both of them to experience the other side of the coin for a short while. A thought occurred to her, something that had her smiling.

"How about bowling?" Lauren asked.

"Bowling?" Allegra blinked.

"Sure, it will be fun. I think we should go somewhere public, you know, so I can make sure you keep your hands to yourself. Try to get you to behave." Lauren winked.

Allegra narrowed her eyes. "I had very little to do with…what happened."

Lauren surged closer to Allegra. "I disagree. You had a *lot* to do with what happened."

Allegra licked her lips and swallowed. Lauren loved how easily she could extract a reaction from her. It was a power play, and Lauren felt no shame in asserting it whenever she felt like it. Allegra clearly enjoyed it. She wondered when the last time was someone flirted with Allegra. She acted like it was a long time ago.

"I'm not sure about bowling," Allegra admitted.

"It will be fun. Something for Hugo to do, as well. I'll teach you." Lauren glanced towards the door and couldn't see anyone around. She leaned in and placed a kiss on Allegra's jawline, as low as she could go before the collar impeded her. She was discovering that traditional dress was a turn-on.

"Fine, but I warn you that I'm no good at bowling," Allegra whispered.

Lauren leaned back. "That's fine. I just want to watch you from behind as you bowl."

Allegra chuckled. "You're shameless."

"You're gorgeous." Lauren closed the gap between them and

kissed her properly on the mouth this time. It was messy, and she wished she had time for more, but she'd already heard the thud of the men's shower room door closing and knew Hugo was on his way.

She ended the kiss as abruptly as she'd started it and walked around the desk at the very second Hugo walked in. Seeing Allegra dazed and attempting to look as if nothing had been happening was a picture. Lauren couldn't help but smile to herself at the perfect timing.

"Hey, Mum," Hugo said. "What's for dinner?"

Allegra blinked a couple of times. "I've...forgotten."

Hugo frowned. "Are you okay?"

"Yes, yes." Allegra reached out and put an arm around him and pulled him in close. It looked like affection, but Lauren suspected it was so Hugo couldn't see his mother's flushed expression.

"How is next Monday?" Allegra asked.

"Sure, I'll book a lane and move my shift so we can go after Hugo's session," Lauren said.

"Lane?" Hugo asked.

"We're going bowling," Lauren explained. "All three of us."

Hugo's eyes widened in excitement and he stared up at Allegra. "Really?"

"Really." Allegra nodded.

"Awesome, I'm going to kick your butt," Hugo told Lauren.

"Hugo!" Allegra admonished.

Lauren simply laughed. "It's cute that you think so, bud."

"You can't be good at everything," Hugo replied.

Lauren stared squarely at Allegra. "Yes, I can."

Allegra swallowed again. "Right, time to go," she announced and angled Hugo towards the door.

"See you on Monday," Lauren said.

Hugo said goodbye. Allegra simply looked at her, presumably unsure what to say. A moment later they were both gone.

Lauren chuckled to herself as she sat down in Jim's chair and realised that she was very much looking forward to Monday.

She looked at the envelope on the desk that Allegra had pointed out. Sighing, she leaned forward and picked it up. She opened it up and took a quick glance at the letter inside. Bold red text came into sight. She quickly folded the letter back up, stuffed it into the envelope, and put it into the desk drawer.

That would be a problem for Anna.

CHAPTER FIFTEEN

Lauren put the phone down and looked around the messy desk. As luck would have it, Billy entered the office at that moment.

"Billy, can you do me a favour? I need to make an urgent phone call," Lauren explained.

"Sure. What do you need?" He stood in front of the desk, eager and ready for a task.

"Can you look through the post and find the invoice from Water City? Then can you take a photo of it and send it to Jim? I would just pay it later, but you know Jim. He wants to check it over first." Lauren hated lying to Billy. He was a sweet kid and willing to do anything for anyone, which was one of the main reasons Lauren asked him to do this sort of thing. It was easy to avoid certain jobs when someone as enthusiastic as Billy was always on standby to jump into action.

"No problem." Billy grabbed a pile of unopened letters and started flipping through them with speed.

"Thanks, Billy. You're a star. I better go and make that phone call." Lauren picked up her mobile and gestured towards the gym floor. Billy distractedly nodded as he continued to seek out the invoice.

Hugo was walking into the gym, and Lauren blinked in surprise. She took a look at the clock on the wall and realised that she'd spent far too much of the afternoon stressing about paperwork.

Anna had called the previous week, moments before she was

due to come in, to say that she was held up and wouldn't make it that day. She said she'd be in touch as soon as possible, but while Lauren waited, the paperwork was building up, and she was having to contact Jim about some of the more urgent matters. She hated to do that.

It was good to get back to her real job.

"Hey," she called out to Hugo.

"Mum's cancelled bowling tonight," Hugo said dejectedly.

Lauren wasn't prepared for the deep disappointment that statement caused. She'd been looking forward to the night out, and now she felt strangely empty.

"Oh. How come?"

"Some last-minute thing in court," Hugo muttered. "She's the duty barrister this week. She said that she'll be there late."

Lauren didn't really understand, but she nodded anyway. "Do you know how late she'll be?"

Hugo shrugged.

Lauren smothered a smile. He was behaving like someone several years younger than he was. She hoped that meant that he was looking forward to going bowling as much as she was.

"Can you call her?" Lauren asked.

He dug around in his school rucksack and took out his phone. He swiped and made the call. "This happens a lot," he told her as the phone rang. "I know that she gets busy sometimes. She does an important job."

"But it's still frustrating?" Lauren guessed.

He nodded. "Hey, Jake, is Mum there?"

He lowered the phone a little. "Maybe we can go bowling instead? Just you and me?"

Lauren grinned. "That kinda wasn't what I was aiming for, sorry, buddy."

Hugo grimaced, but there was a hint of a smile hidden within his expression. Lauren hoped that meant that Hugo was as astute as she suspected him to be, and he'd worked out why she and his mum were spending time together. It would certainly make things easier in the long run if Hugo understood and was on board from the start.

"Hey, Mum. Yeah, I'm fine. No, no problems." He rolled his eyes. "Lauren wanted to talk to you. Okay, I'll hand you over."

He held out the phone to Lauren and picked up his rucksack. "I'm gonna go get changed."

"Cool. I'm gonna steal this top-of-the-line iPhone. See you never." She took the phone and chuckled at his sigh when he left. "Hey there, bigshot. Can't come to the lanes with us mere mortals?"

"I'm sorry. Something came up." Allegra sounded apologetic enough, and so Lauren's fears that she was being blown off were allayed.

"Do you know what time you'll be there until?" Lauren asked.

Allegra hesitated a moment as if the question was unexpected, then said, "I'm not sure. No later than half past six, I imagine."

"I could move our booking," Lauren offered. "If you still want to go after work, that is. I understand if you don't. Just offering. Hugo seems pretty miserable about it being cancelled."

"I bet he is. He's been talking about it all weekend," Allegra said. "If you don't mind starting later, then I can do that. I have a change of clothes in the office, and then I can come to the gym, but that might take a while longer."

Lauren realised that Allegra would have to drive all the way across town to then drive all the way to the other side to get to the bowling alley. It seemed like a lot of wasted time and stress for someone who was working late anyway.

"How about Hugo and I come to you?" Lauren suggested. "Then we can all go on together."

"Are you sure you don't mind?" Allegra asked in a tone that suggested that would be the perfect solution to the problem.

"You concentrate on whatever it is you do," Lauren said. "We'll see you at work later, okay?"

"Thank you, Lauren. I appreciate that. I'll see you later."

Lauren ended the call and felt lighter for having rescued her evening plans. It was only bowling, but she'd been looking forward to getting to know Allegra a little better and maybe putting a plan into action to have a repeat performance of their first night sometime soon. That evening had occupied her thoughts over the weekend, and Lauren was keen to keep the momentum rolling. She was even looking forward to spending more time with Hugo. Even if he was trusting enough to hand a fifteen-hundred-pound phone to a stranger.

She looked down at his phone in her hand and realised that she wasn't a stranger to Hugo any more. It was the first time she'd really thought about it, and it brought a smile to her lips.

❖

Lauren looked around the austere marble lobby of the town Crown Court in wonderment. She'd never been there before and was in a little bit of shock about how big and grand the building was. She was used to public buildings being a little run-down and unloved, but that couldn't be said for the court, which was as grand as it must have been when it had been built over a hundred years ago.

The large echo chamber amplified the important-sounding footsteps of well-dressed members of the bar. Heavy wooden doors lined the lobby, and Lauren imagined that was where the courtrooms were.

Hugo walked over to a bench and sat down as if he was simply taking a seat in a public library. He seemed as at home in the legal environment as he had been on the bus over. The security guard nodded a greeting to him, and Hugo smiled politely back.

Lauren hated to admit to herself that she was a little uncomfortable, but the imposing surroundings were doing exactly what they had been built to do all those years ago—convey seriousness. She stood by the bench where Hugo sat and looked around at the domed ceiling, impressive chandeliers, and magnificent staircase that led to an upper floor.

"Hey, Hugo."

Lauren looked at the young man who had greeted Hugo. He wore a smart suit and held bundles of papers in his hand. He clearly knew Hugo, and Lauren wondered who he was.

"Hey, Jake," Hugo said. "Where's Mum?"

"Court one," Jake replied. "She won't be long. Let me know if you want to wait in her chambers."

"We're good here, thanks, though." Hugo got his headphones and a book out of his bag like he was getting ready for a long but familiar wait.

Jake nodded politely to Lauren and continued on his way.

Hugo looked up at Lauren. "You can watch if you like."

"Watch?" Lauren asked.

"There's a visitor's gallery." Hugo gestured to the stairs with a nod of his head. "Bob will pat you down, but you can go upstairs and watch as long as you're super quiet. It's pretty cool."

Lauren looked at the stairs and then back at Hugo. "You don't want to watch?"

"I've seen it a thousand times," he said. "But you should watch. It can be cool. Sometimes. Sometimes it's boring."

Lauren looked to the stairs again. "You'll be okay here on your own?"

"Yeah, this is like my second home," Hugo said. "I've been coming here since I was four."

He put his earbuds in, attached the lead to his phone, and sat back as comfortably as someone could on a hard wooden bench in a public building. Lauren decided she had the choice of sitting next to him or sneaking a look into the court. Her curiosity had been piqued. She didn't really understand what Allegra did, and the thought of seeing her in her ridiculous wig and gown was appealing. She'd probably get a lot of wig jokes out of it, and she could already see Allegra's half-hearted sigh in her mind's eye. She loved making Allegra laugh, or even smile. The way her eyes lit up was enchanting, and the prospect of getting that response was enticing.

Lauren left her bag with Hugo and headed up the stairs. In the upper gallery she was presented with more large wooden doors, all with plaques above them. She found court one and approached the security guard by the door.

"Visitor gallery?" he asked.

"Yes, please."

"Do you have any weapons or projectiles?"

Lauren smothered a smile at the obvious question and wondered if anyone who had brought anything to throw had ever actually admitted to it. She shook her head.

He gestured for her to lift her arms up and then waved a security wand around her body.

"You been here before?" he asked when he was satisfied that she wasn't carrying anything troublesome.

"Nope."

"Take a seat as soon as you can, no milling about. No talking. No phone calls. Phone on silent. No distracting anyone in the court below."

Lauren nodded. "Got it."

He opened the door for her, and Lauren gingerly stepped into the gallery. Two rows of seats were in front of her, and she was immediately taken back to the one time she ever went to the theatre. The only ticket she could afford was up in the circle with a bird's eye view of the stage. The court gallery had a lot in common with a theatre, and she could hear the mumble of the actors below her.

She made her way to the front seat and looked at her new surroundings. The room was large and imposing with Italian-style columns framing the circular room. The ornately decorated domed ceiling was mesmerising. She looked down and saw the Victorian-style wooden tables and desks. It looked like a television drama, or maybe a television drama looked like reality. She couldn't be certain any more.

Lauren spotted the judge, sitting behind a raised desk in a high-backed leather chair. He wore a curly white wig, a black robe, and a red sash. His glasses were perched on the end of his nose, and he leaned comfortably in his chair, looking imperiously down at the four people in front of him.

A male barrister with his female assistant and Allegra with her own female assistant sat in a row opposite the judge behind their own set of old-looking wooden benches. All wore black gowns and wigs. Lauren had expected to think they all looked ridiculous, but in the serious setting she realised that she thought the opposite. They didn't look out of place at all. She had only travelled a few steps but was suddenly transported into the world of the law where everything she was witnessing somehow made complete sense.

"Mr. Hatton," the judge said, "please do proceed. Briefly, if at all possible. The last time we were here on this matter, counsel didn't go home for seven weeks."

The male barrister, Hatton, stood and spoke. "My Lord, this is of course a straightforward and very simple case. A case as narrow as it is wide, tall as it is long, black as it is white, and indeed as open as it is shut."

Lauren hated him immediately. He was the typical windbag that she'd expected to see in such surroundings. He was saying a lot, but none of it made any sense. Lauren assumed he enjoyed the sound of his own voice.

"Mr. Hatton, please proceed to the point," the judge said.

"If counsel requires any assistance on that matter, I'd be happy to provide him with directions." Allegra stood momentarily as she spoke before taking her seat again.

Hatton looked at Allegra with nothing more than a raised eyebrow before continuing. "The plaintiff, Mrs. Sharon Durrand, or Miss Sharon Shields, as she was at the time when the wrong was indeed committed and her rights were infringed—"

"Alleged wrongs, My Lord," Allegra interrupted as she got to her feet. "And alleged rights."

"Indeed, Mrs. Whittaker, indeed. Please continue, Mr. Hatton," the judge said.

Allegra sat down. Lauren looked at her and frowned. The judge had called her Mrs. Whittaker. Lauren realised in that moment that she didn't know anything about Allegra's past. Was she married? Divorced? Or even widowed? There was also the question as to Hugo's father.

Lauren hadn't thought she'd be around long enough to even want to find out much about Allegra's background. Most of her relationships were shallow, to say the least. Little more than a few sexual encounters. Fun, but never anything that involved getting to know someone on a personal level.

Now Lauren was confused and intrigued. Questions she usually didn't ask were bubbling away below the surface. She supposed that was to be expected if she was going to be involved with a mother. Not that she'd be *that* involved. If she needed any further proof that they were from different worlds and would never work out, then this was definitely it. Lauren was happy to have some fun while Allegra discovered how different they were and how they would never make a good long-term match. Both would have fun for a while and then go their separate ways with no harm done.

Lauren couldn't help but smile as Allegra interrupted Mr. Hatton and his ridiculously long speeches. She sparred gently but respectfully with the judge and made comments that had Lauren hiding a snigger behind her hand.

She was confident and magnificent, a complete change from what Lauren saw when she nervously visited the gym. She realised that this was the real Allegra Whittaker. Capable, intelligent, willing to stand up for the right of her client and say whatever needed to be said.

Most of the events happening below her went right over Lauren's head. But in the middle of it all was the strong suspicion that Allegra was winning the case, whatever it was.

Hatton had spoken for a while, and Lauren realised he was addressing a jury that was seated underneath the gallery so she couldn't see them. She wondered if they were as bored as she was, considering how long he had droned on for.

Finally, Allegra stood. "My Lord, members of the jury, those of us who have homes to return to, admirers of the art of brevity, we who have sat here for the last three hours, and the unfortunate few who parked their cars in the short-term parking lot. Allow me to keep this brief, for it needs very little in the way of summing up."

Lauren smiled and sat back in her chair. Allegra was funny. Not just when playing off Lauren's own backchat but in her own right.

She spoke with ease and comfort, and Lauren felt a sense of deep pride that she actually knew this woman. That she was about to take her out on a date.

She was also extremely turned-on. Knowing how easily she could turn Allegra from this impressive woman into a ball of nerves was thrilling. She watched the rest of the summing up in captivated silence.

CHAPTER SIXTEEN

Allegra entered her chambers with Jake hurrying to catch up. She stopped in the doorway when she saw Lauren standing by the window.

"Um. Ms. Evans said she needed to speak with you," Jake explained.

"I do," Lauren confirmed.

There was a cheekiness to her that Allegra didn't trust but certainly did enjoy. She turned to Jake and took the paperwork from his hand. "Thank you, that will be all."

Jake hesitated for a moment before backing out of the office and closing the door behind them.

Allegra threw the paperwork down on the desk and removed her court wig.

"Where's Hugo?"

"Court six. Bound to get ten years, at least," Lauren joked.

Allegra cocked her head slightly and looked at Lauren for a moment to indicate she expected a real answer sometime soon.

"He's texting with his friend in the lobby. Something about a new update for his game that will take—and I quote—forever to download." Lauren sat on the sofa under the window and grinned.

Allegra winced. "Let's hope it's not like the update last month which took an entire evening. He complained endlessly." She placed her wig on the stand and took off her gown.

"You were great," Lauren said.

"You were in the gallery?" Allegra hadn't seen her, but then she rarely looked up into the gallery any more. For the first six months or so she found the coming and going of onlookers to be distracting, but these days she didn't give it a second thought.

"You were so sassy with the judge," Lauren continued. "I thought you'd be locked up."

Allegra laughed. "Hardly. There's a line, of course, and respect is demanded. But we banter with one another in much the same way you do with your work colleagues. The judges are like a senior management, and counsel is like a colleague I occasionally need to argue with. Sometimes like an irritating younger brother, too."

She shook her head. Lawrence Hatton was a nice enough man, but he did love the sound of his own voice and would rather bore a jury into submission than win the case on merit.

"Who was the guy?" Lauren asked. She pointed to the closed door.

"Jake? He's my clerk. Like an assistant but—"

"I notice he's a redhead," Lauren continued. "Not that it's any of my business."

Allegra didn't know what Lauren was referring to, but judging by Lauren's failed attempt at looking casual, she imagined that it was something rather sensitive. "I'm not sure what you're asking."

A hint of a blush touched Lauren's cheeks. "I mean, well, Hugo has some red in his hair…"

Allegra blinked and then burst out laughing. "Jake? He's…he's barely thirty-five. And he's my clerk!" She continued laughing at the very thought of Jake being Hugo's father. The very idea was quite hysterical.

Lauren stood up and sauntered over. "Okay, okay, it's not that funny."

"It really is," Allegra told her. "You think our eyes met across the tribunal list and we couldn't keep our hands off one another? Lord, he would have been barely twenty-one, and I'd have been… old enough to know better. No, Jake is not Hugo's father. I don't know who Hugo's father was."

"Oh." Lauren stopped in her tracks and swallowed.

"He's adopted," Allegra explained before Lauren's mind went to an unpleasant place. "And yes, he does know."

"You adopted him?" Lauren's face was unreadable.

"Yes. When he was a baby." Allegra couldn't tell what Lauren was thinking. It was as if she'd shut down in some way. Allegra knew that people were often surprised to discover that Hugo wasn't her biological son but wondered what was going through Lauren's mind there and then.

There was a knock on the door that broke the mood. Lauren turned and walked towards one of the bookcases and tapped a statue of Lady Justice that sat on the shelf.

"Come in," Allegra called out.

The door opened and Jake stepped in. "Sorry to interrupt, but Mr. Hatton would like to know if you'd be free for breakfast tomorrow."

"Tell Mr. Hatton that I'll be free if he has a reasonable offer to present me with this time and not just a revisit of what he offered this morning."

Jake nodded, backed out of the room, and closed the door.

"It's a strange world that you work in," Lauren said.

"I might say the same about you," Allegra replied. "A spin class is around twenty people in tight clothes sitting on bikes and pedalling to get absolutely nowhere while someone shouts at them to keep going. To me, that's very abnormal."

Lauren smiled. "True, very true. Why did the judge call you Mrs. Whittaker? I knew you were hiding a husband somewhere in that big house."

Allegra saw through the bluster and cheeky smile to the concern beneath Lauren's gaze. It was clear that she'd swum well out of her comfort zone and into Allegra's deep ocean with its rituals and serious consequences.

"It's a formality. All women barristers are Mrs. in English law—it's starting to change, but our judges are very much stuck in their ways. No husband, or wife, I assure you." Allegra started to pack up the items on her desk. "Do you still want to go bowling, or did the wig put you off?"

"Would you wear the wig at the alley if I asked you nicely?" Lauren quipped.

Allegra smiled at the signal that Lauren was becoming more comfortable.

"No, but I do need to get changed, and that means you need to leave." She pointed to the door. "I'll meet you and Hugo in the lobby."

"Aww. I could stay and help." Lauren wiggled her eyebrows.

Allegra's pulse beat faster at the flirtatious comment. "I have a feeling you'd be more of a hindrance, and my son is waiting for us." She didn't want to leave Hugo waiting, nor did she want to risk being intimate in her chambers in case they were discovered. But she had to admit, the thought was sorely tempting.

"True. I'll go and wait with him." Lauren walked over to her and placed a very soft and respectful kiss on her cheek. "To keep me going," she whispered.

Allegra's resolve was close to splintering into pieces, but she managed to hold on as Lauren left the room. The moment the door clicked closed and she was left alone, she fell into her chair and let out a breath.

From absolute calm and control to feeling like she was tumbling out of control, she should have felt upset by Lauren's effect on her. But she didn't. The unexpected twists and turns of their discussions and how they made her feel were as invigorating as they were terrifying.

It was like being on a ride at the fairground. And she didn't want it to stop.

❖

"Don't tell her about the thing we discussed," Allegra told Hugo in a hushed tone as they exited the car in the bowling alley car park.

Hugo grinned at her before looking over to the other side of the car where Lauren was getting out.

"I'm serious, don't tell her." Allegra tried again.

It was a risk to remind him of the conversation that they'd had that morning and the endless laughter that had ensued at her expense. But the equal risk was that he'd remember later and tell Lauren anyway. Hugo thought it was hilarious how out of touch his mother was, and while Allegra usually wouldn't care about it, this time she was trying to impress Lauren.

"What are you two whispering about?" Lauren asked.

"Mum confused boules and bowling," Hugo announced. "She didn't know which one bowling was until I explained."

Allegra shook her head. "Less than five seconds. Thank you, darling."

Lauren grinned. "Really? You didn't know what bowling was?"

Allegra locked the car and dropped her car keys into her handbag. "As much as this may surprise you, I'm not exactly the bowling alley type."

"I had to tell her to wear jeans," Hugo added.

"I'm glad you did." Lauren looked down at Allegra suggestively, and she felt her cheeks heat up. Hugo was a few steps ahead of them and none the wiser.

"I didn't tell her about the shoes, though," Hugo said. "I'm going to the bathroom—see you in a minute."

The moment they were inside, he ran off. Allegra stopped dead and took in her surroundings. To her right were the bowling lanes, in the distance in front of her was some kind of restaurant, and all around her were noisy arcade machines. It wasn't her thing at all, but she knew beyond a doubt that Hugo would love every moment of it.

She wondered when they had stopped doing things like this. It was certainly longer ago than she could recall. At some point, Allegra had stopped pretending to enjoy things that were out of her comfort zone, and Hugo had stopped wanting to go places.

"Noisy enough for you?" Lauren asked.

"It takes a little getting used to," Allegra admitted. "What was Hugo talking about? Shoes?"

Lauren pointed down at Allegra's shoes. They were as sporty as Allegra got, not a sports brand of trainers but a fashion brand's attempt at some. Mum shoes, Hugo called them.

"As nice as they are," Lauren said in a tone that clearly indicated she didn't think they were nice at all, "they will have to come off, and you'll be given a fabulously stylish pair of lane shoes."

"Lane shoes?" Allegra asked.

"So you can walk on the lane without damaging it, and so you can slide like a pro."

"I don't think I want to slide like a pro."

"You have no choice." Lauren pointed towards a reception desk with rack upon rack of depressing little shoes shoved into unsanitary wooden boxes. "What size are you?"

"But I like my shoes," Allegra said. She wished that she didn't sound like a child but also hoped she would be spared the pain of communal shoes.

Lauren laughed. "If you really don't want to, then you don't have to play, but I think watching Hugo and me play will be boring. They clean them."

Allegra could easily detect a note of doubt in Lauren's tone at the last statement. She looked around at the teenagers and families happily playing on the arcade machines or eating greasy food at the lanes. She was out of her comfort zone, and she wondered if that was the point. Had Lauren deliberately brought her to a place where she'd be a fish out of water to see how she coped?

"Six," Allegra said, deciding that she was going to do her best to fit in despite her concerns.

"Right here?" Lauren asked, wiggling her eyebrows.

"I'm a size six," Allegra repeated, rolling her eyes.

"And the little one?" Lauren asked.

"Seven."

"Aww, he has bigger feet than you, cute," Lauren said.

"I remember when his shoes could fit in the palm of my hand, and now one left in the hallway could easily trip me up." Allegra sighed. Hugo's growth spurt and journey towards adulthood hadn't been sudden nor unexpected, and yet it had seemed to arrive without her realising.

Hugo appeared next to them. "What lane are we on?"

"I haven't checked us in yet," Lauren said. "I had to tell your mum the bad news about the shoes—thanks for dumping that on me, by the way."

Hugo grinned. "Well, if you two start dating, then you'll have to get used to that."

The breath left Allegra's lungs. She'd deliberately said very little to Hugo in the hope that he wouldn't come to such a conclusion. She wondered if Lauren had maybe said something to him to encourage the thought. It seemed doubtful as Lauren was presumably sensible enough not to put ideas into a teenager's head. Not to mention that she still didn't really know where Lauren stood on the matter of…them.

If there even was a them.

"Thanks for the dating advice, Hugo," Lauren said. "Although I think I'm doing okay with my own approach."

Allegra felt more confused than ever. She'd wondered what they were and where they were going, but now the desire to know was causing her to crawl out of her skin. The need to know was so strong that she reached into her handbag and pulled out her purse. She handed it to Hugo while she pointed to the arcade machines.

"Go and play while we check in," she instructed in a tone that left no room for argument.

Hugo took the purse with wide, excited eyes and rushed away.

The moment he was far enough away to be unable to hear them speaking, she turned to Lauren and asked, "What are we?"

She saw the trace of a joke on Lauren's lips, but it quickly vanished again when Lauren's eyes met hers and saw the seriousness within them.

"I don't know, I thought we were figuring that out," Lauren said. She gestured around the bowling alley. "You know, dating and stuff."

"To what end?" Allegra asked. "Because if you want nothing

more than another encounter in my kitchen, then I'd like to know. It's not a problem, but please don't string me along for nothing more than that. Especially if we're to involve Hugo in this. I need to know. What we are?"

Her emotions from the past few days finally bubbled over the top. Allegra liked to know what was happening. She liked plans and schedules, and she liked her life to be neat and tidy. Lauren was not neat and tidy. Lauren was chaos. Fun, sexy chaos. Allegra just needed to know what was going on in Lauren's head. She wanted to know if there was a point in getting emotionally invested in whatever they were doing, or not.

Lauren licked her lips a little nervously. "I don't know. I hadn't really thought of it. I don't usually present a business plan on the second date. What do *you* want from this?"

With the question returned so deftly, Allegra realised she had no idea. The sex had been amazing, and she'd certainly like more of it, but she wasn't the kind of person who had nothing but a sexual relationship with someone. She didn't know how she'd handle that. Her heart automatically engaged in whatever it was she did. It would be impossible to let Lauren go as easily as she'd wormed her way in.

An arcade machine jolted her out of her thoughts with its winning klaxon. It brought her back to the present and where she was and what she was asking of Lauren. Lauren was different to her. She didn't need a schedule and a destination—Lauren didn't have the answers she sought. No one did.

"I'm sorry. I…I don't really know myself. I just…" She sighed and pinched the bridge of her nose. She'd made a mess of things. Her need to be in control was ruining a perfectly nice evening.

"I don't know you very well," Lauren said. "But I can tell you're not the kind of person who usually has sex on a first date. And I kind of get the impression that you haven't seen anyone for a long while."

Allegra scoffed and laughed uncomfortably at the accurate assessment of her woeful dating status.

"I don't know what the future has for us," Lauren continued.

"But I want to get to know you. I don't know how that will end up—that's up to you, me, and Hugo. I kinda see it that the three of us will have some fun, like bowling or going to see a film, and then you and I will have a different kind of fun. If that's what you want."

It was exactly what Allegra wanted. Ideally, she'd have a full plan outlined in advance in the same way Jake arranged her calendar. But she had to be realistic. Life didn't work that way no matter how much that irritated her.

"I'm sorry, I'm a mess," she said. "You're right. I haven't done this kind of thing for a very long time, and I basically thought I wouldn't ever do it again."

She swallowed. She'd never admitted that aloud before. Dating horrified her. The whole song and dance about when to call someone back, when to show interest, when to admit love. It all felt like a difficult game that she'd never managed to master, and she would always end up losing her heart over it.

As a mother, she didn't have the luxury of a broken heart.

Lauren reached out and took her hand. "Let's just see where things go, yeah? Have some fun and see what happens."

Allegra chuckled. "You're the second person to tell me to have some fun."

"Then it sounds like that's what you need to do," Lauren said. "I'll get us all checked in. You go and rescue your purse from Hugo before you have to sell that nice house of yours."

Allegra's eyes widened at the realisation that she had let a teenager run wild in an arcade.

❖

Allegra fastened the Velcro strap of her shoe and shuddered. The shoes were everything she'd hoped they wouldn't be. Ugly, deeply uncomfortable, and moist.

Beside her, Hugo had put his shoes on in an instant and was now picking up bowling balls and giving a running commentary on which colours related to which weights. All of which was going right over her head.

"Bud, how about you set us up?" Lauren suggested, gesturing to a keyboard with her head.

Allegra watched as Lauren removed the inner sole of her bowling shoe and looked at it with a critical eye.

"Problem?" Allegra asked.

"No, just thought I felt a stone or something." Lauren put the inner sole back and shrugged. "So, do you want the lane guards up like the woman in the red top?"

Allegra turned around to see the *woman* in question was three years old at best. "Yes, please," Allegra said. "And that metal ramp device would seem to make the whole thing far easier."

Lauren laughed. "How about, we'll see how you get on? I mean, I'm not saying we won't get you a ramp, but we'll see how bad you are first."

Allegra appreciated how quickly they had fallen back into casual chatter. She was very aware that it was all down to Lauren. She'd tried to reason as to why she felt so stressed about the idea of dating and could only come to one conclusion—she liked Lauren's company. It was a bit of a problem because she knew they were supposed to be casually seeing how things went, but Allegra had always been surefooted about what she wanted in life. Lauren was fun to be around, she challenged the boring status quo of Allegra's life, and Hugo adored her.

Being alone for so long and then suddenly realising what she could have enjoyed all that time was eye-opening. She realised that she'd been missing out and now wanted to experience it all. She was also terrified. Terrified of what someone new in her life meant, what her responsibilities towards Lauren would be, and what the future looked like.

In short, she felt like a teenager. And that irked her greatly because she had spent a lot of time growing older and moving away from such thoughts and the fact that one woman could throw her back into the depths of emotional uncertainty was confusing at best.

"Done," Hugo announced. "I'm first."

Lauren quickly slid on her shoes, did them up, and stood. Allegra watched as Lauren and Hugo stood side by side and chatted about which ball to use and what strategy to employ. It was refreshing to see someone taking such an active interest in Hugo. Allegra had friends who would talk to Hugo, but Lauren was different. When Lauren spoke to Hugo, it was like a friend, but a friend with authority.

A typical teenager, Hugo would now and then try to push the limits of what was acceptable. It was part of the growing-up process and one that Allegra hadn't particularly enjoyed. Sometimes his jokes hit a little too sharply or sometimes his demands were inconsiderate. It had taken a while to learn to navigate this new person, a child slowly becoming a man.

Lauren didn't seem to have such problems. She easily managed the conversation and kept Hugo engaged, happy, and yet still in his place. It was easy to see that Hugo respected Lauren as well as considered her a friend.

And that was incredibly attractive.

"You going to sit there all day?" Lauren asked her playfully.

"It's not my go," Allegra replied, pointing to the screen above. "Hugo, you, and then me. A little more time before I demonstrate my lack of skills."

Lauren narrowed her eyes. "You know, I wonder if you're faking. If you suddenly want to put a bet down, I'm not falling for it. Just so you know."

Allegra laughed. "You saw through me, I'm in a bowling group."

"Uh-huh." Lauren grinned. "They're called leagues."

"Will you two just play?" Hugo demanded with a sigh.

Allegra smiled at the small grin she could see her son desperately trying to hide.

"Go ahead, darling," Allegra said. "Show us all how it's done."

Hugo picked up a ball. He walked to the line, turned to check they were both still watching him, and then bowled.

He'd been bowling a few times with school and with friends, but Allegra was still impressed at the action and the fact that five of the ten pins fell.

"I suck," Hugo announced.

"You got half!" Allegra said. "That's a fifty percent success rate."

"You're not into sports, are you?" Lauren asked her, deadpan.

"That's not the point. He got half."

Lauren smiled. "I really like you."

Allegra blushed and opened and closed her mouth a few times while she figured out what to say to that. Thankfully, Lauren did what she excelled in and took any awkwardness out of the situation by ignoring Allegra's confusion.

Lauren approached Hugo. "It's not about being all macho with a heavy ball—it's about technique. You have the technique, but you're thrown off-track by the weight of the ball. Try the purple one."

Hugo looked uncertain but did as he was instructed.

"Don't look at the dots," Lauren said. "Look at the arrows halfway up the lane—that's what you're really aiming for."

Hugo started his next run up, and Lauren continued coaching him as he did.

"Perfect. Now go low. Lower. Look at the arrows."

Allegra stood to get a better view. The ball trundled down the lane, much slower this time. It inched its way towards the pins, and Allegra found she was holding her breath in the hope that it would collide in the right way and knock over the remaining pins. She'd gathered that complete success was all that mattered in this game. At least, that seemed to be the case with the people she was playing with.

The ball hit its target, causing a chain reaction that saw the remaining pins fall. Hugo jumped for joy, and Lauren high-fived him. Allegra pulled him into a hug and congratulated him. She knew that it was far less cool, but she was his mother, and she'd not lost all hope of the occasional cuddle just yet.

Once the excitement had died down, Lauren was up. She held the ball close to her face and eyed the pins. Just as she was about to take her shot, she paused and turned to face Allegra.

"If I get a strike, will you have dinner with me tomorrow night?"

Allegra's heart fluttered. She wanted dinner with Lauren no matter how many of the damn pins she knocked down.

"Okay," Allegra agreed casually.

Lauren smiled and turned back to face the pins.

Allegra looked at Hugo and whispered, "What's a strike?"

Hugo rolled his eyes. "Mum, you don't know that?"

"Would I be asking?"

"It's knocking all the pins down in one go."

Allegra raised her eyebrows and returned her attention to Lauren. She had released the ball and was watching it speed its way down the lane. Allegra held her breath, never more invested in a ball in her life.

A wisp of a memory of the last dinner they shared flashed in her mind. The sex had been great and whether that was because Lauren was a talented lover or because Allegra was starved for touch she didn't know. Nor care.

All but one pin fell.

She leaned forward with her breath caught in her chest as she watched the pin wobble but eventually right itself. Allegra hated the little block of wood with a passion.

Lauren turned, and for a moment their eyes met in an understanding that the pin was evil. Lauren shrugged. "Maybe next time?"

Lauren made quick work of the pin on her second go, smashing it the back wall of the lane with a precision that made Allegra jump.

"Good luck," Hugo whispered to her as she stood to take her go. His tone suggested that he thought she'd need it.

"Your confidence in me is heart-warming," she said.

"You thought we were going to play boules," he noted with a shrug.

Allegra couldn't argue with him there. She looked at the balls and tentatively picked a couple of them up. She opted for the lightest ball available and tried to put her fingers in the holes, attempting to not think about how many other fingers had done so before hers.

"Know what you're doing?" Lauren asked, suddenly right behind her and whispering in her ear.

"Throwing a ball down that lane and hitting pins?" Allegra asked.

"Do you know how to throw the ball?"

"Overarm?" Allegra grinned.

"Right, I'll be over there, cowering," Lauren said, indicating the seat as far away from their lane as possible.

Allegra approached the line and looked down at the long lane and then at the pins in the distance. She didn't know how to throw a ball but reasoned it couldn't be that difficult. She'd spied a little girl no older than six looking as comfortable as professionals with her sliding action. Allegra wasn't going to slide. That was how you ended up falling over and needing rescuing.

She crouched a little lower and threw the ball. It meandered down the lane like a lost old lady in a supermarket that had recently been redesigned. Eventually, it gave up all hope of reaching the end of the lane and slipped into the gutter.

She turned around and looked at Lauren and Hugo who were barely able to control their sniggering.

"So, I get another go, yes?"

Lauren nodded.

Allegra picked up another ball. She looked up at the screen and calculated that ten goes, at two balls a go, meant twenty opportunities for her to be the laughing stock. She determined there and then to get her own back by challenging them to a chess match one day. Unless Lauren was also an expert chess master. She did seem to have hidden depths.

Strong arms reached around her, and Allegra stopped dead. Her heart started to beat so loud and so fast that she felt for sure Lauren would be able to hear it.

"The key is to glide the ball in the direction you want it to go," Lauren said. She placed one hand on Allegra's stomach to guide her in the right direction, and the other gripped Allegra's wrist lightly.

She allowed herself to be walked back to the line with Lauren much closer than she needed to be.

"The lower you go, the better you can aim," Lauren continued. Lauren manoeuvred her limbs to demonstrate the desired technique, and Allegra happily followed the instructions. Familiar nerves bubbled up within her, fear of being too eager, worry about ruining a precious moment.

"Dinner tomorrow?" Allegra asked, aware that she sounded breathless.

"I didn't get a strike," Lauren whispered in her ear.

"I don't give a fuck," Allegra whispered in return.

Lauren chuckled.

"What if I get a strike?" Allegra asked.

"You can't—you've already had your first go. If you knock them all over now, it would be a spare."

"The rules to this game are ridiculous," Allegra muttered. "Dinner?"

"I'd love to. Now…focus."

Lauren again walked her through the action. When she let go and stood back, Allegra felt cold and saddened by the loss of contact. She pushed the feeling to one side and focused on everything Lauren had told her.

She approached the line, crouched, swung her arm, and let go of the ball. This time the ball was on course and looked like it was going to impact at the exact right spot. It didn't, but it was close, and eight pins fell.

She'd never felt such elation from sport but suspected that was because she'd never really excelled at any sport. She gave a little jump for joy.

A second later she was swept into a hug and clear off her feet by Lauren.

"That was amazing!"

"I had a good teacher," she said.

"Shall I come over at six tomorrow?" Lauren asked as they walked back to the seats.

Hugo eagerly rushed around them to have his next go.

"Perfect," Allegra agreed. She lowered her voice. "Hugo will be at a sleepover at a friend's tomorrow."

Lauren nodded. "Good to know."

Allegra stared at Lauren, who in turn was watching Hugo

play. She had wanted to know what the situation would be and had deliberately dropped a hint that she thought told Lauren that she would be very interested in a repeat performance of their last dinner. But Lauren was giving her nothing to indicate that she'd taken the clue on board.

She felt well out of her comfort zone and didn't know how else to broach the subject.

Determined not to make a further fool of herself, she quashed down the feelings and focused on the game. Hugo deserved to have her be fully present and cheering him along even if she knew he'd take the odd opportunity to laugh at her. And it was mostly warranted as she wasn't known for her sports ability.

Before she knew it, they were reaching the end of the game. Just a couple more frames would show whether she might be able to score half of what Lauren had. Hugo sat comfortably in between them on the score front in what Lauren had described as a very respectable position.

Allegra had already agreed to Hugo's request to come and play again soon. She had to admit, the shoes and questionable hygiene of the balls aside, it was quite a fun activity.

She stood to take her go, and Lauren handed her a ball.

"I think you should keep the shoes," Lauren said.

"I'd rather not."

"I can see you wearing them in court."

"I think the judge would have something to say."

Lauren opened her mouth to reply but frowned. Allegra realised she was looking over her shoulder.

"What is it?"

"Does your son often sit like that?" Lauren asked.

Allegra subtly turned to see Hugo slouched so low he was nearly horizontal. His cheeks were red. He looked uncomfortable and anxious. Allegra had barely moved an inch towards him when Lauren put a hand on her arm to stop her.

Lauren was looking up the bowling alley to a group of boys. "You know them?"

Allegra shook her head. "I don't think so."

"I think Hugo might be hiding from them," Lauren said.

Allegra looked at the boys again. She didn't recognise them, but they looked like the rowdy sort that Hugo wouldn't be friends with. They were loud, and the staff at the bowling alley were watching them closely.

"I gotta go to the bathroom," Hugo announced. He ducked his head and hurried away.

Allegra watched him run away. Her heart clenched at the sight of him clearly going to hide.

"I'm going to assume you don't want me to go over and chat to those boys?" Lauren asked, her gaze narrowing as she stared at the rowdy group.

"I would very much like for you not to be arrested for assault or intimidation during our date," Allegra confirmed.

"I know a kick-ass solicitor," Lauren said.

"Barrister. Unless you know a solicitor as well?"

Lauren shook her head. "What's the difference?"

"We'll talk about the intricacies of the legal system another time. What should we do about this situation?"

"Leave," Lauren said.

"Are you sure?"

Lauren nodded. She took the ball from Allegra's hand and tossed it down the lane. All the pins fell as the ball struck in exactly the right place at exactly the right speed. It was obvious she'd been holding back her true skill throughout the evening.

"Hugo's not comfortable. I'm sure the boys will tease him if they see him here with his mum—no offence."

Allegra wanted to take offence but couldn't as she knew it was true. Children were cruel.

"We can go to a coffee shop?" Lauren suggested. "Hugo can have a cake. I'll tell him what the calories are, and he can work it off tomorrow. It will be a learning experience, and we don't have to end the night early. What do you think?"

Allegra sagged in relief that Lauren wasn't at all fazed by the situation with the boys. She was also pleased that Lauren didn't want to end the night early either.

"That sounds like a good idea. I'm sorry about this."

Lauren picked up another ball and threw it down the lane, resulting in another ten pins scattering to the back wall.

"Don't be sorry. This kind of thing happens with kids. I don't want him to have a bad time."

Allegra smiled at her. She picked up her phone to text Hugo that they were leaving and to meet her out by the car. She made up an excuse about hurting her wrist so as to save his blushes. "You're sweet. And I've hurt my wrist."

"Oh?" Lauren frowned.

"Just an excuse for Hugo. A reason why we're stopping," Allegra clarified.

"Ah, I see. That's good. After all, you might need that wrist tomorrow." Lauren looked at her suggestively before picking up another ball and throwing it down the lane.

Allegra didn't see what happened to the pins that time.

CHAPTER SEVENTEEN

S o, there I am, defending a man who was quite literally a bank robber. Trying to appeal to the jury by saying, *Who hasn't wanted to try to pick the lock of a cash machine while drunk in an attempt to get enough money together to get a cab home,*" Allegra said.

Lauren was practically crying with laughter. When she'd first asked Allegra to tell her about her work, she hadn't expected the hilarious stories that would ensue. Allegra was a master storyteller and had seemingly been a barrister so long that she had seen everything.

The waiter delivered their meals, and they both thanked him.

Lauren shook her head. "So he just wanted a ten-pound note to get home?"

"That's what he said."

"And he thought it would be a good idea to steal it from a cash machine on a crowded high street?"

Allegra held up her fork. "Borrow," she corrected. "He wasn't stealing, he was borrowing."

"Tell me the jury didn't buy that nonsense. I'll lose all faith I have in the court system," Lauren said.

Allegra sighed. "Alas, they thought he was extremely guilty. Can't win them all."

"You just said yourself that he was a bank robber," Lauren pointed out.

"Even bank robbers deserve a fair trial and a crack at justice." Allegra picked up her knife and started to eat her food.

Lauren chuckled. She picked up her own cutlery and started to eat her delicious looking salad. Allegra had found a restaurant in town that had genuine healthy eating at the heart of its ethos. They focused on sustainable, nutritious food without all the extras that made food appealing to the masses. It was perfect for Lauren. She could order a salad and know that any dressing would come on the side, and there wouldn't be a hint of cheese unless she asked for it.

They'd been dating for four weeks and seeing a lot of each other. At first they mainly dined at Allegra's home, but after the first week Lauren had been keen to prove that she could wine and dine Allegra by taking her to a nice restaurant.

The problem with nice restaurants was that they used a lot of butter, oil, cheese, and mayonnaise in almost everything they made. Food had to be sumptuous to be considered luxurious, and sumptuous meant unnecessary fat and other nasties that Lauren didn't want to eat. More than that, Lauren hadn't eaten rich food for so long that by the second meal out she had become sick. Allegra had been horrified by the incident and had found a restaurant that would serve Lauren the type of food that she was used to.

Hugo had taken to spending more time at either his friend's or uncle's house in an obvious attempt to give them more space. But when Hugo was at home, Lauren was happy to eat at Allegra's kitchen table as a family.

There had been no further discussions about what they were or where they were headed. Since Allegra's comments at the bowling alley and Lauren's attempt at a reply, they'd agreed to simply see where things went. As it happened, things went very smoothly.

"Will you come to the house tonight?" Allegra asked softly.

It was Allegra's way of asking if they would be having sex that night, and Lauren found it adorable.

"Would you like me to come to the house tonight?" Lauren replied.

"You know I would," Allegra said.

"Then I'd love to."

"Will you be staying the night?"

Lauren paused. She'd stayed the night just once before. The softest sheets she'd ever known, a spare toothbrush waiting for her use, and a wake-up call in the shape of a naked and lustful Allegra had made it a wonderful night and even better morning.

While it had been everything that she could have dreamt of, she was also keen to make sure it didn't become a habit. They were having a lot of fun and good times, but Lauren knew that it wouldn't last forever. Their relationship was still firmly in the honeymoon phase, and Allegra had yet to fully grasp how different they were and how it could never work between them.

Mainly because things were working out so well between them.

Lauren had felt for certain that the cracks would have started to show by now. She'd thought that her own need to exercise would bore Allegra, but instead Allegra had started to take an interest in her workout schedule. She'd not wanted to exercise herself but had asked about activities and times so she could shape her own calendar around Lauren's.

And Lauren thought for certain that hearing about legal cases would be boring, but they were fascinating. The things people went to court about were mind-boggling. Just the previous week Allegra had talked about a case about an overgrown tree that was unresolved and had already racked up twenty thousand pounds in legal fees.

But the most unexpected thing had been the fun family times they had together. Watching movies or playing Monopoly as a group had gone from something she saw on television to something she enjoyed herself. She didn't feel like an addition to the family unit but like a part of it, as if it wouldn't exist unless she was there, which was ridiculous because obviously Allegra and Hugo watched television and played games without her.

"Lauren?" Allegra prompted, a worried look on her face.

"Sorry?" Lauren pretended she hadn't heard the question. She had, but she had no idea how to answer it. Now time had drifted by and there was a potential for awkwardness unless she fixed it.

"I asked if you'd be staying the night."

"Sure, if that's okay with you?"

She knew she shouldn't be staying over if she wanted to keep a distance between them and make sure that no hearts were broken when the inevitable end came. But she reasoned that the odd night here and there wouldn't hurt too much. They were already seeing a lot of each other, so what did it really matter?

Allegra smiled. "That's very okay with me."

Lauren could tell that she was holding back from what she really wanted to say. Initially, Allegra had been very keen to explain to Lauren that she was welcome to visit and even to stay over whenever she liked. She had even cleared out a drawer for Lauren to keep her belongings in. Lauren had never used the drawer. She had wanted to kindly indicate to Allegra that they weren't in that kind of relationship, and the message seemed to have gotten through. Since then, the drawer remained empty and ready for her to use, but the offer had never been repeated.

She suspected that Allegra wanted more from the relationship, but she hoped that desire would diminish in time as Allegra got over the elation of being back in the dating game and moved onto the disappointment at realising how they weren't right for one another. They'd have a conversation, cry a little, and then Allegra would hopefully feel confident enough to find someone that would suit her better. Lauren knew that Allegra would be a wonderful partner to someone. Just not her.

"Did you manage to get out of the hot yoga session later this week?" Allegra asked.

Lauren shook her head. "Nope. I'll be sitting in a sauna looking for my inner peace on Thursday."

"At least your pores will look great."

"My pores always look great," Lauren joked. "You should come."

"To hot yoga?" Allegra laughed. "No, thank you. But I do hope you enjoy yourself."

Lauren's hatred of hot yoga was well known. She wasn't a big fan of yoga in general, much preferring Pilates. But yoga in a warm room was positively torture. Unfortunately, Erin was unwell, and Lauren was the only other person qualified to instruct the class.

"I asked Hugo, and he laughed in my face. I see where he gets it from," Lauren said.

"I didn't raise a fool," Allegra replied. "Besides, you spend far too much time complaining about hot yoga. Did you really think he'd want to?"

"I suppose not. Maybe if I put his PlayStation in there?"

Allegra grinned. "He loves that machine more than us. He'll kill if it gets overheated or waterlogged."

"That reminds me." Lauren put her knife and fork down and looked seriously at Allegra. "Who, precisely, is MumWithAGun?"

Allegra's cheeks reddened. "I have no idea what you're talking about."

"Oh, I think you might, Mrs. Whittaker," Lauren said. "I put it to you that on the night of…last Wednesday, the witness, me, was told by the…other guy, Hugo, that you once had your very own profile on said PlayStation where you shot up a small French town—"

"*Fictional* town," Allegra corrected.

"Aha! You admit it!" Lauren laughed. "Did you really steal everyone's grenades and just lay waste to the whole town?"

"Of course not. I used my own rocket launcher, which I paid for with my own money," Allegra said.

Lauren laughed. "MumWithAGun…wow. I thought I knew you."

Allegra shrugged. "It had been a hard day at work, and Hugo wanted me to become more interested in his game. I showed him what real warfare was all about. Strategy. And rocket launchers." Allegra held out a piece of her sea bass meal on a fork. "Try a bite of this—it's divine."

Lauren chewed and nodded in appreciation.

"Did I tell you about the time I represented a fisherman who was convinced that his son's vegan girlfriend had hidden his fishing nets?" Allegra asked.

Lauren felt her eyes widen. "No! You've been holding out on me. Tell me everything."

Allegra launched into the tale of the netless fisherman, and Lauren listened intently. At the back of her mind, she was starting to wonder how much longer their time together could last. When they'd first met, she would have said less than a week. Soon it would be five weeks since their first date. Not that she was counting.

Don't get too close, she reminded herself. *It cannot last.*

CHAPTER EIGHTEEN

Lauren slowly lowered herself into Jim's chair with her mobile phone to her ear. She listened to her boss explaining all that he knew about the situation with his granddaughter. Which was precious little, aside from the fact that he would be gone for some time yet.

"So they basically don't know what's going to happen," Jim said.

Jim had never been a man to express many feelings, but the repressed emotions were starting to break through if the cracking in his voice was anything to go by. Lauren couldn't blame him. Illness in children was tough, but to be comforting your own child while your grandchild was sick and likely dying was more than Lauren thought was fair to put on anyone.

"I'm so sorry," she said.

"Well, it is what it is. We carry on," Jim said. He'd always been the pragmatic sort or at least wanting to appear that way rather than breaking down. "How is everything there?"

"Great," Lauren replied immediately. "No problems, few more sign-ups to classes. Everything's fine."

While there were a few new members to be happy about, other things were piling up thick and fast, and Lauren was quickly becoming overwhelmed. Anna had repeatedly said she'd come by but seemed to always cancel at the last minute. Lauren had tried to keep things light and breezy, asking Anna to pop in as soon as she could. She didn't have time to find a new freelance administrator, had no idea what to teach them, and didn't want to run the risk of someone else discovering her issues with reading.

Instead she tried to hold down the fort and convinced herself that Anna would be by any day now to fix everything. But the last thing she wanted to do was to tell Jim that. He needed to be with his family. He needed to feel that everything at work was fine, so he could focus his energy on being with them and not worrying about what was happening at work.

"You're sure? I thought the guy for the fire extinguishers was supposed to be coming by soon for the paperwork. Did that happen? Did it, you know, go okay?"

"All fine. I got Seb to deal with it," Lauren said.

"Okay, great. And everything else? It's not too much? Anything you need help with?"

Lauren rolled her eyes. Sometimes Jim's fatherlike tendencies warmed her heart, and sometimes they were frustrating. She imagined that was what it felt like with a real father, so she didn't say anything.

"Everything is fine," she maintained.

Everything wasn't fine, but she was sure that she'd figure it out somehow. She'd been figuring things out for years, and now would be no different. Lauren had ways and means around things that she couldn't do, and she had no doubt that she'd manage. She might achieve the highest amount of stress in her adult life to date. But she'd manage.

"Okay, great. Thank you again, Lauren," he said. "There's no one else I trust."

Lauren's heart swelled with pride. "I am pretty awesome," she joked to take the edge off the compliment.

"Did I hear correctly from Luke that you were on a date the other day?" Jim asked.

Lauren chuckled. "Oh, has the gossip mill started already?"

"You know what it's like in that place—you can't do anything without at least four people noticing. So, is it true?"

Lauren couldn't help but smile at the memory of the dates she'd been sharing with Allegra, the woman who was her polar opposite but also somehow a match made in heaven.

"Yes, it's true. We've been seeing each other for a couple of weeks. Had a few dinners and stuff. She's Hugo's mum."

"Hugo?"

"The kid who joined the gym by stealing his mum's credit card."

"Oh, him!" Jim laughed. "Wow, these are some extreme measures you're going to so she doesn't sue us."

Lauren chuckled. "Well, you know, got to take a hit for the business, right?"

"Seriously though, how's it going?" Jim asked.

"It's going well," Lauren admitted. "We're having a good time."

"Does she know?"

Lauren tensed. Of course Allegra didn't know Lauren struggled to read. And could never know. It was the reason why Lauren was one foot in and one foot out of the relationship. She knew, and had known all along, that it could never work out. Jim would never be able to fully understand that. He wouldn't be able to grasp that Lauren would never have it in her to admit her biggest secret to anyone other than him. The only reason he knew was because he'd seen through her bluster and cornered her about it. That would never happen again. She was far too careful.

"No."

"Tell her," Jim encouraged.

"Anyway," Lauren said, deftly changing the subject, "as I said, everything is fine here, so don't feel the need to rush back. Or check up on me by calling Ruth because I know you did that. And you shouldn't be trusting Ruth to keep your secrets."

"Hey, I built that business from scratch. You can't blame me for worrying about things."

"I'm hanging up now," Lauren said.

"Okay, I'll call you tomorrow."

"Okay. Give my love to your girls."

"I will."

Jim hung up the call and Lauren let out a big sigh before doing the same. She looked at the desk and shook her head. More and more post and paperwork was accumulating all the time. She'd managed to give some of it to Seb and Luke, but the boys had their own work to do. She needed Anna to come and help, or she was afraid that something would get missed. Not that she'd ever admit that to Jim. She wasn't about to confess that she couldn't cope.

She picked up the phone and dialled Anna's number. The call immediately bounced to voicemail. Lauren sighed as she listened to Anna's recorded message.

"Hey, Anna! It's Lauren from the gym. Could you give me a call when you get this, so we can arrange when would be a good time for you to come in? Thanks. Speak soon."

She hung up the call and stared at the phone for a minute. Anna was usually reliable. It was unusual for her to cancel so often, and especially last minute.

"Afternoon."

Worries slipped from Lauren's mind as Allegra confidently entered the office as if she belonged there. She couldn't have been further away from the adorable woman having a mini meltdown at the bowling alley five weeks ago. She'd grown in confidence each time they saw each other, and Lauren loved this new self-assured woman who she was privately referring to as her girlfriend.

Lauren walked around the desk and greeted her with a kiss. She closed the door to the office so the rest of the staff knew not to disturb her. She struggled to keep her hands off Allegra and didn't need to shock some of the younger staffers.

"I thought I wouldn't see you today," Lauren said.

"My case was postponed," Allegra said.

"The bus driver case?" Lauren asked.

"Yes. Apparently, he is very sick." Allegra rolled her eyes. "Probably sick at the likelihood that he'll be sacked from his job the very moment he's found guilty. Which he will be."

Allegra didn't tell Lauren everything about her cases, but she did say enough so Lauren knew what was happening in her day-to-day work life. It had opened up a whole new world to Lauren. She'd had no idea how many people were in and out of court every single day and for the strangest of reasons.

Allegra placed her briefcase on the desk and unclipped the two brass locks. "I have a question for you."

Lauren sat on the edge of the desk. "Yes, you do look hot in that skirt."

"A serious question," Allegra said, ignoring the flirting but smiling at the compliment. She took out two pieces of paper and handed them to Lauren. "Which one of these wearable fitness trackers is best? I thought I'd pick one up, but I'm completely at a loss for what all the technical details and specs actually mean. And I can't compare them because they seem to use different terminology."

Lauren glanced at the papers and then looked up at Allegra again. "They are all basically the same. Get the one you like the look of."

"But they seem to do different things," Allegra said, tapping on of the pieces of paper.

Lauren took the papers and put them on the desk. "Same things, different words. They all do the same thing. Just get the one you like the look of, trust me."

She tugged Allegra closer to her, and Allegra willingly stood in front of her and draped her arms over Lauren's shoulders.

"But do I want the one with the breathing feature? What even is that?" Allegra asked.

"Do you often forget to breathe?" Lauren asked.

"No."

"Then you don't need it. But if you'd like it, fine. They all have the same basics."

"Do I need GPS?" Allegra attempted to reach for the paperwork again.

Lauren pulled her back. "I enjoyed dinner last night," she said, changing the subject. "Especially dessert."

Allegra blushed and looked down at Lauren's shirt. They'd

gone to dinner and then to see a play at Lauren's insistence. She'd wanted to prove that she was interested in cultural events and could afford to pay for them, despite being a lowly fitness trainer.

She'd convinced herself she was doing it for Allegra but had been surprised at just how much she had enjoyed the play herself. Afterwards, Allegra had insisted on driving Lauren home, which had resulted in a very hot make-out session in Allegra's car on a very public street where they could have been seen by anyone.

"You are a bad influence on me," Allegra said.

"Okay, I'll stop." Lauren grinned knowingly.

"Well, you don't need to go that far."

"You like that I want you," Lauren said. "You like that I encourage you to do things you wouldn't usually do. You're a good girl with bad girl desires."

Allegra looked like she wanted to disagree but knew she didn't have a leg to stand on.

"Maybe we can have dinner again at your place soon," Lauren suggested.

Dinner almost always ended with either sex or kissing, which meant asking for dinner had connotations that made Allegra equally blush and nod in good measure. Allegra was so completely different to other people Lauren had dated in the past—she was classy and almost prudish. Lauren had gone from wanting to knock her off her pedestal to realising there was no pedestal at all. It was all just nerves and perceived expectations of what people thought and required of her. The feeling of wanting to take the hoity-toity woman down a peg or two had changed into a desire to guide Allegra into wantonness while still ensuring she felt safe.

"Do you cook?" Allegra asked. "Really?"

Really had become a frequently used word in Allegra's vocabulary. At the start of their relationship, Lauren had either been flippant when replying to questions or changed the subject completely. Now that they had been together for longer, Allegra was wanting real answers. And Lauren surprised herself by sometimes giving them.

"I do." Lauren toyed with the buttons holding Allegra's jacket together. "But nothing you'd like. It's just protein shakes and meals that are nothing more than fuel at my place."

Allegra made a face. "I'll take my chances with the meal service."

Lauren had never really cared much about food in the past. Once it was broken down into its core components, it became quite boring. She'd been eating bland but nutritious food for years and had almost forgotten the joy of eating lovingly crafted home-cooked meals.

Even if Allegra wasn't the one actually cooking them.

"Sounds good to me," Lauren admitted. "Will Hugo be there?"

Allegra's mood suddenly changed. Lauren felt cold despite having her near. She suspected that something was coming.

"I wanted to talk to you about that. I can't keep sending Hugo away for the night. Or hope that he'll want to go somewhere," Allegra said, her voice suddenly shy. "It's not fair."

Lauren nodded.

So far, they'd been lucky that Hugo had embraced the frequent suggestions that he go and stay with a friend or family member, but soon that would end. Soon there was a very real chance that he'd feel pushed out and not wanted, and Lauren wanted no part of that.

"He should get used to you being around," Allegra said, suddenly focusing her attention on the collar of Lauren's shirt. "If you're going to be around."

The penny dropped, and Lauren realised they were having the discussion. The *What are we and where are we going?* conversation. She should have expected it, considering Allegra's personality and how much they had seen each other over a short period of time.

It had quickly become more than casually meeting up. It had become full on dating, seeing each other multiple times a week. So it was no wonder that Allegra was now asking the question of what they actually were.

Lauren knew that now would be the right time to end things. They couldn't become more, and the happy times would have to end soon. Allegra was emotionally prepared right there and then for Lauren to end things. It was clear now that she'd deliberately come to the office at a quiet time to ask a question that had been weighing on her for a while. Allegra's body was tense, and she refused to make eye contact with Lauren. The air was charged, and Lauren wished she'd had the time to prepare herself.

Lauren knew that it would be best if she ended the fling right then. Kindly, of course. But she didn't want to. She was having far too much fun. She felt a part of the Whittaker family these days. On her own, in her quiet apartment, she had lain awake on more than one occasion, wondering if she'd forgotten what a real connection with someone meant. During the long and lonely nights, she had come to the frightening conclusion that being alone forever wasn't going to be as simple as she had thought.

She'd become too closely attached to these people. And she wouldn't change a thing. Getting to know Allegra and Hugo had been the best thing that had happened to her for years.

The knowledge that it was temporary hung heavily around her shoulders. She could never be fully open with Allegra. She could never confess the secret that kept her awake at night. But she wasn't ready to break the connection yet either.

Lauren continued to play with the buttons on Allegra's suit jacket. She raised her gaze and looked at the formal collar of Allegra's barrister's shirt. It was a constant reminder of just how different they were.

Surely it couldn't last much longer. At some point the differences would have to change from cute quirks to annoying distractions. Allegra would surely realise soon that being in a relationship with an uneducated fitness fanatic wasn't right for her.

And then, with considerable kindness and apology, Allegra would be the one to end things. Lauren was certain of it. Allegra would eventually see sense and put a stop to the relationship.

Which meant that Lauren didn't have to be the one to break Allegra's heart right there and then. Allegra would realise the situation on her own in time and do what was necessary. Lauren could carry on until that time. It was the right thing to do, she convinced herself.

Lauren raised her head and smiled warmly. "I'm not going anywhere," she promised.

CHAPTER NINETEEN

Allegra stared at the ceiling. The sun was beginning to rise, and she was just about able to make out the shape of the ceiling light above the bed. She'd been lying on her back, wide awake with her eyes open, for at least an hour. The day would start soon, and she wasn't looking forward to it.

"Can't sleep?" Lauren asked, her voice husky.

Allegra turned her head. "I'm sorry. Did I wake you?"

"By lying completely still? No." Lauren edged a little closer. "What's wrong?"

"Work."

"Ah."

Allegra didn't speak about the details of her work while a case was active because of privilege rules, not to mention strategic risks. It wasn't that she didn't trust Lauren. In fact, she trusted Lauren far more than most. It was just that the discipline of not discussing active case details was ingrained. No matter how stressful the case details sometimes were.

Lauren understood. She never pushed and made sure Allegra knew that she was there if she wanted to talk and even if she didn't.

"Do you want to talk? Or do you want distraction?" Lauren asked.

"Distraction."

Lauren edged closer. "I'm an expert at distraction."

Allegra couldn't help but smile. "That you are."

She felt Lauren's hand ghost over her bare thigh. She'd recently started sleeping naked, something she'd never done before. When Lauren stayed over, it seemed like a waste of time to put on nightwear. There was also the fact that Lauren was always delightfully warm. The once-cold bed was a perfect temperature when Lauren was in it. Allegra wished she'd stay over more but knew not to push too far too fast.

"Do you want to play I Spy?" Lauren teased.

Lauren's hand trailed to Allegra's inner thigh, a place where she was simultaneously ticklish and ravenously turned on when touched. Lauren had discovered that fact quickly and then proceeded to exploit it at every opportunity. Not something that Allegra complained about.

"It's not very high on my list of wants."

Lauren shuffled closer still. She was now as close as she could be, her body pressed against Allegra's side.

Lauren's touch turned from teasing to deliberate. Allegra gasped. Not for the first time, she wondered how she had gone so long without the touch of a lover. It had seemed so obvious at the time that being alone was the only choice she had. Now she looked back and cursed herself for wasting her life.

Thankfully, she was soothed by the knowledge that it had been worth the wait. Lauren knew exactly how to please her and seemed eager to do so as frequently as possible.

"We could play charades, but we'd have to turn a light on," Lauren continued.

Allegra growled and spun herself around, pushing Lauren onto her back as she did. She understood that she only ever managed to overpower Lauren because Lauren allowed her to, and Lauren often assisted her in whatever goals she had. In this instance, she wanted to straddle Lauren and stop her smart mouth from making any more ridiculous jokes. Even if she did enjoy the teasing.

Lauren lay beneath her, looking up with a cheeky grin.

"That mouth of yours," Allegra said.

"You have a suggestion of what to do with it?"

Even in the partially lit room, Allegra could imagine that her blushing cheeks were visible to Lauren. She had some suggestions but didn't know how to ask. She wasn't as comfortable as Lauren when it came to talking about sex. Luckily, Lauren always seemed to understand. She knew exactly what to do and when, all while making Allegra feel safe and loved.

Strong hands gripped her hips. A few moments later they gently tugged, encouraging Allegra to move higher.

"I…" Allegra started, although not sure what she was going to say.

"Shh." Lauren's grip tightened a little and she pulled again. "Come on. Up here. Let me."

Allegra sat a little higher and edged closer to the headboard. At the same time, Lauren slid lower. Confident hands guided her hips down, and she felt Lauren's mouth connect with her.

She gasped before quickly covering her mouth with her hand. The house was large, but she would be mortified if she woke Hugo. She used her other hand to brace herself against the headboard.

Lauren set a familiar pace. She let go of Allegra's hips and brought her hands up over her stomach before settling on Allegra's breasts.

Thoughts of work flew from her mind, and all she could think of was hanging on to the pleasurable feelings for as long as possible. Which she knew from experience wouldn't be that long. Lauren knew exactly how to touch her. Allegra didn't know if all women were programmed the same way and Lauren had deciphered some universal code, or if she had quickly deduced what Allegra needed. Whichever was the case, Allegra planned to enjoy as much as she could before she inevitably collapsed in a pleasured heap.

Lauren's tongue was moving like lightning, and Allegra wondered if she was trying to beat some kind of record. She didn't mind—she was the winner no matter. She knew Lauren would take her time after. The hour between then and when the alarm would ring would be filled with Lauren's best distraction techniques.

"I'm close," she whispered.

Lauren's hands kneaded her breasts. Allegra gripped the headboard tighter still. Moments later she shuddered uncontrollably, half wondering how Lauren managed to take her from a dark place to ecstasy so quickly.

Lauren somehow managed to manoeuvre them so they were lying down and spooning, Lauren behind with her body pressed against hers.

"That was incredible," Lauren whispered in her ear.

"You did all the work." Allegra took a deep breath to try to calm her racing heart.

"Trust me, that is never work." Lauren held her close. "Did we get all the nasty thoughts out of that overactive brain of yours?"

Allegra chuckled. "Some are lingering," she lied.

"We'll have to see what we can do about that."

Allegra shut the file and let out a sigh. She was used to the worst of case files. You didn't get to the criminal court without having seen some things. But even so, some of the cases were harder than others, and some hit home.

A welcome knock on her door had her pushing the file and its nightmare-inducing contents to one side.

"Come in."

Roberta stuck her head around the door. "Am I interrupting?"

"Not at all, I was just planning to take a break." Allegra tossed her reading glasses on top of the file.

"Buckley case?"

Allegra nodded. "I believe in justice for all, but sometimes the amount of evidence against someone is so staggering that we should just save the taxpayer some money."

The case had already been through the circus of media attention, both when the young woman was murdered and later when Stuart Buckley had been arrested for the crime. It was now approaching trial, and Allegra was dreading it. Reliving the details of the case, knowing the full details of events, having to sit in the same room as a man who was clearly guilty, and the increase in press activity were all going to equal a very trying time at work.

Roberta entered Allegra's office, closed the door, and sat down. "You need to make sure you take some time for you during this. I mean it, Allie. This is going to be a tough one, and you don't want to be taking that home with you every night. Do some gardening, start a project, take up art. Do something."

Barristers were a hardy sort, but even they could be known to crumble under the pressure of a particularly difficult case. Allegra had only ever taken personal time off once in her long career, but she knew many others who were in therapy or took early retirement.

"And make sure you talk to someone—you know my door is always open," Roberta added.

"Thank you, I appreciate that," Allegra said. "I don't think distraction will be too much of a problem. I'm still seeing Lauren."

Roberta's eyebrow rose. "That's been…a month?"

Allegra nodded. "Longer. Around six weeks? We're going steady or whatever term the youth use these days."

"Oh, exclusive? Girlfriends?" Roberta teased.

Allegra wrinkled her nose. "I'm not sure I like the term, but I suppose we are, yes."

Roberta smiled brightly. "I'm really pleased for you. You deserve some fun."

Allegra shifted a little in her seat. She'd never been one for girl talk and baring her soul, but she needed to talk to someone and trusted Roberta implicitly. "I'm nervous."

"About?"

"I don't know," she confessed. "Everything?"

Roberta threw her head back and laughed. "You crack me up. I don't think you know how to relax. Seriously, you're so uptight I'm surprised you don't crackle as you walk. Didn't we have this conversation about just having fun? Enjoying some time with someone with no expectations?"

"I know, but I can't help but think of the future. I mean, take Hugo, for example. He really loves spending time with Lauren, and Lauren seems to like him, too. What if it doesn't work out, and we split up? Hugo's a sensitive boy, and he's never experienced something like this before."

Roberta shrugged. "Do you never get on a flight in case you might crash? Never eat fish in case of a bone? You take risks because life is boring without them. Yes, it's safe, but have you ever really lived if you exist in a bubble?"

"But am I asking Hugo to take a risk for me?"

"Have you spoken to him about this?"

Allegra shook her head. "I don't think he needs the added pressure of whether or not his mother's relationship will work out. Nor to know how neurotic I've become."

"Then is it even worth worrying about? You're going to date Lauren anyway. It might work out, in which case I'm totally your maid of honour. It might not work out, in which case you had a lot of fun and then you'll feel sad for a few days, a week at the most, because I'll tell you to get over yourself and then you'll move on, having lived your life."

Allegra knew she was right, but she still couldn't shake the feeling. The Buckley case had put her on edge, and her emotions were all over the place. High-profile murder cases didn't come up often, and when they did, they were deeply unsettling. Every time Allegra tried to comfort herself with the thought of her safe and secure home life, something caught in her mind. But she couldn't grasp what.

"I just feel...I don't know." She leaned back in her chair, let out a breath, and drummed her fingers on the desk.

"What is it?"

"There's...something."

"Something?"

"I can't put my finger on it. But I feel like there's something. Almost like..." She paused, not knowing if she wanted to bring reality to her niggling fears. "As if she's keeping something from me."

"Like what?"

"I have no idea. I see fragments of something. But then she shakes it off, and there's a joke and we laugh and it's gone. Or she tries to distract me, but I can't fathom what she's trying to distract me from. Maybe I'm dreaming."

She knew that she wasn't dreaming. There was something that Lauren was keeping from her. Allegra had been happy to ignore it for a while, but now she was working on a case where it was her job to analyse and question everything. Doubts crept into her mind everywhere she went. Had the barista really used sugar-free syrup? Had Hugo really cleaned his room? Had the garden hose really developed a tear, or had the gardener simply wanted to charge her for something that she didn't need?

It was an unfortunate side effect of working in the law. At some points in your career, you started to question everything, just for a week or even a month. Harsh reality made you see things that you ordinarily would have ignored. And it was hard to put the genie back in the bottle.

Roberta worried her lip a little. "I want to tell you to leave it alone. Let the girl have her secrets. But then I know you won't let it go just like that. I wouldn't either."

Allegra nodded. "Years of being a barrister. You see when people are hiding something, don't you. I've been trying to tell myself that it's nothing. But the longer we see each other, the more I feel that there is something."

She watched the tree outside her window flutter in the wind. There was nothing particular about Lauren's behaviour that she could identify. It was a gut feeling she had, more than anything. But it could well be one born of general fear and anxiety rather than rooted in anything specific and real.

Lauren didn't speak about herself much and easily shunted aside questions. Allegra didn't want to pry, but she also couldn't hold herself back from wanting to know more. They were supposed to be dating, an item, or whatever strange terminology people currently used.

"Just remember that you're only recently back in the dating game. And she's younger than you," Roberta said. "There are bound to be differences between you. And most importantly you're just having fun. No need to Sherlock Holmes your way to singledom. Not yet."

Allegra had to agree. Ignoring her feeling was definitely the easier path. It was just a matter of whether or not her curiosity could be kept under control. Something which she somehow doubted.

Her personal mobile rang. Hugo's school was calling her.

"Allegra Whittaker," she answered formally.

"Ms. Whittaker, I'm afraid I'm going to have to ask you to come and pick Hugo up."

❖

Allegra rushed through the school gates and into reception. She couldn't remember there being a reception when she was at school, just a main door and then classrooms. It seemed that these days there was a need for receptions, administrative offices, and a whole battalion of people to get through before you could see your own child.

"I'm here to pick up Hugo Whittaker," she told the young woman on the desk who looked like she'd only recently left school herself.

"I think the headmaster might want to speak with you, one moment." The woman picked up the phone and told someone that Mrs. Whittaker had arrived. Allegra itched to correct her but didn't want Hugo to be labelled as the boy with *that* mother.

The phone was lowered. "Yes, Mr. Symonds would like to see you."

Allegra turned and marched towards the headmaster's office. She knew where it was, as she'd been in the office in the past during her short-lived stint as a member of the school board of governors. The day a debate had broken out about what length the playing field grass should be left to grow to before it was cut was the day Allegra decided she had better uses for her time.

She rounded the corner and stopped dead. Hugo sat on a chair outside the office with blood down the front of his uniform and an angry looking split lip.

"Oh my goodness." She knelt in front of him. "What happened? Who did this?"

As she examined his face, she could see a bruise on his cheek which indicated that more than one blow had landed on him. She softly took hold of his hands and turned them over to reveal undamaged knuckles.

Time sifting through evidence at work told her that Hugo had been struck more than once and hadn't fought back. It hadn't been a fight as she'd been told on the phone. It had been an attack.

The headmaster's door opened, and Lawrence Symonds stepped out. "Ah, Allegra. Would you like to come in and sit down?"

"Sit down?" Allegra raged. "I want to call the police. My son has been attacked. Has this been documented for evidence?"

"Mum," Hugo whispered, the first thing he said since she'd arrived. "Don't."

"Maybe we'll have some more privacy in my office," Lawrence suggested.

"You said a fight." Allegra stood and glared at him. "A fight indicates two participants at least. I can see no evidence that Hugo played a part of this."

Not only was there no physical evidence, Allegra also knew that Hugo wasn't the sort to get involved in a fight nor attempt to start one. He'd never been one for even play-fighting as a child. She'd attempted to engage him in karate and the like when he was six, but he quickly declared that he didn't like hitting things or throwing people about. The most violent he became was via video games where he would happily punch and even shoot whatever monster was presented in front of him. Beyond that he was a pacifist.

"The teacher that broke it up—"

"Stopped the attack," Allegra corrected.

"Said that both boys were fighting," Lawrence finished.

"I'm taking this through the complaints procedure," Allegra said. She knew it was robust and would get to the bottom of what had really happened. She'd helped to overhaul it before she had left her governor duties.

"Mum, please don't," Hugo whispered again.

She looked at him. His head was still low, and his posture looked defeated. She knew exactly why he wanted her to stop. He knew that she'd take it as far as it could go, an official report, the demands of an investigation, and, ultimately, an apology. He didn't want that spotlight shone on him.

"Is he free to go?" she asked Lawrence.

Lawrence nodded.

She took the car keys out of her pocket and handed them to Hugo. "Go and wait in the car. I'll be just a moment."

Hugo didn't argue. In fact he didn't say anything. He grabbed the keys and threw his bag over his shoulder as he left the room.

Allegra wanted to hold him and tell him everything would be okay. More than that, she wanted to go back in time and prevent it all from happening at all. She wanted to protect him and keep him safe in a world that was anything but, at times. But that wasn't feasible.

She looked at Lawrence with her best stare and enjoyed the way he withered.

"You have a duty of care, Lawrence. One which you have clearly failed on. The only reason I'm not going to take this through a very robust complaints system is because my son has asked me not to. This once, I'll accept that request. Next time will be different. You know Hugo—he doesn't fight. He was attacked, and you're trying to make it look like a boys-will-be-boys disagreement. Do better."

She turned and left, not interested in a word Lawrence had to say in reply. She'd always considered the man incompetent, but the school had the best ratings in the area, and the rest of the faculty were excellent. Working in the law, she knew what it was like to have an idiot boss seated atop an otherwise well-oiled machine.

When she exited the building, she almost didn't see Hugo in the car as he was slumped so low in his seat. She inhaled a cleansing breath. She knew that the last thing he'd want was her anger or her pity.

She got in and noticed the car keys on the centre console that separated them. Hugo faced away from her. She couldn't see his face, which was probably for the best because she worried that she might cry at the damage she saw. He wasn't irreversibly maimed or anything, but even a tiny scratch made her well up at the injustice of not being able to keep loved ones safe from any harm.

"I didn't take it any further," she told him. "But if you want to tell me what happened, then we can talk."

"No, thank you," he said, his voice barely audible in the deafening silence of the car.

"I promise I won't do anything with whatever you tell me. It will just be between the two of us," she added.

"I don't want to talk about it."

She knew she was unlikely to get anything else from him and started the car.

"Okay, maybe you can talk to Lauren about it when you see her later."

"I don't want to go tonight."

Her hands tightened around the steering wheel. Hugo loved his gym sessions with Lauren and would talk about them extensively before and after, whether Allegra wanted him to or not.

"If you're sure," she said, not wanting to pile extra pressure on him.

She wanted to say that it was better to get on with life as a way to let the mental wounds heal and to reassure him that Lauren would think no less of him. But she had no idea what was going on in his mind. Any such statements could possibly lead to new fears and doubts. It was times like this that she really felt as if she was just making it up as she went along.

"I just want to go home."

"Home it is."

❖

Allegra paced the kitchen. Hugo had gone straight to his room once they had returned home. After an hour had passed, she'd decided to check on him and see if he wanted to speak. Instead of being at his desk playing on his games console, he had been in bed and staring into nothing. Not asleep, not even trying for sleep.

She'd sat on the bed and brushed her fingers through his hair as she had done when he was a child and felt unwell. She'd asked if he wanted to talk about it but was greeted with silence as he continued to stare into the distance. In the end she'd told him some stories about funny things that had happened at work over the last week, day-to-day things that usually made him laugh. After ten minutes and not even a giggle, she told him she'd leave him alone until dinner was ready.

It would be four hours until dinner, and Allegra had no idea what to do with herself. Anger bubbled within her that someone had hurt her son. The fact that she had no idea who, on top of the fact that justice wouldn't be met, made the matter worse. She'd gone into law when she had realised as a teenager that she had a problem with injustice. Seeing or hearing of a wrong undid her usually calm composure and sent her into a fit of rage. She'd decided to dedicate her life towards righting those wrongs and fighting for justice. It was become a charity worker or go into law. She reasoned that her education afforded her the ability to go into law where, some might argue, she could possibly do more good.

The problem was that her itch to fight injustice had only strengthened over the years. Losing a case put her in a mood for days, and seeing someone who was obviously guilty receive no sentence because of a lack of evidence frustrated her. Seeing her son cowering in his bed with a bloodied lip incensed her. But there was absolutely nothing she could do.

Remembering that she needed to contact Lauren about Hugo's decision to stay home that afternoon, she picked up her phone. She noted the time and, assuming Lauren would be with one of her other clients, texted instead of calling.

She sat at the table and composed a message explaining briefly what had happened and saying that Hugo wouldn't be at the gym that afternoon. She finished by saying that she'd call her later that evening when Lauren was off work. She read through the message twice before sending it.

She drummed her fingers on the tabletop as she wondered what to do with her afternoon. She'd left in such a hurry that she hadn't brought her work folders home with her. She wondered if she should ask Jake to bring some things to the house or if she'd rather spend the time doing something non-work related as Roberta had suggested.

Her phone rang and the selfie which Lauren had mischievously taken when Allegra had left her phone unattended came up on the screen.

"Hello, I thought you had a coaching session now," Allegra said.

"I've put him on the treadmill," Lauren said.

"You make him sound like a puppy you need to keep entertained while you do something."

"Well…" Lauren laughed. "So, what's up?"

"Did you read the message?"

"No, my phone is playing up again. Just saw that I had a text from you, but it vanished somewhere."

"You need a new phone," Allegra said. "Does it just eat my text messages, or is it everyone?"

"Everyone. I might have pushed something. You know me and technology. Anyway, what's up?"

"Hugo won't be coming tonight. There was an incident at school." Allegra swallowed nervously. Saying the words was harder than typing them. She felt a lump in her throat at having to explain verbally that her precious boy was injured and distressed.

"What kind of incident?" Lauren asked.

"I don't know all the details—he won't tell me. Won't speak to me at all, actually. I was asked to come and get him because of fighting, but it's fairly obvious to me that he was attacked. He—he has a split lip and bruising…" She trailed off, worried she might start to cry if she carried on.

"I'll be there in fifteen," Lauren said. There was a cold determination to her voice that was nothing like the light and airy tone Allegra was used to.

"But you're working," Allegra said.

"Fifteen minutes."

The line went dead. Allegra lowered the phone to the table and was aware of the ghost of a smile on her face. Doubts might have lingered in her mind that Lauren was hiding something, but her protectiveness of Hugo was obvious and something that couldn't be faked.

She called Jake and provided him with a list of things to bring to the house for her to read through that evening. They rearranged her schedule for the next couple of days and spoke of upcoming cases and whether Allegra wanted them or not.

Before she knew it, she'd been on the phone for a quarter of an hour, and the doorbell was sounding. She hung up with Jake and rushed to the front door.

"Hey, how is he?" Lauren asked.

She stood just outside the door astride her bike. A small sheen of sweat covered her neck, and her hands gripped the handlebars tightly. Allegra was struck by how this woman had so easily dropped everything and rushed to Hugo's aid.

"Come in," Allegra said.

Lauren jumped off the bike and easily carried it into the hallway as she so often did. At first she had offered to leave her bike outside, but the wary look in her eye led Allegra to assume that it was expensive, and she was concerned about leaving it unattended. Even in Allegra's nice neighbourhood.

Allegra closed the door and was immediately swept into a hug.

"How are you?" Lauren asked.

"I'm…a bit shaken, to be honest," Allegra admitted.

"I could tell by your voice. What happened?" Lauren stood back and gave her room to breathe, think, and talk. Allegra couldn't help but marvel at how well Lauren fit into her life and knew exactly what she needed, even when stress levels were undoubtedly high.

Allegra quickly recounted what had happened, from the ridiculous call about Hugo having been in a fight through to the sight of him outside the headmaster's office.

"He won't talk to me," she finished. "I don't want to push him."

Lauren looked thoughtfully at the stairs. She worried her lip. "Can I try?"

"Of course. Don't be surprised if he's not too happy to see you, though. He looks up to you and probably doesn't want you to see him like this." Allegra folded her arms and clutched at her own upper arms in a comforting move she had done since she was a child.

"I'll be careful," Lauren promised. "I wouldn't say no to a cup of tea when I get back down here."

Allegra smiled at the cheeky request. "I bet you wouldn't. What about work?"

"They aren't expecting me back tonight."

"Then maybe you could stay?" Allegra suggested.

"You'll not be able to get rid of me," Lauren said. She kissed Allegra's cheek and then bounded up the stairs, two at a time.

Allegra watched her go and realised that she was finally comprehending what it felt like to have a second parent around. It had been something that she'd wondered about ever since Hugo came into her life—what would it be like to have a partner in the parental business? She was finding out that it was pretty marvellous.

CHAPTER TWENTY

Allegra felt guilty. She was enjoying resting on the sofa with her legs on Lauren's lap. They were both bathed in the glow of the television, and Allegra imagined they looked like any one of the millions of typical couples up and down the country. It was nice, but something was missing—hence her guilt.

Hugo had come downstairs only briefly to eat dinner before disappearing again. His mood had clearly indicated that he was still struggling and wanted to be left alone. Allegra couldn't blame him, but she was missing the time they spent together as their new little family unit.

She looked at Lauren out of the corner of her eye. She was engrossed in the nature documentary onscreen, which gave Allegra the perfect chance to stare in wonderment at the perfect partner that she'd somehow managed to find. When she thought back to their first meeting and how close they had come to being at permanent odds, it sent a shudder down her spine.

They'd become so close so quickly that the thought of Lauren not being a part of her life now seemed like a distant memory, despite it only really having been a terribly short period of time.

Maybe time moved differently when you were happy. Maybe happiness was fleeting and you needed to chase it, while sadness got its hooks into the fabric of time and caused it to drag.

Lauren hadn't divulged what was said during her chat with Hugo, and Allegra didn't feel she needed to know. If anyone else had spoken to Hugo, then Allegra would have fished for details, but she trusted Lauren and didn't feel as though she needed to know whatever might have been said. For once she was content to just let things be.

Or maybe she just wanted to think she was, so as to keep the peace and maintain the idyllic life they had built up for themselves. Because the more she tried to ignore the questions that niggled at the back of her head, the more persistent they became.

She's allowed to have her secrets, she reminded herself.

"I can feel you worrying," Lauren said without taking her eyes from the screen.

"I am," Allegra agreed.

She wouldn't tell Lauren that she was worrying about whatever secret Lauren was choosing to keep hidden from her, but she wouldn't hide that she was worrying either. She knew that Lauren knew her too well. To deny that she was worrying was pointless.

"Remember that you promised not to report it to the school," Lauren said. She paused the show and turned to look at Allegra. "I know you want to handle this for him, but it's not going to help him in the long run if you go in and make a big deal about it all."

"It is a big deal," Allegra said. "I want him to know that assault is a very serious thing. But I won't report it. I promised him that I wouldn't, and I won't."

Lauren smiled. "I know you want to be protective of him, but he has to deal with this in his own way. And he has to be able to trust you. You don't want to make things worse for him. Or even make him skip school because of this."

"He wouldn't do that," Allegra said with certainty.

Lauren shrugged. "You never know what's going through kids' heads."

"Hugo likes school too much. I remember when he was first conscious of what school was and desperately wanted to go. I kept telling him that he was too young and had to be bigger, and he'd be so mad with me. He would sit and sulk for the longest time for a three-year-old. I had to make a fake school for him to attend."

Lauren leaned her head against the back of the sofa and looked at her wistfully. "I wish I knew him back then."

Allegra laughed. "To enjoy the long sulks?"

"To see him grow."

Allegra saw real sadness in Lauren's eyes. She stood up and held out her hand. "I can't turn back time, but I can show you the family photo album."

Lauren took her hand. Allegra led her through the downstairs of the house to a room that she was only now realising Lauren had never seen before. Her home office was a place of work, which she kept locked away from the rest of the house. Allegra never considered it a part of the house. When she was in her office, she was at work.

She opened a drawer in the telephone table in the hallway and removed her office door key.

"Is this the way to the dungeon?" Lauren asked. "I thought the whole innocent thing was an act."

"It's my office," Allegra said. She'd started ignoring Lauren's little teasing comments simply because she'd realised that they were designed purely as a way to make her blush. Replying to them simply upped the ante, and Lauren would always win.

She unlocked and opened the door. She stood to one side and gestured for Lauren to walk in first. For the first time since knowing Lauren, Allegra saw real hesitation. Small steps and wide eyes seemed so out of place on someone ordinarily so comfortable.

"That's some book collection," Lauren commented.

Allegra glanced at the wall of books and nodded.

"You've read all of these?" Lauren asked as she ran her finger along a row of book spines.

"Yes. Many multiple times. Quite a few are reference books."

"Reference books?"

Allegra opened the cupboard and looked for the keepsake box she wanted to show Lauren. "Yes, for cases. English law is very complicated, and not every scenario is covered, so sometimes you have to look at old cases to see if you can find an example of what a previous judge might have thought about something similar to what you're working on. It's really a case of the more you know…"

She located the box and brought it over to her desk. "I told you that I adopted Hugo, but we never spoke about the details of why."

Lauren nodded. "I didn't know if it was something you were comfortable talking about or not."

"It's not something that I often talk about. Not through a need to keep it secret—it was just so very long ago. It feels as if I was a different person back then." She got the key out of her office drawer and unlocked the keepsake box. "I was pretty fresh-faced in the criminal court and one of the few women. My boss assigned me this case, an urgent relocation of a child."

She took out the initial police report and held it out to Lauren.

Lauren didn't take it. "I don't have my glasses with me. You read it."

Allegra blinked. "You wear glasses?"

Lauren chuckled. "I look terrible in them. I usually wear contacts, but I took them out earlier. I can see okay, but not well enough to read."

Allegra lowered the report to her desk. "I never knew that. I find out something new about you every day."

"You can talk." Lauren laughed. "You're in the process of telling me Hugo was a part of some case? Come on, tell me everything."

Allegra gestured for Lauren to sit down and took her own seat behind the desk.

"I received a call one night. Well, I suppose it was morning, to be honest. Around two o'clock. I was on duty, and the police officer told me that a woman had been arrested for attempting to leave a baby in a bathroom. She denied the baby was hers, but a member of the public had seen her do it."

Lauren's grip on the arm of the chair tightened. "Why would someone do that?"

"People do strange things," Allegra said. "When I arrived at the police station, it was chaos. It was a Friday night in London. They were dealing with all kinds of things, and in the middle of it all was this sergeant with a baby in his arms. He was the only officer in the station who had children and knew how to hold a baby."

She looked in the keepsake box and pulled out the photograph of Hugo as a baby, wrapped up in the blanket he'd been abandoned in. She handed it to Lauren.

"I'm not sure if you'll see this without your glasses but—"

"I see him. Those eyes! They haven't changed." Lauren stared at the photo.

"No. He's always had a soulful expression," she agreed. "Anyway, the woman was identified in the system as having a criminal record. A rather long and concerning one. She denied knowing the baby."

"What a monster." Lauren continued to stare at the baby photograph. "Why would someone do that?"

"She probably knew that child abandonment comes with a custodial sentence. By that point it was obvious that the baby would be taken into care, so I imagine she wondered why she should add a prison sentence to her problems."

Lauren looked up. "You took him in?"

Allegra laughed. "Not exactly. I'd been assigned to the case, and the baby was now in the care of the state, so I was legally obliged to wait to see him handed from the police station to the social care officer. Social services were called, but the duty officer was on another call and her deputy couldn't be found. Hours went by. The sun came up, and the sergeant's shift came to an end, and he had to go home to attend to a family matter."

"And then you took him in?" Lauren asked as a grin started to curl at her lips.

"I held him while we waited for the social services officer to finally arrive," Allegra said. "No one else knew how to hold a baby. I'd had experience with my sister's children. Eventually, the care officer arrived." Allegra pinched the bridge of her nose at the memory. "She was a disaster. I don't mean to sound snobbish or judgemental, but she smelt as if she hadn't washed for a while. Her hair was matted—not just messy, but actually matted. She wrote her notes as if she was cataloguing books in a library rather than taking in a baby. Actually, I believe a librarian probably cares more for the books than this woman did for Hugo. She was a strange woman, and I felt a deep sense of unease about her."

"How did she get a job like that?" Lauren asked.

"I have no idea. I asked one of the officers about her, and apparently she was in charge and had been for some years. There had been…questions about her commitment and conduct. Nothing I can substantiate," she added.

"So you took him in?" Lauren asked again.

"It wasn't as quick as that. There was a lot of paperwork and time that passed. But yes, I took him in. I couldn't leave him in her care. I raised my concerns, and an investigation into her work started shortly after. She resigned before she could be removed from her post."

"Always righting wrongs, aren't you?" Lauren smiled. "So you never intended to have a baby, and you suddenly did. That must have been hard."

"Very. My boss wasn't pleased. I was new, and now I was taking maternity leave to settle in with a new baby." Allegra remembered the terrible sinking feeling that she was making a mistake and ruining her career and her life. Only the year before she had chosen not to adopt a dog because of the amount of care it needed. But even now, years later, she shivered at the thought of that terrible woman taking Hugo.

"I wish I'd known someone like you when I was a baby," Lauren said.

Allegra frowned. Lauren had very deliberately never spoken of her background. Hugo had mentioned in passing that Lauren had been in foster homes, but Allegra had waited for Lauren to feel comfortable enough to bring it up herself. "Did you need rescuing?"

Lauren nodded. "Sort of. I suppose I had a lot of people try, but none of them were quite right. I went through a lot of foster families."

"I'm sorry to hear that."

Lauren waved the comment away. "I ended up fine. Wasn't all

that bad. Just wish that I'd had what Hugo had. Someone like you to step in and be there throughout, you know?"

"Maybe I can do that now."

Lauren smiled tightly. "Maybe."

Allegra realised that she had pushed too far. She thought about changing the topic, and her mind immediately went back to the subject of Lauren's vision. "So, these glasses of yours—how terrible do you look in them? Will I get a chance to see them?"

It was meant as a playful comment and one similar to what Lauren might say. It was obvious that she'd missed the mark as Lauren looked even more uncomfortable.

"My sister had this made for me." Allegra picked up the memory book in a last-ditch effort to fix whatever it was that she'd done wrong. "It's a sort of origin story that she wrote for Hugo to have when he's older. It talks about him and the case and then about our time together through the first few years of his life. It's a good insight into everything. I read it now and then to remind myself of those times. You may enjoy it."

She held the book out. Lauren didn't take it. Instead, she looked at her watch and then made an attempt at an apologetic look that didn't quite make it to its destination.

"I'm sorry, I have to get back to the gym and check on some things."

Allegra felt cold. Something had happened. Something had changed between them, and it seemed huge, but Allegra had no idea what it could be. A chasm had suddenly opened between them, and Allegra was left disorientated at how they'd gotten to this point so suddenly.

"Did I say something wrong?" She stood at the same time Lauren did.

"No, not at all," Lauren said brightly, but the smile didn't meet her eyes. "I just realised that I have stuff I need to do and lost track of time."

Lauren hadn't mentioned anything she needed to go and deal with that evening, and Allegra wondered why the sudden change. She wondered if she'd brought up bad memories of foster families and Lauren was retreating because of that. She rounded the desk. "I'm sorry if—"

"Really, there's nothing to be sorry about," Lauren said. "I'll see you tomorrow, okay?"

Allegra nodded. Lauren had yet to fully meet her gaze. "Okay."

Lauren cupped Allegra's face in her hands with incredible care and deftness of touch, almost as if she was a bubble, and Lauren was afraid to break her. Their lips connected for a few seconds, and Allegra wondered if she was imagining it or if Lauren was actually shaking.

As quickly as it had started it was over, and Lauren showed herself out.

Allegra looked down at the keepsake box and its contents and wondered what she had done wrong.

CHAPTER TWENTY-ONE

Lauren shoved the front wheel of her bike into the bike rack and sighed when it came loose a second later. She did it again and waited a moment to see if the bike was going to be her enemy that morning just like the alarm clock, the toaster, and the mug, which broke in two when she accidentally hit it against the kitchen tap.

She was having a terrible start to her day, and while she would love to blame all the inanimate objects in her life, she knew there was one common theme. Her.

She'd not slept because she'd set her alarm clock in tears the night before and had accidentally set it for the middle of the night. It had woken her shortly after she'd finally managed to get to sleep. The toaster fell off the counter because she pressed the button too hard. The mug broke because she wasn't looking at what she was doing.

She was distracted and embarrassed by how she'd left things with Allegra the night before. She hadn't even texted Allegra to say goodnight, which she always did.

It was the end of the relationship. Lauren was absolutely certain of that much.

An evening that had started off so well had quickly become an eye-opening disaster for Lauren, and now the relationship was in tatters. It was always going to happen, but she hadn't realised it would happen last night.

Sitting on the edge of Hugo's bed and telling him that all bullies would get theirs had morphed into being surrounded by the library that Allegra called a home office and lying about needing glasses. It was a lie she had deployed in the past but never with someone she was actually dating. It had been a stupid lie, and the moment she'd said it she realised she'd made a huge mistake.

But her secret had been close to coming out, and she had felt the familiar cold fear creep up her spine. Allegra was an intelligent woman, and Lauren knew it could only be a matter of time before she started to demand answers. Answers that Lauren would never give her.

As much as it hurt, she'd rather break up with Allegra than admit her failings, failings that seemed to be growing by the day. She was ashamed to admit to herself that she'd become too comfortable as she waited for Allegra to realise that she wasn't what she wanted in a partner. Something that didn't seem to be coming over the horizon any time soon.

Their relationship had gone from being fun to being something more serious, and Lauren had allowed that to happen. She'd stayed over when she shouldn't have done so and had become involved in Allegra and Hugo's family life. It had always been her intention to keep things light, a few dinners, some night-time company, and little more.

She'd allowed it to become so much more, and now she was paying the price. More upsetting was that Allegra was paying the price, too. Lauren had kept her guilt at bay by telling herself that it would always be Allegra who would put a stop to their relationship.

Her hope had been that the vast differences in their education, work, and even upbringing would drive a wedge between them, and they'd naturally fizzle out as so many relationships did. But that had never happened, and if anything, they'd gone from strength to strength.

Now Lauren finally realised that she was as far as she could go. Lies were mounting up. Allegra wasn't making any noises about slowing things down. The time had come, and Lauren was tragically ill-prepared for it.

While nothing had been exactly said the previous night, she hoped that Allegra would understand that it was over. Or certainly on the way to being over. Lauren still held on to a small amount of hope that Allegra would officially put an end to things, especially considering the way Lauren had behaved the previous evening. Surely the rude way she had left things would cause Allegra to want to cast her aside.

Lauren could only hope.

She also hoped that Allegra wouldn't pull Hugo from his sessions. She'd be within her rights to, but Lauren knew that would double the amount of pain she was feeling.

She shook the thoughts away. There was no point in worrying about things until they had happened. She removed her rucksack and walked through the back door of the gym, wondering what awaited her that day.

Jim was still away, Anna hadn't returned her calls, and Lauren's to-do list seemed to grow all the time. Most of it was impossible, and she was fast running out of people to assign jobs to.

"Lauren, LivingFit called. They need those certificates today, or they'll come and take the rowing machines," Billy said the moment he saw her.

Lauren laughed. "They're bolted to the floor. I'd like to see them try."

Billy chuckled. "Just passing on the message. Didn't you send the certificates the other week?"

"I did." Lauren let out a sigh. "Paperwork, eh? Someone is always losing it. I'll send it again. Thanks for the message, Bill."

She entered the office and bit her lip so hard that she worried she might have cut into the skin. She threw her bag to the floor and took a deep breath to keep herself calm. She peeked through the blinds to see who was in the gym that day, wondering if there was someone who she hadn't called upon multiple times to help her.

She flew back in surprise at the sight of Allegra entering the gym.

For a brief second she wondered if she had time to sneak out of the office and disappear. While she knew the break-up was going to happen, she wanted at least a few more hours to come to terms with the fact before it became a very real reality.

It was just like Allegra to be up bright and early to deal with the matter. Lauren wondered how Allegra even knew that she was in the gym that morning as the schedule had her starting much later in the day.

Lauren backed up towards the desk. There was no escaping it. Her heart pounded, and her head started to ache.

Heels clicking on the tiled floor outside got louder and louder. Lauren used to love that sound, but now it only brought sorrow and heartache.

A moment later and Allegra stood in the doorway. She looked exhausted and emotionally wrung out. Lauren automatically wanted to apologise and to try to fix things but knew she had to hold her ground. Things couldn't work out between them, so trying to patch this incident now would just lead to even more heartache later.

Allegra blinked in confusion. "I thought you started later today."

Lauren realised then that Allegra hadn't been coming to speak to her. She'd been hoping to avoid her.

"Shift change," she lied. She didn't want to admit that she'd been unable to sleep and desperate to distract herself from unwanted thoughts of how foolish she'd been to let this whole relationship go on for far too long.

Allegra held out an envelope. Lauren took it and frowned.

"Open it," Allegra encouraged.

She did as she was told and took out a greeting card. Inside was a handwritten essay, presumably Allegra's heart and soul poured onto two rectangles of white cardboard. Lauren swallowed and closed the card up again.

"I'll read it later," she said.

Allegra looked as though she'd been punched.

Lauren realised then that she was holding a peace offering, and Allegra wasn't there to end things—she was there to fix them. Lauren hadn't calculated for that turn of events. Part of her wanted to cry. Why couldn't Allegra see that they were plainly wrong for one another? Why couldn't she understand that it could never work out?

But another part of her wanted to soothe Allegra's emotions. Seeing her in distress was heartbreaking, and Lauren ached to fix everything. At the same time, she would not lead Allegra to think that things were about to be repaired. The matter still remained the same—they couldn't be together. Allegra could never be happy with her. As if someone like Allegra would ever want to be with someone who couldn't read. Lauren shivered at the thought of Allegra finding out her biggest secret.

"I'm sorry," Lauren said. "I'm dealing with a bit of a paperwork emergency. I need to send some insurance documents to the machine rental company, or they're going to take away some of the machines."

Allegra looked down at the overflowing desk. "Well, I did suggest filing as you went."

Lauren chuckled. "You did. But Jim will want to see everything when he gets back—I told you what he's like. Always leaving things lying around or somewhere you'd never expect. He wants everything to hand, and it all just ends up being a big mess. Anyway, I need to find these bits of paper. I'm sorry."

"What do they look like?" Allegra asked.

"Something with Harrington Insurance written on it." Lauren made an effort of looking as if she was searching through the piles on the desk, but really she wasn't looking at anything. All she wanted was for Allegra to leave so she could grieve what had been between them and figure a way out of the mess she'd created at work.

"Is that it?" Allegra pointed to the cork pinboard behind the desk.

Lauren turned and reached out for a piece of paper.

"No, the one next to it," Allegra said.

Lauren swallowed and moved her hand to one side. All she wanted was for this painful moment to be over.

"No, the other side...Lauren? I know you said you needed

glasses, but is there something wrong with your eyes? Is that what you're not telling me?"

Embarrassment and frustration boiled over. "I made a mistake, okay? Wow, Allegra, we can't all be perfect, you know? Don't you have other things to deal with? Other people's business to interfere with? Why can't you just stay back for five minutes?"

The moment the words left her lips, she regretted them. Allegra shrank back in surprise. Her gaze fell to the floor and she turned to leave.

"Allegra, wait," Lauren said. "I'm sorry. I'm just..."

Allegra paused in the doorway and looked at Lauren. "Just...?"

Lauren couldn't come up with any more words. The walls had gone up, and even if her heart had wanted to tell Allegra everything right there and then, she didn't think that she'd be able to verbalise a single word as her body rebelled. She felt tense and unable to move. Unable to speak. Unable to do anything but feel cold and numb as Allegra looked at her as if she was utterly lost.

"Lauren?" Allegra asked.

Lauren stared at the floor. She felt utterly broken.

"If you don't want to be with me, just say that," Allegra pleaded.

"It's not that," Lauren said automatically. She quickly bit the inside of her cheek as her self-control reasserted its dominance. It was easier now to just remain silent and let the conversation take its course.

Allegra sighed. "Please tell me what's going on. I know there's something, but I can't help you if you won't let me in."

Lauren maintained her fixed stare on the ground. It was nearly over. Allegra was nearing the breaking point, and then it would be done. She just had to hold on a little longer.

"I suppose this is it, then," Allegra whispered. "I don't know what happened. I hope you'll read my note. I mean every word of it, even now. Of course I'll continue to send Hugo to his sessions unless you'd rather I didn't. I just don't think he should be punished for, well, whatever this is."

"I'd like to continue working with him," Lauren said, unable to face the possibility of no longer seeing either of them. At least seeing Hugo meant some connection to what she had lost. What she had ruined. It was greedy, but she couldn't let go of all of it. Not yet.

"Very well. I..." Allegra let out a faint breath. "Goodbye, Lauren."

CHAPTER TWENTY-TWO

Allegra kept her head held high as she walked through the gym and into the car park. She was aware she stood out in the gym. She was there frequently, wore office attire, and never used the machines. It was natural that some people would watch her as she made her way back and forth from the office.

And so walking out of the gym for the very last time and knowing eyes were on her was one of the hardest things she had done in a long while. Especially as her legs shook and her heart slammed against her ribs with a ferocity that scared her. Breath came in dribs and drabs, and she felt as though she had lost all control of her body.

Now she remembered why she hadn't dated for so long. When things didn't work out, a broken heart was often the result, and it felt like you were dying.

She got into the car and grabbed hold of the steering wheel just for something to ground her. A thousand thoughts flew around her head as she wondered what on earth had happened and if it was all her fault.

Had she stuck her nose in where it wasn't wanted? Had she pushed Lauren too far?

She had no idea.

She'd played the conversation of the previous evening over and over in her mind, and she still was no closer to understanding what had gone wrong. She'd poured her heart and soul into the card with every intention of leaving it on Lauren's desk in the hope that she'd read it later in the day and call her so they could talk. She didn't even know if Lauren would read it.

And on top of everything else she had to tell Hugo that the relationship was over, and she didn't even know why. At least Lauren hadn't cast him to one side, too. Something had stuck in all the time they'd shared.

"How could you have been so stupid?" she asked herself.

She'd gotten emotionally invested in something that Lauren clearly saw as a casual fling. She'd thought they had something special. Something mutual. She wondered how she could have misread a situation so badly.

She gripped the wheel and tears started to fall down her cheeks.

Lauren rubbed her eye. She'd been covering up crying fits throughout the day in her determination not to go home. She was trying to convince herself that she wasn't the kind of person who had to go home to lick their wounds when they were dumped. Even if she knew she probably should have given herself some time and space to work things through. Now her eyes were red and sore and she knew she must look a mess.

She felt close to completely falling apart but would hold herself together if it killed her. She knew she deserved every bit of pain she felt. Knew that Allegra was feeling it as keenly—if not worse—than she was.

You couldn't have just left well enough alone, could you. You knew Allegra wasn't like that, knew she wasn't used to anything casual. Knew she'd want something more. You idiot.

Thankfully, she had been able to hide in Jim's office for the day and pretend she was getting on with the mountains of paperwork. In reality she hadn't done a single thing. She couldn't have worked her way through it all even if she'd wanted to.

Allegra's card sat in front of her. The front was an artistic watercolour of a teddy bear and probably was from a posh stationery set. It was such an Allegra thing to own. Lauren could barely manage to scrounge up a sticky note.

Lauren had no idea what the inside said. Would probably never know. It wasn't as if there was anyone she could ask.

She picked the card up and put it in her bag.

Heartbreak was a term she'd never really understood in the past. Yes, she'd been sad when some relationships ended, but her determination to never put too much of herself into one had kept her relatively well protected over the years. She'd seen movie depictions of heartbroken protagonists grieving an ex-partner as if they'd died and had never really understood the strength of emotion.

Until now.

Her heart ached in a way that made her wonder if she should call a doctor. Surely it wasn't normal to struggle to breathe? Surely it wasn't right that her chest felt so tight and that tears might come at a moment's notice?

She looked up at the clock and realised that the second most difficult thing in her most heartbreaking day on record was due. Hugo would be arriving any moment now.

She went to the ladies' bathrooms to have a look at her reflection and was horrified by what she saw. She looked ill. In fact, she'd looked better when she'd had flu two years ago. There was little she could do about it aside from drying her eyes and attempting to do something with her hair. Holding her head in her hands all afternoon had done her no favours.

When she exited the bathroom, the first person she saw was Hugo. Her heart skipped a beat. She was surprised to realise that she felt a little scared of him and what he might do or say. She had no idea what Allegra had told him, or if she'd maybe left the task to Lauren.

She hated herself for not fully considering Hugo's emotions while she played her games. She'd assumed that a break-up would be a simple thing, a drifting apart that everyone would be happy with. Now she looked back and realised how stupid that idea was.

She approached him in the warm-up area. "Hey."

He looked up at her with a tight expression. "Hi."

He knew. Lauren didn't know if that made it easier or harder.

"I'm sorry," Lauren said.

He shrugged.

"Do you want to talk about it?" she asked while praying that he didn't.

He shrugged again. "She said I can still come here if I want."

"You can. Do you want to?" Lauren held her breath.

"I suppose."

It wasn't a ringing endorsement, but then, he was a teenage boy, and they didn't specialise in them.

"Great. Shall we get started?" Lauren attempted to inject a bit of pep into her tone but knew it fell flat.

It would be an uphill struggle to try to rebuild her relationship with him. In fact, she didn't even know if she could. She didn't deserve his forgiveness and wouldn't ask for it.

CHAPTER TWENTY-THREE

Lauren lifted the empty water bottle from the dispenser and dropped it to the floor. It made a sound louder than she'd expected, and she turned around to apologise to anyone she might have disturbed.

Kim made eye contact with her and smiled. "Don't know your own strength, huh?"

Lauren tried to smile at the comment, but her heart wasn't in it. Her heart had been missing in action for the last two weeks. Realising what heartbreak actually felt like had been a terrible and eye-opening experience that had left Lauren re-evaluating a lot of her life.

If she'd ever left anyone feeling this way after a break-up, then she owed them more than just an apology. She was certain that her lifespan had been shortened by the heavy feeling of sadness that had affected her mood, appetite, and sleep pattern for days on end now.

"I've not seen you much lately," Kim said. She got off the exercise bike and wrapped her towel around her neck.

Lauren returned her attention to the water cooler as she realised that Kim was on her way over to snoop or offer some unwanted advice.

"I've been around," Lauren said. "Just busy."

"How's Jim?"

Lauren lifted the fresh water bottle onto the cooler. That was another weight on her shoulders. "Not great," she confessed. "His granddaughter is really sick."

"Oh no, that's terrible." Kim leaned against the wall and took a long swig from her can of energy drink.

"Yeah." Lauren didn't want to say too much more as it wasn't really her place to do so. Not to mention, she didn't really want to talk to Kim. The jokey banter they shared and the questionable life advice Kim distributed weren't really what Lauren was looking for at the moment.

"Uh-oh," Kim muttered.

Lauren was still wrestling with the water bottle and couldn't look up. "What?"

"Your girlfriend looks furious."

Lauren forced the bottle into place and swung around. Her gaze settled on Allegra for the first time in two weeks. She looked stunning but absolutely panic-stricken. Lauren was stunned that Kim couldn't tell that she was frightened and not angry. It either spoke to Kim's inability to read people or Lauren's connection to Allegra.

Allegra wore her work clothes including her black gown, which Lauren had never seen her wearing outside of the courtroom. Allegra's gaze raced around the gym, and Lauren could only think that she was looking for her, even if she couldn't understand why.

She raced over to Allegra. "Hey, everything okay?"

Allegra's wide eyes met hers. "Hugo left school an hour early along with a group of other boys. Is he here? I can't get hold of him. Please, tell me he's here."

"He's not here. He left with other boys?"

Allegra nodded. "A teacher saw them walk out of the gate. Why the gate was open, I couldn't tell you. Why something wasn't done, who can say? He won't answer his phone, and now I'm wishing I'd installed some kind of tracking device because I have no idea where he is, and he could be dead."

Lauren gently held Allegra's upper arms to ground her. "Listen to me. He isn't dead. We'll find him, okay?"

Allegra nodded ever so slightly. She clearly didn't believe that if her expression was anything to go by.

Lauren let go of her as she realised that she didn't have the right to do such a thing any more. Hugo was missing. The thought shook her. She'd known that Hugo had never really given up on his yearning to be able to fight off his bullies. They made him feel so low and helpless, which had sparked an unbending need to prove himself. After the unprovoked attack two weeks ago, Lauren had wondered if that need within him would increase. He'd not spoken about it, but now she wondered if maybe she should have brought it up.

"The playing fields up by Ridge Farm," Lauren said. "That's a quiet place where a lot of kids go. It's walking distance from his school."

"Where's that?" Allegra demanded.

"I'll grab my coat and meet you in the car."

Allegra nodded sharply. She spun around and rushed outside, her gown flowing in the wind as she did. Lauren watched her for a second before shaking out of her daze and rushing to the office to get her jacket.

Guilt gnawed at her.

The moment Allegra said that Hugo had left school with the other boys, Lauren had known exactly what that meant. Hugo was on his way to a fight. What really worried Lauren was the possibility that Hugo had been the one to plan it. For all Allegra's assertions that Hugo was a pacifist, he was still a teenage boy who had been pushed into a corner and felt the need to prove he could defend himself.

Lauren had known that all along, but she'd never really spoken to Hugo about the importance of non-violent conflict resolution. She'd touched on the subject, but at the back of her head she'd often wondered if the words were going in and registering with him. She'd known this was a possibility, and she hadn't done a thing to stop it.

She raced through the gym only pausing to speak to Elliott to hand over and explain she was leaving the building for a while.

When she opened the car's passenger door, she noticed something was on the seat. She reached down and picked up a barrister's wig. Now she realised that Allegra must have been in court when the call came in. She must have raced to her car in her full barrister get-up and had only thrown the wig off as she was driving.

Lauren got in the car and handed Allegra the wig. "Here's your dog."

Allegra put the wig on the back seat. "I don't have time nor strength for your jokes."

Lauren tensed at the cold tone. She wasn't used to Allegra reacting badly to her jokes—they'd always worked to break the ice. She'd wondered what Allegra's reaction would be to her after their break-up. Now she knew.

"Sorry."

"Where are we going?" Allegra asked.

"Out of here and then turn left," Lauren said.

"Could you text Hugo? See if he replies to you?" Allegra requested as she sped out of the car park.

"I'll FaceTime him," Lauren said. They had always spoken via video chat before the break-up. After that she had just stopped calling him. She wasn't entirely sure why, other than it seemed inappropriate. She saw him every weekday in person but no longer felt she should call him before school or at the weekend. Now she wished she'd stayed in touch with him as that might have prevented whatever had happened.

Lauren held the phone up and called him, but she didn't expect him to answer. While she waited, she gave Allegra directions.

"What are these playing fields anyway? Hugo's never mentioned them."

"He might not be there," Lauren said. "I just know a lot of kids go up there because it's out of the way. They can do kid things."

"Drink," Allegra said.

"And fight," Lauren added.

"Do you think Hugo can defend himself?" Allegra asked.

"Depends who the kid is. Or how many there are."

"You think they'd gang up on him?"

"You think they'd play fair?" Lauren asked.

For someone who dealt with criminals in her working life, Allegra was delightfully naive sometimes. Lauren hated that she had to bring her down to reality with a bump.

They arrived at the field, and Lauren unclipped her seat belt.

"I'm going to run to the top of the hill to see if anyone is up there," she explained. "Keep trying to call him."

Lauren got out of the car and sprinted up the hill. She didn't want to tell Allegra that she had spent a lot of her own youth here. It was a great place to get away from the stresses of school, and almost no adults came up there.

If someone had told teenage Lauren that she'd be returning to the site years later to check on a boy who had practically become a son to her, she would have never believed it. Even back then Lauren knew she'd spend her life alone.

As she approached the apex, it became painfully clear that Hugo wasn't there. Lauren stopped and looked around just in case they were on the way but had yet to arrive. After a few seconds of looking around she decided that all routes up to the hill were clear.

"Shit."

She turned and jogged back towards the car.

"Anything?" Allegra asked the moment she got in the car.

"No. Nothing."

"What now?"

Lauren thought for a little while. "The industrial park over by the river—I know kids hang out there."

Allegra put the car into gear and pulled away. "You seem to know a lot about where kids hang out."

"I was one."

"Were you? You never mentioned."

Lauren winced at the cold words. She deserved the quip. Allegra had tried to ask about her past, but Lauren simply pushed the questions to one side. She'd soothed her rebuff of Allegra's questions with either a joke or a kiss. Anything to distract Allegra from digging around in the past.

She clamped her mouth shut, not wanting to give Allegra any further ammunition to develop an argument nor to apologise and pave the way for a reconciliation that could never be.

"Turn right up here," Lauren said.

Allegra did as she was told and turned the car onto the industrial park that could be used as a pedestrian cut through to several retail parks.

The tension in the car was thick enough to cut with a knife, and Lauren was struggling to cope with it. Time with Allegra had always been precious and easy-going. Feeling the air charged with anger was unwanted confirmation of how much she had ruined things and caused Allegra unnecessary pain.

Apologise. Just say sorry.

She bit her lip and focused on the passenger window.

She couldn't apologise. To apologise would mean to explain, and she couldn't do that.

Something caught her eye. Her breath caught.

"Stop the car."

Before the car had even come to a full stop, Lauren was out of the vehicle and running towards the crowd of boys. She'd only just noticed them in between two abandoned warehouses but knew a fight when she saw one. As she got closer, she saw Hugo in the middle of the group.

"Hey!" she shouted.

The boys jumped back and looked at her in shock.

"What's going on?" she demanded.

Luckily the boys were sheepish. Lauren could tell they wouldn't give her any grief. She glanced at Hugo, who looked a little shaken up but uninjured.

"You good, H?"

He nodded, and the boys looked from him to Lauren in surprise.

"You know him?" one of the boys asked her.

Lauren walked right into the middle of the group and stalked the boys, getting a good look at them as she did. They were nothing more than privileged little brats who wanted to prove themselves. None of them would have lasted a minute in her old school.

"I do," she said. "None of you were thinking of giving him any trouble, were you?"

She towered over the boys except for one who was nearly as tall as her but so skinny that she reckoned she could blow him over with a deep breath. They were bullies but had no substance to them and only held any power because of their number. She imagined that none of them knew how to fight, and the group would disperse at the first sign of trouble.

They all started to shake their heads and did their best to avoid her gaze.

"None of you would know who assaulted Hugo a couple of weeks back, would you?" Lauren asked. "Because I have a few words I'd like to say to them."

The denials were louder this time. Lauren would never lay a finger on any child, but she was more than happy to scare the hell out of them. She determined one of the boys was the leader by the sideways glances some of the boys were giving him.

Lauren stood in front of him. "You don't happen to know anything, do you?"

He swallowed, looked up at her, and shook his head.

"I think you all need to run along." Lauren stared at each one of them. "Now."

The boys turned and sprinted in different directions. Lauren's heart pounded even though she knew the moment had passed. She pushed aside thoughts of what might have happened if she and Allegra had turned up later.

"What did you do that for?" Hugo demanded.

Lauren looked at him and raised her eyebrow. "Excuse me?"

"I was about to take Tristan down," Hugo said. "End all of this right now."

"You planned this?" Lauren asked incredulously.

Hugo nodded. His cheeks were flushed, and he was practically shaking with the adrenaline flooding through his body.

"For someone so smart you can be really stupid," Lauren said. "You really think the rest of those boys would stand to one side while you beat their friend up? If, and it's a big if, you could beat one of them up, then you would be enjoying that moment for less than two seconds before someone else landed one on you."

"I could take—"

"No, Hugo! You couldn't!" Lauren shouted at him. "I honestly don't think you could take down one of them. And I know you would end up in hospital if all six of them decided to teach you a lesson. Losing some weight and gaining some stamina doesn't make you a boxer."

"Hugo?" Allegra called out, having finally arrived at the scene. "Are you hurt, darling?"

"Why can't you just keep your nose out?" Hugo shouted at his mother. "I was dealing with this! Why did you call her?"

Allegra paled and took a step back in shock. Lauren took hold of Hugo's arm and pulled him in front of her.

"Listen to me," Lauren said as she pulled Hugo practically on tiptoe so she was eye to eye with him. "You never, ever speak to your mother like that again. You never, ever speak to any woman like that." She let go of his arm and put her hand on his shoulder to push him to the ground. "Sit down. You're staying here for five minutes to calm yourself down. Then you will come over to the car and apologise to your mum. Don't push me. Not today."

Hugo sat in a heap. His cheeks were red, and his breathing came in sharp pants.

Allegra still looked shocked and horrified at Hugo's reaction. Lauren imagined that she'd never seen her little boy so hopped up on testosterone and adrenaline. She softly took Allegra's arm. "Come on, let's get you back to the car."

Allegra allowed herself to be walked away from Hugo, only occasionally looking over her shoulder to check on him.

"I've never seen him like that," Allegra whispered.

"He's never tried and failed to defend himself like this before," Lauren explained. "He's full of emotions right now. He'd organised this fight and was probably realising deep down that it was a bad idea and he was about to get his arse handed to him."

"Organised this fight? You think this was his idea?" Allegra sounded shocked.

"Pretty sure." Lauren glanced over her shoulder towards where Hugo sat on the floor. Fury radiated from him, but she knew it wouldn't take long for it to fade and reality to kick back in. He was a good kid but under a lot of pressure. More pressure than she'd known.

They arrived at the car, and Lauren leaned against the door and folded her arms. She watched Hugo pick up a small stone and throw it. She'd been him once, so angry at the world that she couldn't see straight. She wondered what she'd been so furious about. Being a teenager was an ordeal.

"Thank you for breaking it up," Allegra said. "I don't know what would have happened if you weren't here."

Lauren had an idea what would have happened. Allegra would have marched over, and the boys wouldn't have responded so well. She shivered to think what the outcome might have been.

"It's fine. It will be fine," Lauren told Allegra—and herself.

Allegra stood stoically by the car with her arms folded and her gaze firmly on Hugo. Lauren could see that she was shaking a little. She itched to comfort her but knew it wasn't her place.

"Well, thank you, anyway," Allegra said. "I never would have found him without your help. I'm certain I wouldn't have been able to break it up if I had found them. I can't imagine what might have happened."

A shudder raced up Allegra's spine, and the shaking increased. Lauren pushed herself away from the car and pulled Allegra into a hug. She didn't care whether it was the right thing to do or not. She couldn't stand by and watch Allegra suffer, so obviously in need of comfort without asking for it.

Allegra didn't hug back. Her crossed arms were so tight against her body that Lauren wondered if that was all that was keeping her together. But Allegra did lean in to the hug.

"Thank you. I'm sorry."

"No need to apologise," Lauren said. Lauren closed her eyes and allowed herself to appreciate the smell of Allegra's perfume. Her hands touched the silky material of Allegra's barrister's gown, and it instantly reminded her of the equally silken underwear that she knew lurked under the modest suit.

She gave her one final squeeze and stood back. If she stayed much longer, then she wasn't sure what she'd do. Her throat burned with words she wanted to say but knew she couldn't.

"I meant everything I said in the card," Allegra said.

"I know," Lauren replied.

She hadn't read it. Couldn't read it. But she knew that Allegra needed to think that she'd read it. To admit that she hadn't would be like another punch to an already bruised gut.

"He's coming over," Allegra said.

Lauren looked up to see Hugo rushing towards them with tears streaming down his face and his arms outstretched towards his mother.

"I'm sorry!"

Allegra's relief was palpable. She threw her arms open and pulled him into a tight embrace.

"I'm sorry. I'm so sorry," Hugo repeated. "I don't know what I was thinking. It was stupid. I shouldn't have said that to you. I'm sorry."

Allegra made soothing noises and ran her fingers through his hair. "It's okay."

Lauren decided she needed to have a long talk with Hugo about toxic masculinity and the feelings of helplessness he must be feeling. Sometimes being a fitness instructor also meant being a kind of therapist.

She watched mother and son and knew she wasn't part of that picture any more. She'd helped out in a tense situation just like anyone else would have. But they weren't her family, and she needed to leave.

"I'm glad you're both okay," she said. "I'm going to leave you to it and walk back."

Allegra loosened her grip on Hugo immediately. "I can drive you."

Lauren shook her head. "It's fine. We're just around the corner."

"I don't mind," Allegra said.

Lauren looked at Hugo. "I'll see you tomorrow?"

Hugo nodded. "I'm sorry, Lauren."

"You can apologise to me by treating your mum well and avoiding those boys. The best tactic for winning a fight is avoidance, okay?" She held his gaze until he nodded and broke the connection to stare at the ground. She'd be hammering that lesson into him every day until she was sure that he understood and agreed.

"Please, let me drive you back," Allegra said. "I feel terrible for wasting your afternoon and then just leaving you here."

"It's literally around the corner," Lauren said. "And you didn't waste my time." She stuck her hands in her pockets in an attempt to look casual but really to mask that she was now the one shaking. "See you tomorrow, Hugo."

She turned and walked away, determined not to look back.

Allegra watched Lauren walking away and pulled Hugo back towards her to continue the embrace. He happily wrapped his arms around her, and she held on tight. She wished that Lauren had allowed her to drive her back to work if only to alleviate some of her guilt at dragging Lauren into this mess.

When the school had called she hadn't known what to do. The chance of Hugo being at the gym had been a small one, and Allegra had to wonder if she had—at least on a subconscious level—gone there to seek support rather than her son.

Seeing Lauren again had been both a balm and a curse. Being reminded how strong, capable, and calming Lauren could be in any given situation had ripped open the barely healing wound of their inexplicable break-up.

Allegra's life was governed by rules, facts, and figures, and so it was all the harder for her to accept that she had no idea what had happened and why they were no more. Lauren had seemingly made the decision that they were over and had then stopped talking.

Even the faintest idea of why would have soothed the pain

Allegra felt on a daily basis as she woke up to remember that she was, once again, alone.

She'd put her heart into the card she'd planned to deliver when Lauren was out of the office. She'd admitted things she hadn't told other people and told Lauren how special and perfect she was. It had clearly been the wrong thing to do because it had brought about no response from Lauren at all. That was something she was going to have to learn to live with.

"Am I in trouble?" Hugo asked.

"Massively so," Allegra replied while squeezing him close.

"Good," Hugo said.

"Good?"

"I should be," he said softly.

Allegra kissed the top of his head. While it was very clear that she wasn't made for relationships, she did have a hope that she was occasionally doing moderately well at being a mother.

"Noted," she said.

"I'm sorry." He leaned back out of the hug and looked up at her. "Really. I wanted to show them that I can beat them. Just for once. It was stupid. I see that now."

"We need to talk about this," Allegra told him. As much as she wanted to give him space, now wasn't the time for silent sulks.

"I know," he agreed.

"We'll deal with this together," she promised. "Let's go home."

CHAPTER TWENTY-FOUR

Lauren threw all of her strength into the punch. Her fist was aching, but she fought through the pain as she lunged forward and struck the punching bag again. In the back of her mind she knew that she needed to ease up or risk a real injury, but she wasn't about to stop now. Her emotions were boiling over, and the only safe place for them was the padded middle of the bag.

She hadn't returned to work immediately after leaving Allegra and Hugo at the industrial park. Instead she'd walked aimlessly around for hours with her head in the clouds and wondering how she had allowed her ordinarily controlled life to become such a mess.

By the time she had returned to the gym, it was late in the evening, and the evening rush was over. Billy was on duty and wisely kept out of her way as she wrapped her hands and took her anger out on the heavy bag.

She lunged at the bag once again and struck it with all her fury at the unfairness of life. This time she cursed as pain ripped through her knuckles.

"Okay, I'm timing you out."

Lauren rolled her eyes and sighed at the sound of the familiar voice. The last thing she needed right then was Kim. "All good. Thanks."

Kim wasn't one to take no for an answer. "You've been tenderising the bag for an hour. If it was anyone else, you'd be telling them to take it easy." She stood by the side of the bag, not directly in Lauren's path but definitely in the way.

"I'm good. Thanks," Lauren repeated. She focused her attention on the bag and waited for Kim to move.

Kim didn't move. "You need to take a break. What's wrong? You look like someone has taken away your birthday."

Lauren didn't want to talk, and she certainly didn't want to talk to Kim. "Look, I appreciate what you're trying to do, but I'm fine. Just…let me train."

"It's the barrister, isn't it?" Kim asked.

Lauren gritted her teeth. She wasn't going to talk about her broken-down relationship with anyone but certainly not with Kim.

"Broken hearts are a painful thing," Kim said in a tone that Lauren guessed Kim thought sounded wise. In truth it sounded patronising.

"No broken heart here," Lauren said. "It was just some fun. Bit of a laugh, you know how it is."

Kim smirked. "I know precisely what you mean." She took a long swig of her drink. "So, if you're over and it was all just a bit of fun, do you mind if I have a crack at her? Seriously, those legs. I don't need to tell you about those legs, do I? And that backside in those skirts she wears. I want some of that. Text me her number."

Lauren vibrated with rage. The thought of Allegra being within five hundred metres of Kim and her disrespect was enough to make Lauren see red. She flexed her fist and was *thisclose* to knocking Kim to the floor but managed to hold herself back.

Kim put her can of drink on a shelf and walked over to Lauren. She grabbed her wrist and lifted her clenched fist. "If you want to kill me for saying that, then I have news for you. It wasn't just a bit of fun." Kim let go of her but stayed in her personal space as she spoke in a low tone. "Look, I know we don't really see eye to eye that much, but I like you, Lauren. You're a good person. And I hate to see a good person in so much pain. You've been hollow these last couple of weeks. I'm not going to pretend I know what's going on or that I have all the answers, but I saw the way she looked at you, and I saw the way you looked at her, and if there is anything, and I mean *anything* you can do to try to fix whatever happened, then I think you should do it. Love like that doesn't come along often, and you have to fight for it when it does. Not spend your evenings in here breaking your hand."

"It wasn't love," Lauren whispered.

"Bullshit," Kim said. "I can't believe how one of the strongest women I know has somehow turned into one of the weakest. I've seen you bench-press weights that grown men struggle with. I've watched you do marathons for charity on these treadmills. I even gave you twenty pence when you rowed the English Channel on that machine over there."

"It was forty pence," Lauren corrected.

It had been a shitty joke when Kim had balanced the two coins on the end of the rowing machine, but the anger Lauren had felt had spurred her on. The paltry amount of money and Kim's irritating smirk had given Lauren the extra energy she needed to row even faster and beat her personal best. It wasn't until much later that Jim told her that Kim had actually donated fifty pounds, and the whole forty pence thing had been a gag.

Lauren had thought she had misjudged Kim until the next day when she came in bragging about buying a new car and bedding someone half her age.

"I've never seen you run away from a challenge." Kim shrugged. "Actually, you're not even running. You're hiding."

"I'm not hiding," Lauren said.

Kim tilted her head and looked at her. "Yes, you are. I've seen you fight with everything you've had, and I can tell when you haven't even tried. I don't think you've worked hard enough to earn the right to sit this one out. Do you?"

Kim didn't allow Lauren the chance to answer. She just turned around and snatched up her drink before heading back to the mirrors.

Lauren hated to think that Kim was right, but she was. She hadn't given it everything she had. She'd barely given it a chance. If it had been a fitness challenge, then she would have given it her all and not stopped until she was completely spent.

Fear was stopping her, a fear that had stopped her throughout her life, and Lauren was beginning to think that she couldn't live under the weight of that terror any longer. She needed to give it everything she had, and at least try. How could she ever look herself in the mirror again if she didn't?

She unwrapped her hands as she jogged towards the staffroom. She pulled her backpack from her locker and swung it over her shoulder. It was time. It had to be time. She couldn't continue to live in fear. Didn't want to be alone forever.

No matter what happened next, at least she would know that she had done all she could. If Allegra discarded her, then at least Lauren would be able to stand proud and know that she'd lived her truth at last and broken a cycle that had lasted for years.

She left the gym and felt the cold winter air whip around her bare arms. She quickly decided not to go back for her coat because every second that passed was a second where she could potentially change her mind. Bravery was in short supply when it came to this particular topic, and she needed to conserve it while she could.

She unlocked her bike and cycled to Allegra's home at the fastest speed she could manage. She didn't allow herself to think of what she would say when she arrived. She knew that thinking about it was the quickest way to talk herself out of what she was about to do.

Instead she planned to knock on the door and say the first thing that came into her mind. Anything to start the conversation and finally tell someone the truth.

Throughout the ten-minute journey, she only stopped to plug the visitor code into the keypad on the gates. It was then that she realised how late it was. The streetlight was barely enough illumination to allow her to see the digits on the keypad, but she managed to enter the code through muscle memory alone.

The gate opened, and Lauren cycled through and towards Allegra's house. She jumped off the bike while it was still moving and came to an ungraceful stop. She realised then that the ground was wet, and it had been raining. She looked down at her body and realised that she was soaked through and had cycled through the rain without realising it. It was a miracle she hadn't gotten into an accident.

She rang the doorbell and knocked on the door at the same time.

Her nerves were frayed and her bravery was running thin. She needed to see Allegra right away to say what she had to say. Any delay, and she worried that she'd do what she always did and cover up the truth with a joke or some expert distraction.

She knocked again and this time made sure it was louder and more insistent but still with a tune that she hoped Allegra would recognise as friendly. She didn't want to scare her, but she did need her to answer the door quickly.

As the seconds ticked by, she wondered what she was even doing there. Familiar negative thoughts bubbled just beneath the surface, and she fought to keep them down. Doubts were beginning to emerge and drown out everything else.

She'll never want you now, the negative voice in her head sounded clearly through the swirl of emotions. *What's the point in trying?*

She rang the bell twice more.

The door opened, and Allegra stood in the doorway with wet hair and a damp robe clinging to her body.

"Lauren?" she asked in obvious confusion.

Lauren pulled her backpack off her back and ripped it open. She pulled out the handwritten card that Allegra had given her and held it out towards her. "I didn't read it."

Allegra frowned and slowly reached out to take the card from her. Confusion was written all over her face.

"I didn't read it because I can't," Lauren said.

The words were almost out but she knew she hadn't quite reached the summit yet. She swallowed down the nerves and the guilt and prepared to say what she had to say. But nothing came. She was so close but also at a tipping point where she knew she could retreat to safety. A quip, a lie, a distraction, and she could get away with it all.

She wondered if she could have Allegra and her secret.

"Because of your eyesight?" Allegra asked.

Lauren sucked in a deep breath and closed her eyes. She had to be honest. It was the only way that she'd feel free. The only chance she had at happiness. It was time.

"I can't read it," she said and then paused. Her whole body shook. "I can't read it because I can't read."

CHAPTER TWENTY-FIVE

A llegra had no idea what she was being told. She'd heard the words that Lauren had spoken but couldn't decipher what she actually meant. She was fresh from the shower, her adrenaline running high after hearing what sounded like a maniac hammering on her door. Thankfully Hugo had his headphones on while playing a videogame with his friends and was none the wiser to what was happening at the front door.

As Allegra had rushed to the door and pulled tightly on the knotted belt of her robe, she had considered calling the police. It was a peek through the spyhole that showed a distraught Lauren Evans standing on the other side of the door that had convinced her to answer.

Lauren was soaked and shaking, but Allegra didn't know if she was shaking because of the cold or because of the obviously distressed state she was in. Allegra held the card in her hand and could do nothing but stare blankly at Lauren.

Whatever did Lauren mean, she can't read? *What am I missing?*

The silence clearly dragged on for too long, and Lauren let out a small sigh and started to turn away. Allegra stepped a bare foot onto the front step and grabbed her arm.

"Wait, I'm sorry, I'm a little…I'm just out of the shower, and I'm trying to catch up with whatever it is that's happening here."

Lauren's gaze was glued to the floor, and Allegra knew she had little time and few words to figure out whatever was happening and to make it right.

"Let me dry off and get some clothes on," Allegra said. "Can you give me a moment?"

Lauren gave a short, sharp nod. Allegra immediately recognised it as a lie and knew that if she left Lauren there alone for a few seconds, then she'd vanish again.

"Actually, come with me," Allegra said. She pulled on Lauren's arm.

"My bike is muddy," Lauren said.

"Then leave it outside. I'll buy you a new one if it gets stolen," Allegra said. "I'd just like to not be standing in my robe in the front garden for much longer."

Lauren leaned the bike against the wall, and Allegra was relieved that she was actually complying. The atmosphere was charged. She knew that one false move would be disastrous.

She took hold of Lauren's hand and pulled her into the house. She closed the front door and gestured for Lauren to go upstairs. Lauren kicked off her trainers and walked up. Allegra followed closely behind her and tried to collect herself enough to figure out what was going on.

They passed Hugo's bedroom, and the sound of him chatting to his friends filtered through the door. Allegra was satisfied that he had no clue what was happening in the rest of the house and would leave them in peace.

Lauren stood in the doorway to Allegra's bedroom with wide and uncertain eyes. Allegra gestured towards the tub chair by the window.

"Please, sit down. Let me just dry off and get some clothes on."

Lauren hesitated for a second but did as she was told. Allegra walked into the en suite and left the door open so she could see if Lauren tried to leave. She threw her robe into the laundry basket and grabbed a towel to dry her hair.

I can't read. Did Lauren mean what Allegra thought she meant? Allegra knew she had precious few moments to understand what Lauren meant and to find the right words to reply. It seemed improbable or maybe even impossible that Lauren couldn't read, but that was what she had said, and Allegra couldn't think of how she might have misunderstood those words. She tried to think of a time when she'd seen Lauren read and realised she couldn't think of one occasion.

Allegra put on her underwear and recalled talk of glasses and contact lenses that she was sure never existed. Her memory went to Lauren's tendency to always FaceTime rather than text. In fact, she frequently claimed text messages went missing. Allegra had thought it strange that texts sent to Lauren's phone seemed to vanish but had never thought too much of it. She never looked at restaurant menus, always asking either Allegra or the waiter for a recommendation instead.

Allegra was suddenly struck how all the seemingly innocent actions were amounting to a lot of hard evidence. She remembered the way Lauren brushed off Hugo's sponsorship form in such a casual way, joking that she would charge an administrative fee for filling it in. Then there was the bowling alley. She'd fidgeted with her shoes for some time and then suddenly finished with them the moment Hugo had set up the game on the screen.

Allegra couldn't believe that she'd been so oblivious to something that was right in front of her all along. She'd encountered people with literacy issues in the past but never someone like Lauren. Some had learning difficulties or were in care or were much older than Lauren. It seemed that Lauren masked her difficulty so well that Allegra would have never known.

She finished getting dressed and returned to the bedroom in time to see Lauren pacing like a stressed wildcat. Allegra gestured to the end of the bed.

"Please, sit down. Talk to me. You can tell me anything."

Lauren hesitated a moment before sitting on the very edge of the bed. Allegra sat next to her but gave her plenty of room.

"I know," Lauren whispered. "I just wish I didn't have to tell anyone."

Allegra waited patiently for Lauren to speak. She knew that any interruption from her could disrupt Lauren's flow or even prevent the truth from coming out at all.

"I was in and out of foster care from a young age," Lauren said, her voice whisper soft. "Because I was a quiet kid, no one really worried much about me, and they let me get on with things. I guess I just flew under the radar. Each new family meant a new school, and each school thought I knew things that I didn't know."

Lauren worried her hands in her lap and started to shake. Allegra went to the wardrobe and grabbed a soft wrap that she often favoured on chilly nights and silently draped it over Lauren's shoulders.

"Teachers looked horrified when I couldn't spell something and then when I couldn't read..." Lauren shook her head. "I hated seeing that look, so I learned to pretend that I could. Or I distracted them. Sometimes I asked them a question about something else, and sometimes I did something to get sent out of class." Lauren pulled the wrap closer around her shoulders. "Then came the bullying. In the end, I just stopped attending classes. I arrived for registration and then gave teachers contradicting information about where I was supposed to be during the day. It was actually really easy. I avoided the teachers and the other kids and did my own thing all day. Social services always hoped I'd be adopted, so they pulled me out of foster care a lot to put me in new places where I might be more likely to find a forever family rather than a temporary one. I got fed up with being moved on just as I got settled, so I started to act out. In the end I was known as a troubled child no one would want."

Lauren finally looked up at Allegra. "By the time I was in high school, I couldn't read and knew the shame of that. I pretended I could read so I didn't attract any attention to myself. I bunked off as many classes as I could. I didn't attend my exams and left with no formal education. Just slipped through the gaps in the system like a knife through butter. It was so easy." Lauren sniffed and wiped her nose with the back of her hand. "So, there you have it. I'm an idiot."

Allegra scoffed. "You most certainly are not." She stood up and plucked a tissue out of the box on the bedside table and handed it over. "I've known you for a while, and I've also known a few idiots, and you most certainly aren't one of them."

Lauren wiped her eyes with the tissue. "Allegra, I can't read."

"So I'm beginning to realise." Allegra sat back down. "Give me a minute to catch up."

Lauren nodded and lowered her head again.

"Who else knows?"

"Jim," Lauren whispered.

"Is that all?" Allegra couldn't imagine keeping such an enormous secret from everyone. She imagined it meant a very solitary life as it would be impossible to keep such a secret from anyone close.

"Yep."

"Do you have problems with your eyesight?"

Lauren looked up apologetically. "No. I'm sorry I lied about that."

"It's okay. I imagine you've lied about a few things to protect yourself."

Lauren shuddered and looked away.

Allegra edged closer. "I'm not judging you. I understand why you would feel the need to keep this to yourself. I can't imagine the strain of carrying this secret around."

She reached into Lauren's lap and gently ran her thumb over the back of one of Lauren's hands.

"I can't imagine how you've managed to cope for so long while keeping this a secret," Allegra continued.

"You find ways," Lauren said. "I get help from Jim with some things. I find ways to talk to people rather than read things. Bravado gets you a long way."

Allegra smiled a little. Lauren had the ability to charm the birds from the trees, and it had clearly been a tactic she'd relied on.

"But with Jim gone and the paperwork in the office building up…" Lauren shrugged.

"You were under pressure," Allegra finished.

"And then there was you. I didn't mean for us to become serious. I thought it would be some fun, and then we'd kinda drift apart because we're so different." Lauren turned her hand over and grasped hold of Allegra's in her lap. "And then we didn't drift apart, and I got scared."

"Scared of…?"

Lauren looked up. "Of having to tell you this," she said as if it was the most obvious thing in the world.

"What did you think would happen when you told me?" Allegra asked.

Lauren swallowed. "You'd laugh. Or dump me. Probably both."

"So you dumped me first?" Allegra smiled.

"I wasn't exactly thinking straight," Lauren replied. She rolled her eyes and shook her head, and Allegra felt a small tick of relief at the tension slowly leaving the room. "You have a library downstairs, Allegra. Like, more books than the actual local library. You're a barrister. Reading and writing are a big part of your job, and I'm a pathetic nobody who can't—"

"You're not a pathetic nobody," Allegra said firmly. "You're more than this gap in your knowledge. You have a career, and you're good at what you do. This doesn't define you, Lauren. I don't know anyone who knows more about the science of fitness than you. You can look at a sandwich and calculate its fat content and then calculate how many hours I'd need to run on a treadmill to work off just the mayonnaise. Which is really something no one needs to know. But you can do it. Because you're incredibly smart. You convert kilograms to stone without a second thought. You were let down by the system. You are not to blame. And you are not diminished in any way."

Tears slipped down Lauren's cheek. "Thank you," she whispered.

"How did you get into fitness anyway?" Allegra asked. She was keen to take some of the emotion out of the situation and give Lauren the chance to calm down while she in turn took the time to catch up.

"Jim gave me a job as a cleaner," Lauren explained. "He'd just opened the gym, and I went in there and told him it was filthy and no one wanted to work out in a filthy gym. I was just being mouthy.

I wanted him to need me and to ask me to help him rather than ask him for a job. I'd struggled because of application forms and things at other places and decided I needed someone to hire me, so I could bypass the paperwork. Jim gave me a job and quickly saw through me and just asked me outright if I was dyslexic."

"Are you?"

"I don't think so." Lauren shrugged. "Maybe. I don't know."

Allegra filed that away for a later date. "So, from cleaner to assistant manager?"

Lauren smiled. "Jim's a good guy. I told him everything, and he took me under his wing. I'm kinda like his second daughter. He trained me up and helped me become an accredited trainer. I have a certificate. Can't read it, but I have one." Allegra hesitated to ask the question on her lips. Her hesitation was clearly felt by Lauren, who looked up at her. "You can ask whatever you like."

"How much can you read?" Allegra asked.

"I can read things I see a lot. Like, I know what a fire exit is. I know when to push a door or when to pull it. Well, about half the time, but that's nothing to do with reading. I know place names locally. I know where the buses go. But I couldn't read a book. I can't read a word I haven't seen before." Lauren's lip quivered. "I couldn't read your card. I'm sorry—I wanted to, but I couldn't. And I couldn't tell you that."

The dam finally broke on Lauren's emotions and she burst into body-shaking tears. Allegra wrapped her in a hug, held her close, and gently rocked her.

"It's okay. It will all be okay," Allegra promised.

Lauren just cried and cried. Allegra suspected that the outburst had been a very long time coming and had probably built up from a time long before Allegra was in her life. All she could do was hold on to Lauren and whisper affirmations into her ear.

After many minutes and thousands of tears, Lauren seemed to finally be calming down. Allegra knew that they'd discussed enough for now and didn't want to drag Lauren through even more emotional turmoil.

"Let's get you in bed," she suggested. "It's time to rest."

Lauren didn't argue, and Allegra took that to be confirmation as to just how tired she was. She pulled back the covers and helped Lauren out of her wet clothes.

"I'm sorry," Lauren said as she got into the bed. She looked tiny, drained, and so frightened. Her eyes kept drifting closed, and Allegra knew that sleep would take her away soon.

"Don't apologise. You've been so brave, and I'm so proud of you. Everything will be okay." She placed a kiss on her forehead and waited for Lauren to close her eyes and slip off to sleep.

She sat on the edge of the bed for a few moments and watched Lauren's chest rise and fall in a steady rhythm. She was still processing what she'd heard and was still in a degree of shock. She didn't know what came next, but did know that she had a lot of research to do. Lauren would need support, both emotional and educational.

After a while she stood up, placed a kiss on Lauren's forehead, and then left her to her sleep. In the hallway she smiled at the closed bedroom door, knowing that her dreams of a family might just be coming back together again.

She went downstairs and picked up the garage keys from the hook. She slipped on her welly boots and walked Lauren's bike around the house and into the garage. She parked it up in between Hugo's muddy bike and her own pristine one, then looked at the three bikes in a row and couldn't help but smile.

When she entered the house again, Hugo was in the hallway, looking at her with confusion.

"Where have you been?" he asked.

She closed the front door and kicked off her boots. "Lauren is here. She's had a bad day, and she's asleep in my room. I was just putting her bike into the garage."

"Is this because of me?" Hugo asked.

"Not at all. It's just something that I think has been bubbling beneath the surface for a while." She ran her hand through Hugo's hair and kissed him on the forehead. "She just needs a bit of time to work through some things."

"Is she staying?" Hugo asked.

"I hope so." Allegra walked into the kitchen to make some tea.

Hugo followed her and opened the cupboard where his protein shakes were now kept. "Is she going to be okay?"

"I hope so," Allegra repeated.

"Is there anything I can do?" He asked.

"Just be yourself." She pulled a mug out of the cupboard and dropped a teabag into it. Her mind was spinning with possibilities and questions, and she knew that she currently had no answers and no direction. Ultimately, Lauren would choose the path in front of them, and Allegra knew that was for the best.

"I'm glad she's home," Hugo said softly.

Allegra couldn't help but smile. "So am I. But this may be temporary. Let's just wait and see."

"Are you okay?"

Allegra looked up at him and saw mature eyes looking questioningly back at her. From a boy who had been willing to start a fight to a man checking on the emotional well-being of his mother—it had been a day of ups and downs.

"I am," she said.

And she was because a mystery had been solved, and now she could do what she did best—try to fix things.

❖

Allegra held the mug of hot tea close to her chest and looked to her side with a fond smile. Lauren was still sleeping and hadn't noticed when Allegra returned to the room, got into bed, or opened her laptop. She'd typed softly at first but soon realised that Lauren was completely dead to the world. Since then, she'd gotten a refill of tea twice as she dived deeply into her research.

She'd been stunned when she'd started looking into modern-day literacy rates. The first official website she came across proclaimed that one in six people in England were thought to have very poor literacy skills. A quick calculation told her that was over seven million people. In the USA it was forty-three million people.

Obviously, the range of the issue was a wide one with the term *literacy* defined slightly differently depending on the study. But regardless of the specific detail, it was very clear that Lauren was not struggling alone. It was an enormous problem that was being hidden through shame and misinformation.

News sites were filled with people's personal stories. A top chef who struggled to read or write but could cook to award-winning standards, a builder who got into the bricklaying trade as a way to avoid a job that involved a need for reading.

Allegra had represented people who struggled to read or write, and she'd always assumed them to be in a tiny minority. It was becoming clear to her that wasn't the case. Millions of people struggled to read on some level and many of them hid that fact.

The next step was for Allegra to understand more about what Lauren's situation was and—most importantly—how she wanted to tackle things. Did she want Allegra's help directly or simply as a support network?

These were things that needed to be discussed once Lauren was awake.

And then there was the status of their relationship. Allegra hoped and assumed that Lauren's admission was born out of a desire to continue seeing each other. Again, that would wait for the morning.

She looked down at the sleeping woman next to her and smiled sadly. She couldn't imagine the pressure Lauren must have been under over the course of her life. Allegra shivered at the thought of being so absolutely alone for so very long.

Thankfully, she wasn't alone any more.

CHAPTER TWENTY-SIX

Lauren opened her eyes and wondered why the window had moved. She was on her back, but the stream of sunlight through the window was coming from her left rather than her right.

She lifted her hand to shield her eyes.

Things weren't making much sense, but she was too exhausted to figure out why.

The light disappeared. Lauren lowered her hand and squinted.

"Sorry, I keep the curtain open to wake up with the morning sun," Allegra explained. She fastened the curtains closed and checked that the light was no longer blinding Lauren. "Better?"

Lauren nodded slowly. Her brain was sluggishly putting the pieces together and attempting to answer questions. Like, why she was so exhausted, and why she was in Allegra's bedroom?

"I'll get some coffee," Allegra said. "I'll be back shortly."

Lauren watched her leave the bedroom. Once the door was closed again she rubbed at her eyes and willed the tired haze to lift from her memory. As it did and she recalled what had happened, she suddenly wished it had remained in place.

She sat up. Her heart pounded and her throat felt immediately dry.

"Shit, shit, shit," she muttered.

She'd told Allegra. And then apparently had fallen asleep.

She jumped out of bed and rushed into the en suite, slamming on the light switch as she passed it. Her reflection told her everything she needed to know—she'd cried herself to sleep. She ran her hands over her face in frustration. There was no going back now, and she didn't know what that meant.

The only option was to get out of there. She had to run.

"Hi."

She spun around at the sound of Allegra's soft greeting. Allegra stood in the doorway blocking Lauren's only route of escape and looking at her with knowing eyes.

"Hey," Lauren said softly. "Um. I gotta get to work."

"You don't even know what time it is," Allegra replied.

Lauren swallowed. Her main line of defence was beginning to be dismantled before her eyes. Allegra not only knew her secret but also her coping mechanisms. Distraction and lies weren't going to shield her any longer.

"I'm not going to force you to talk about anything you don't want to talk about," Allegra said. "But I do want you to know that I'm here for you, that I don't think any less of you, and that I'll help you—or leave you alone—in whatever way you require. I have some thoughts on next steps, but that's up to you."

"Next steps?" Lauren asked.

"Yes."

"What kind of next steps?" Lauren pressed.

"Well, I've broken them down into three sections," Allegra said.

Lauren smiled. There was something reassuringly familiar about Allegra taking a problem and turning it into a roadmap of actions. "That sounds like something you'd do. What are these sections?"

"Reading, immediate solutions, and...well...us." Allegra suddenly looked a little less confident, and with that Lauren's own confidence start to grow.

"I like the sound of that last one," Lauren admitted. She'd come so far that she figured she might as well put it all out there. The desire to run away niggled at the back of her brain, but Allegra's calm presence was keeping her in situ and providing her the bravery she needed to carry on. She'd done all this for Allegra. For them.

It would be pointless to come this far and not try to fix things. "If you'll have me back."

"I never wanted you to leave in the first place," Allegra pointed out.

Lauren looked away. She was still too tired and shaken up to think about what the future might look like. She wanted Allegra in her life but just couldn't see how that would look at the moment.

"I have a suggestion," Allegra said. "It's entirely up to you. I don't want you to feel that I'm overstepping."

Lauren let out a shuddery breath. "What is it?"

"Let me come to the gym with you today and help you with that mountain of paperwork that must be giving you heartburn. No judgement. Just clearing paperwork and giving you a tidy desk. It would be doing me a favour because even the thought of it gives me sleepless nights."

Lauren smiled. She appreciated Allegra's attempt at a joke. It felt so right. So them.

"I'd like that," Lauren confessed. "But I don't want you to skip work because of me. Because of this."

"I've already informed Jake that I won't be in today," Allegra said. "If you don't let me help you, then I suppose I'll be forced to watch daytime television."

Lauren laughed. "That I'd like to see. Would you be wearing sweatpants?"

"Darling, I don't own any sweatpants." Allegra grimaced at the thought.

Lauren felt a tingle of warmth at the familiar term of endearment. She felt a rush of embarrassment, and the urge to run spiked once again. "I...I'm bad at this," she confessed.

"This...?" Allegra asked.

"Feeling...I don't know." Lauren turned away and bashed her fists against her thighs in frustration.

"Vulnerable?" Allegra guessed.

"I suppose. Yeah."

"That's to be expected," Allegra said. "You've been running

from this a long time, and you're only now confronting it head-on. The next step is to overcome it, and I believe you can do that."

Lauren slumped against the wall. "What makes you think I can do that?"

"You're one of the strongest people I know. Not just..." Allegra gestured to Lauren's body and reminded Lauren that she was wearing only a sports bra and panties. "I think you're stubborn enough to do anything you put your mind to. I wonder if part of your issue is a mental block of some kind. Can I ask you something?"

Lauren nodded.

"Have you ever tried to learn how to read? Perhaps Jim has tried to help you?"

Lauren bit her lip and looked at the floor. Embarrassment washed over her. "You know people who don't go to the doctor?" she asked. "Like, they've had a giant lump for months, but they don't get it seen to? Probably worried that it's going to mean they're dying, but actually if they'd just gone the moment they saw it, then it would have been fixable. But they left it so long that now it's a big problem?"

"You've been putting it off, and now it's a big problem?" Allegra asked.

"I guess. Getting help means telling someone. It means saying the words to someone and making it real. And I've been doing okay without ever having to put myself through that. Jim wanted to send me to night school, but I told him I didn't want it. Told him I'd never speak to him again, actually."

"And now?"

Lauren stood up straight and walked over to her. "Now I have no idea what I'm doing or what I'm going to do. But the idea of losing you was killing me, and I had to let you know. Even if it did mean losing you." She stood in front of Allegra and smiled sadly. "You can walk away. I'll understand if you do, and I appreciate all that you've said and done, but—"

Allegra silenced her with a kiss. Lauren wanted to pull back to tell her that she meant it and that she didn't want to be in a relationship grounded in pity. But she soon allowed herself to push the feelings of inadequacy away and allowed the love to flow in.

She slipped into an easy embrace and remembered how damn good Allegra was at enveloping her in a safe cocoon of affection.

When the kiss finally ended, Allegra placed her fingers under Lauren's chin to encourage her to meet her gaze. "I'm all in, if you want me."

Lauren just stared silently at her. How she'd managed to get so lucky as to find someone like Allegra was beyond her. She didn't know what the future would look like, but when she tried to see it, she couldn't imagine Allegra and Hugo not being there. Pushing the thought away wasn't going to work. She was invested, heart and soul.

"I'm all in," she whispered.

Allegra's smile lifted her heart.

"Weren't you making coffee?" Lauren asked cheekily.

"I was, but I could sense that you were planning to make your escape, so I came back," Allegra said. "Was I right?"

Lauren shrugged a little. "Maybe. Few more seconds."

"Understandable," Allegra said. "I'm going to go and make that coffee. Come down when you're ready. Maybe put some clothes on, so you don't scar Hugo."

Lauren chuckled and pressed a kiss to Allegra's cheek before she left the room. She turned and looked in the mirror once more. She looked brighter and happier already—from looking as though she'd recently awoken from the dead, to looking somewhat at peace. Or at least on the way to it.

She knew there was a long road to travel in front of her, but she also knew that for the first time in her life she had support in that journey. She didn't need to hide any more because she had found that most elusive of things—someone to stand shoulder to shoulder with, no matter what.

She didn't know if she'd ever be able to thank Allegra enough for what she had done, but she did know that she was going to try to stop being afraid and start living her life.

CHAPTER TWENTY-SEVEN

Lauren looked on as Allegra started to flip through the stack of paperwork in front of her and quickly organised it into three separate piles. She felt a little useless. As Allegra sped through the first pile, she gestured for Lauren to pass her the second pile.

"Where's the rest of it?" Allegra asked without looking up.

Lauren pointed to the desk drawers silently.

Allegra opened the drawer and a couple of envelopes fell to the floor. Lauren braced herself for the telling off that she was convinced would be coming.

"Could you take these and open the envelopes, and then we'll add them to our piles," Allegra said. She handed over handful after handful of unopened envelopes to Lauren and made a small space on the corner of the desk for her to do the work.

"Sorry," Lauren mumbled.

"No need to apologise," Allegra said. "This can all be fixed. Don't worry."

Lauren pulled up a chair and started to open the envelopes. These letters were the ones that scared her the most, the letters that other people had pointed out as being bad news or ones that had angry red text on the front.

They'd gone into the desk drawer to be away from prying eyes and out of Lauren's sight. It was classic avoidance. She could see that now. But at the time it had seemed the right thing to do.

"Can it, though?" Lauren asked. "Jim's going to kill me."

"I'm sure Jim will be fine," Allegra said. "He knows the situation. He must have expected this."

"No, he thinks Anna has been here and everything is fine. I didn't want to tell him the truth. Not when he needs to be there for his family."

"Who is Anna?"

"She's a freelance administrator who usually comes in to help Jim with stuff at certain times of the year. She's our fail-safe. When he goes away, then Anna comes in and does all the paperwork."

"But not this time?" Allegra frowned.

"She's been avoiding coming in. She kept saying she'd come and then not showing up. Bill mentioned that the last time she came in, she left with Kim." Lauren sighed. When Bill had mentioned that interesting fact, Lauren had instantly known what had happened. Kim had used poor Anna up and spat her out, and now Anna was avoiding the gym.

"Poor woman," Allegra said. "But not to worry. It's only paperwork, not a nuclear bomb. We just need to clear through it so we can put it in the right order to be dealt with. Simple."

Lauren winced at the amount of underlined bold red text on the letter she opened. "Even this one?"

Allegra looked at the letter. "What does it say?"

Lauren glared at her.

"Seriously, I want to know how much of it you can read." Allegra continued going through her piles of paper as she spoke.

Lauren looked at the piece of paper and tried to focus on the letters that made up the words. She'd spent so long automatically looking away from words that it felt strange to be really staring at them for a change.

"Well, I know our business name and the address."

"Can you write that down?" Allegra asked.

"Yeah, if someone isn't watching over me as I do it."

"What about the rest of the letter?"

Lauren blew out a breath and focused hard on the piece of mail. "I can see some dates. Some numbers. I get from the context that this is an unpaid bill."

"How do you know that?"

"Because it's all formal and red letters. Numbers." Lauren put the letter down and opened the next one. "I don't know, I just *know*. You learn to adapt."

"I don't mean to make you feel uncomfortable. I'm just trying to understand." Allegra continued to sort through papers, and Lauren was grateful that she didn't make eye contact. She was struggling to keep her emotions in check. This was the first time she had ever really discussed the issue. It was easy enough to shut Jim down and pivot the conversation to something else. But Lauren knew that Allegra wouldn't be shaken off the point so easily.

"I've never really thought about it," Lauren admitted. "I've been too focused on ignoring it rather than dealing with it. If that makes any sense."

"It does. May I ask you a question?"

Lauren continued to open envelopes but braced herself for what might come next. "Sure."

"You've never told anyone about this before. Presumably you never intended to tell anyone either."

"Right."

"And you presumably knew that being in a committed relationship with someone would make it very difficult to keep this secret."

Lauren felt a sinking feeling. "Yes."

"So why were you dating me?"

Lauren breathed out a long sigh. The question had been asked calmly enough, but it was a potential hand grenade thrown onto the table.

"I didn't think we'd work out," Lauren admitted. "I thought we'd date a little, and then it would be over. I didn't expect we'd become as close as we did."

Allegra paused in her paperwork stacking and looked at Lauren with confusion. "Why didn't you think we'd work out?"

Lauren licked her lips and smiled. "You're kidding, right?"

Allegra shook her head. "No, I'm not sure I follow your line of thought."

"I'm a six and you're a nine, at least. Nine point five," Lauren said.

Allegra frowned. "I have no idea what that means."

Lauren laughed. She'd missed Allegra's ability to be completely removed from cultural references. Allegra lived in her own little bubble. Now and then she had to learn about slang or something that had happened online for a case, but on the whole she let it all pass her by.

"You're better than me. I was waiting for you to realise that," Lauren said.

Allegra laughed. "I am not better than you."

"You are."

"Poppycock." Allegra shook her head and picked up another stack of paper. "What a ridiculous idea. I don't know why you would think something like that."

"Well, for one, you say things like poppycock, which I'd only ever seen someone say on television before I met you," Lauren said. "But you have to admit that you've noticed that we're a bit different."

"Of course I've noticed that. You're young and fit, and I am old but thankfully blessed with a fast metabolism that keeps up with my ravenous need for cheese."

"You do eat more cheese than anyone I've ever met," Lauren admitted. "But I'm not talking about age or fitness."

Allegra looked surprised. "You weren't?"

It was then that Lauren realised that Allegra had a completely different viewpoint when it came to their relationship. Whilst Lauren thought of the differences in their status, careers, and upbringing, Allegra was far more concerned about their age difference.

"You do know how different we are, right?" Lauren asked. "Aside from age and your refusal to even own sportswear."

Allegra paused and thought about the question for a moment. "I suppose. I'd just always assumed that I'd be different to the person I was dating. Otherwise you'd have two identical people sharing a meal, and I can't think of anything more dull."

Lauren had never thought of that before. But now that Allegra mentioned it, it made so much sense. Of course people would seek out different personalities. Dating someone just like you would surely lead to disaster somewhere down the line. Being with someone you found interesting, or who even challenged you, on a daily basis was surely healthier for a relationship. Lauren couldn't believe that she'd never considered that before.

"So, you planned to end things but never got around to it?" Allegra asked.

"No, I assumed that you would end things."

Allegra chuckled. "You would have been waiting a while."

Lauren felt tears prick at her eyes at the acknowledgement of how happy Allegra had been.

"What I thought on day one and what I felt later were very different things," Lauren explained. "By the time I was in a relationship with you, it was too late. I shouldn't have gotten involved with you from the start. I'm sorry for that."

"Don't be sorry. As terrible as it was to be without you, it was only because being with you had been so wonderful. And I think—hope—that we're able to…at least be friends. I know you said you wanted to get back together, but I don't want you to feel any pressure on that front. Know that I'm here for you in whatever capacity you need."

Allegra was clearly trying hard to not push Lauren into defining what they were. It broke Lauren's heart that she felt the need to be so careful. Lauren had spent most of their relationship fluctuating between push and pull, and so she wasn't surprised that Allegra was now so confused and treading on eggshells.

"I want to go back to how we were," Lauren said with as much clarity as she could. "Closer than we were. I want to be with you, Allegra. If *you* want *me*."

Allegra put the paperwork down and turned to face her. "Of course I want you. I'm in love with you."

Lauren felt her mouth fall open.

Allegra snapped her attention back to the desk. "I'm sorry. I shouldn't have said that."

"You love me?" Lauren repeated.

Allegra picked up a piece of paper. "Is LifeFit for the treadmills or the cross-trainers? I forget."

Lauren had spent her life not letting anyone close, and so she'd never heard anyone say that they loved her. Of course she sometimes said the words in a casual manner to her work colleagues, or even to Jim if she was feeling particularly generous. But actual love, real romantic love between two people, was something that she had never thought she would be able to experience. Knowing that she would never be able to get close to someone meant trying to hold her emotions back. Flipping a switch on the ability to be able to love. If that was even possible.

Hearing that Allegra loved her was a shock and something that was taking a while to settle in her mind. It wasn't that she thought she was unlovable, more that she'd never put enough of herself into a relationship to be loved. But she had been more involved in her relationship with Allegra than she had with anyone else before. And that had translated to love.

She thought about the pain she felt while they were separated. How Allegra came to her in dreams every night when she was finally able to get to sleep. How in the early morning hours she sometimes daydreamed of a life together. She remembered how close they'd gotten, even when the voice in the back of Lauren's mind told her that she shouldn't get so invested. She hadn't been able to help herself. And now it was clear why. She was in love.

"Forget I said anything," Allegra said. "This invoice? Treadmills or cross-trainers?"

Lauren pulled the piece of paper out of Allegra's hand and placed it back on the desk. She took hold of the office chair and turned Allegra to face her.

"I've never been good at relationships," Lauren explained. "For really obvious reasons. I decided that I would probably be alone for the rest of my life. I know that doesn't sound very likely to you, but it was what I believed. It was what I was aiming for. I thought that I'd rather be alone than tell someone my secret. Believe me when I say I have never considered the possibility of someone loving me or me loving someone. But the pain I felt when we were apart, and the joy I felt when we were together, is something I have never experienced before. And I can only find one word for it. Allegra, I'm in love with you. I don't know what that means yet, or anything, really. But I...I'm sure that I do love you."

Allegra looked as if she was torn between multiple emotions. Happiness mixed with sorrow mixed with confusion. She swallowed and slowly nodded her head.

"I think this is a little new for all of us. I think this conversation is best parked up for a time when we've both had the opportunity to reflect on what all of this means and what we want," Allegra said. "I don't want to ruin what we have just managed to rebuild."

Lauren understood Allegra's fears. She smiled and nodded her agreement. Allegra was frightened and for good reason. She'd lost a lot and then had been plunged into this mess that Lauren called a life. Lauren knew that no amount of conversation now was going to make any difference. Allegra was right—they needed time. Lauren decided there and then that she would give Allegra all the time she needed as she slowly rebuilt Allegra's trust in her and demonstrated that she wasn't going anywhere.

"Um, Lauren?"

She sighed and turned towards Billy. "Yes, Bill?"

He stood awkwardly in the doorway. "Sorry. Um, there's a call for you on line one. It's Fitness First."

"Okay, I'll grab it in here. Can you put it through?" She felt panic washing over her.

"What is Fitness First?" Allegra asked.

"They maintain the weight machines. I'm going to guess they haven't been paid." Lauren sucked in a deep breath and placed her hand over the phone.

"Let me." Allegra removed Lauren's hand and answered the call. "Hello, I'm sorry but Lauren is in a meeting at the moment. I'm Allegra, can I help?"

Lauren could hear the sharp tone of the Fitness First staff member who had been leaving her voicemails for the past week. She hated that she'd not been able to pay them, but the invoice amount changed week to week depending on what work they had done, and

Lauren had no idea where their invoice was. Jim hadn't been calling as regularly and Lauren didn't want to bother him. She'd made such a big deal of being able to cope that she felt deep shame at admitting that she'd made such a mess of things.

"I see," Allegra said calmly. "I'm sure I will be able to sort that out for you. We've been having a problem with our computer system, and a lot of our post has unfortunately gone missing. But I can rectify this for you today. Can I take note of the amount due and your bank details? I assure you that I can get this over to our accounts payable department immediately, and the money will be with you by the end of the day."

Lauren stared at Allegra. She'd made it seem so easy. In a few words, the situation was on the way to being resolved. Lauren didn't know why she'd allowed things to get so out of control. Fear and a desire to bury her head in the sand, she guessed.

Maybe Allegra was right, and they would be able to work together to deal with the huge backlog that Lauren had allowed to build up.

Allegra jotted down a note before apologising again and hanging up the call. She turned to Lauren and said, "I think we'll start by paying everything that needs to be paid. That way we can at least get the more pressing issues dealt with. And if we do them all in one go, then surely that will be easier."

"I'm sorry," Lauren said.

"Listen to me," Allegra said. She turned to face Lauren to ensure that she had her attention before continuing. "There is no need for you to be sorry. This is a situation that we can easily deal with, and there is no need for you to feel guilty in any way. We all make mistakes, and most of them can be fixed. I'm happy to help—just don't feel the need to constantly apologise. Maybe you can think of another way to thank me?"

Lauren bit her lip teasingly. "I have no idea what you mean."

Allegra raised an eyebrow. "Oh, I think you do."

Lauren loved the return to their usual playful conversation. It was a sign that things were maybe returning to normal, if normal had ever really existed between them.

"Can I come over tonight?" Lauren asked.

"I'd be very glad if you did," Allegra said.

They both returned to their piles of paperwork.

"Maybe I can leave a few things at yours?" Lauren suggested softly, hoping that the offer of the empty drawer was still open to her.

"Absolutely," Allegra said. "I'll clear a drawer for you."

Lauren felt a burst of warmth at the knowledge that she might be able to get things back on track. She felt helpless and battered after recent events and knew that she needed time before she would be able to feel like herself again. But at least now she felt she was on the path to that.

"Right," Allegra announced. "We have three piles. Filing, junk mail, and to be actioned."

"I haven't finished opening my envelopes yet," Lauren said.

"I think we can assume that all of them are to be actioned, can we not?" Allegra said. "You hid them away for a reason."

Lauren smiled. "You know me well."

"I'm getting there," Allegra said. "I'm looking forward to finding out more."

The statement would have ordinarily sent Lauren into a spin, but this time she just smiled.

"But first, let's get all of this dealt with." Allegra gestured to the mountain of paper. "I'm looking forward to seeing the desk under this lot."

"Organising turns you on, doesn't it," Lauren said, laughter in her voice.

"No. But disorganisation might turn me off," Allegra said with a meaningful look.

Lauren stood up and grabbed hold of a pile of paper. "Let's get started."

CHAPTER TWENTY-EIGHT

Allegra opened the kitchen cupboard and frowned. She reached for a mug that she didn't recognise and turned it around in her hand. It was a large and clearly well-loved mug with the logo of a fitness company on the side. It was evidently Lauren's, and it was in her kitchen cupboard.

She smiled and put it back. Slowly but surely Lauren's beloved possessions were appearing in the house. It had started with a few clothes and then progressed to a few toiletries. The small weight rack appeared beside the television one evening and now a mug in the cupboard beside her own favourite teacup and saucer.

She reached to the shelf above and plucked two wine glasses from the shelf. Lauren had introduced her to an alcohol-free, sugar-free wine that tasted a lot better than it sounded. It also meant that she could share a bottle with Lauren.

Hugo entered the kitchen, got a tumbler from the shelf, and filled it with water. "Hi, Mum. You smell nice. Is that perfume? How was work today?"

She unscrewed the cap of the wine bottle and poured two glasses. He obviously thought she had been born yesterday. "What do you want?"

"Nothing!" he exclaimed in a manner that clearly indicated *something*.

"Darling, the sooner you cut to the chase, the quicker you can argue your case and try to convince me. All you're doing now is making me suspicious and more likely to say no."

"Can I go to France with Simon and his family?" Hugo asked.

"Absolutely not." She placed the wine glasses on the table.

The front door closed, and Allegra smiled at the knowledge that Lauren was home. It had only been a week since they'd gotten back together but she had quickly presented Lauren with a front door key and explained how she'd like to pick up where they had left off.

Thankfully, Lauren felt the same way, and they quickly fell back into their old routine. Except this time Lauren was a lot more engaged, and the heavy feeling of a mystery between them had vanished.

"Please?" Hugo pleaded.

"Please what?" Lauren asked as she entered the room. She immediately came over to Allegra and greeted her with a kiss on the cheek.

"He wants to go to France with Simon and his family," Allegra explained.

"Are they paying?" Lauren asked.

"That is not the point," Allegra said.

"They are paying," Hugo said. "Please, Mum?"

"Why are we saying no to this?" Lauren asked. She opened the oven door and peeked in to see what was for dinner that evening.

"Because…he's too young," Allegra said. She was on the spot and didn't have a better answer. She knew how silly it sounded.

"Simon's parents are adults," Lauren pointed out. "Simon's dad is a doctor."

"Yes, I know that," Allegra said. Her argument was gone, and her high ground was crumbling. Suddenly the idea of having a second parent was a silly one. Lauren was about to tear right through her walls of worry.

Lauren looked at her and frowned. "Hugo, set the table. We'll be back in a moment."

Hugo rushed to his task as if he sensed the winds of change were in his favour.

Lauren pointed out of the kitchen and towards Allegra's study. Allegra trudged into the room and waited for Lauren to follow her and close the door behind them.

"You're in charge, but I need to know why we're saying no," Lauren said.

"I'm not in charge," Allegra said.

"Cool, then I'll tell him that he can go." Lauren grinned in a way that said she knew she'd easily cornered Allegra and was enjoying it.

"Simon's mum once left Simon in a taxi," Allegra said.

Lauren's eyes widened. "Go on…"

"She told me that she'd once left him in a taxi when he was about four years old. She got out and slammed the door behind her, and the taxi driver called out and asked her if she wanted to take her child," Allegra said.

Lauren smothered a smile. "So because of a moment of distraction ten years ago, you don't want Hugo to have a nice free holiday with one of his closest friends?"

"It sounds silly when you put it like that," Allegra admitted.

Lauren held out her arms, and Allegra walked into the comforting hug.

"It is silly," Lauren said. "But if it really worries you, then we'll come up with a real excuse and say no. But I kind of think it might be nice to have the house to ourselves, don't you?"

Allegra felt a pleasant shiver run up her spine at that thought. "Well, maybe."

"I know you're trying to spend more time with him, but taking away quality time with his friend isn't going to help." Lauren's hand rubbed soft, soothing circles on her lower back and she felt it lull the stresses of the day away from her. "How's the case going?"

Allegra rested her head on Lauren's shoulder. "Fine."

"How's the case going?" Lauren asked again, seeing right through Allegra's nervous tension and to the root cause.

"Hard," she admitted. "But I'm not bringing work home with me."

Lauren took a step back and smiled softly. "You're not talking

about it. But you're still bringing it home because it sits up here."
Lauren softly tapped Allegra's forehead.

Allegra knew that was true on some level. As much as she tried to distinguish between work and home, it was sometimes impossible to separate the two. Of course work would come home when it was a difficult case that took up all her energy.

"I'm going to look after you tonight," Lauren said.

"You don't have to do that."

"I want to." Lauren kissed her cheek and whispered in her ear, "What do you say to a nice night in front of the television watching that crime show you pretend to hate but secretly can't get enough of? A nice glass of wine—"

"Real wine?"

"Real wine. With all the sugar and all the alcohol they can possibly inject into a tiny little defenceless grape. I'll massage your feet because you were cross-examining today, so I bet you've been standing up for hours."

"I have," Allegra admitted, hating how pitiful she sounded, but the idea of an evening of relaxation and pampering sounded divine.

"And then I'll make sure you get off to sleep at an appropriate time, and I'll make sure your mind is on nothing but fun things when you do."

Allegra licked her lips. "How will you do that?"

Lauren leaned in close to whisper in her ear.

"When are we eating dinner?" Hugo shouted out from the kitchen.

Lauren laughed and Allegra sighed.

"Let's send him to France tonight," Allegra suggested.

Lauren pressed a quick kiss to her lips. "Maybe if we agree that he can go with Simon to France, then he'll want to go and see Simon tonight to discuss it. Unless you'd rather he was home tonight?"

Allegra couldn't get over how well Lauren could read her. With the final barrier between them broken down, the corridors of communication flowed freely. Allegra had never felt so transparent in her life. Every worry, idea, and desire seemed to be easily picked up by Lauren, and it felt wonderful.

"I'd like to encourage him to stay home, if possible," Allegra admitted.

"No problem. Let's eat before he turns wild," Lauren said.

Allegra chuckled, and they returned to the kitchen. Hugo was eager to help serve dinner, and Lauren encouraged her to sit down and be waited upon. Hugo opened his mouth to ask a question, and Lauren placed her hand on his shoulder to silence him. He looked at her, and an unspoken conversation happened between them in a split second. He smiled and nodded his understanding at whatever was conveyed.

Allegra imagined it was a suggestion that now wasn't the time. Which it wasn't. Lauren was right that Allegra had brought the case home with her, and worries gnawed on her frayed nerves. It was part of the life of being a barrister, and she knew that it would all be a distant memory by next week when the case was over and the judge had ruled.

For now, she was happy to spend quiet happy evenings with the two people who mattered more to her than anything.

EPILOGUE

Lauren stood on the pedals of her bike and enjoyed the feel of the wind against her face. The route from the college back home was mainly downhill. It was like a reward for the hard work she'd put in during the hour-long afternoon session.

She picked up a lot of speed on the first big hill, and the adrenaline rush was fantastic. Her backpack felt heavy with schoolbooks, and in that moment, Lauren felt as though she could take on anything.

Deciding to cut through the park and cycle along the canal path, she realised that she was finally using the word "home" when she thought of Allegra's house. It had taken some getting used to, and she still wasn't ready to think of it as their home even though she did live there these days.

Allegra had welcomed Lauren into her life fully and without a second thought. It hadn't been easy for Lauren to break the habits of a lifetime, but she had eventually started to break down some of the walls she had spent so many years building. A slow sprinkling of her belongings at Allegra's house and a few miserable evenings back in her own apartment had quickly highlighted that Lauren didn't want to be anywhere else.

She'd been staying over for three full weeks when Allegra had pointed out that she lived there now, and that meant maybe having her post redirected and possibly telling her landlord that she didn't need the apartment any more.

That was two months ago, and Lauren was still getting used to the fact that she lived in the snobby Gables development. Although none of the neighbours had been at all snobby. They'd all been kind and welcoming, and Lauren had instantly lost all of her jokes about the posh neighbourhood, which she'd enjoyed telling to make Allegra roll her eyes.

She slowed down as she entered the development and sedately cycled towards the garage. The main garage door was open, and Hugo was in there using her weightlifting bench as he often did after school these days. With exam season upon him, his schedule was becoming busy, and he didn't always have the time to go to the gym. The fact that he went running in the morning with Lauren and lifted weights in the afternoon made her feel proud at his determination.

"Hey," he greeted. He sat up and wiped his hands on a towel.

With focus and hard work he had managed to build up quite the upper body strength. Allegra had initially complained that her little boy was turning into a bodybuilder but had quickly seen that he was happy with the new body shape he was developing.

"Make sure you're not using your back," she instructed as she parked up her bike.

"I won't, Mum," he replied with a cheeky grin. He only called her *mum* when she was mothering him. But Lauren had to admit that she enjoyed hearing it.

"Good boy," she said in much the same way she would to an excitable puppy.

"School go okay?" he asked.

"Yep." She didn't talk much to Hugo about the fact that she was back in school and learning how to read. The embarrassment still stung no matter how understanding he was. She still felt a pang of guilt about her inability.

"Cool. You got homework?"

"Every damn time." She laughed.

"At least you only go twice a week," he said. "I get homework every day."

"Well, make sure you do it all, or you'll be like me and revisiting it years later," Lauren replied.

"It's not your fault." Hugo lay back down on the weight bench. "You were a kid and let down by the system. It's the system's fault. Don't blame yourself."

He easily picked up the bar and started to lift. Lauren hesitated for a moment but knew he wouldn't want her hanging around and watching over him. He was able to train without her these days, and while that sometimes hurt, it was nice to see that he'd taken on everything she'd taught him and was moving onto the next stage in his fitness journey.

"I'll see you later," she said.

He grunted what she thought was a farewell.

She entered the house and dropped her bag onto the kitchen table. She got a couple of pieces of fruit from the bowl and grabbed a glass of water. She pulled her exercise books from her bag and opened them to the lesson they'd been learning that day. The familiar shiver of fear ran up her spine, and she did her best to shake it off.

Allegra had said from the start that some of Lauren's issues were rooted in fear and the fact that she pushed anything to do with reading or writing away without a second thought. That had been a breakthrough for Lauren, and now that she knew that she did that, she could work on overcoming that initial hurdle.

She tackled her literacy issues in the same way she'd train for a gym challenge. She had a plan, and she stuck to it like glue, not allowing herself a day off and enjoying each moment when she could mentally tick off a waypoint that she had reached. Since thinking of the issue in a different way and having the support of both her family and the college, she was coming along in huge strides.

In the evenings of the days that Lauren attended college, Allegra often whispered to her before they went to sleep that she was proud of her. Each time, Lauren's heart welled up with love and emotion, and she felt strong enough to carry on her journey. She knew it would be a long road, but she also knew that she would reach her goals.

She flipped through her exercise book to the envelope at the back and took out Allegra's handwritten card. She opened it and took a deep breath. She could read the contents now. Some of the words she had needed Allegra's help with a few times, but nowadays she could read it without much hesitation. It had been slow going, but she enjoyed savouring the words.

Allegra didn't confess in the card that she was in love with Lauren but she said everything but. In many ways it was a precursor to the biggest statement of them all. Lauren was pleased that Allegra hadn't been able to say that yet. It meant that she had a card filled with Allegra's thoughts and feelings, which would have otherwise been distilled down into the one small sentence.

She heard the front door open and the familiar sound of heels on the tile floor. Her heart skipped a beat as it often did when Allegra came home. She was somewhat surprised that she still felt that way but hoped that the feeling would never go away.

"Hello?" Allegra called out.

"In the kitchen," Lauren replied.

After a few seconds during which she imagined Allegra was taking off her coat and kicking off her heels, Allegra appeared in the doorway.

"How was class?"

"Great, I'm asking Sam to help me write a letter to you explaining how impressive your breasts are," Lauren said. She'd always used jokes to lighten the mood when she felt hesitant or vulnerable, and that would never change.

"I look forward to receiving it," Allegra replied, playing along. She filled up a glass of water at the kitchen sink. "Sam will know what to say, as she has seen them back when we dated."

"What?" Lauren blinked in shock, and her mind ran at a mile a minute at this new information.

Allegra turned around with a wicked grin on her face. "You're not the only comedian in the family, darling."

Lauren slumped in relief. "That was mean."

"No. That was funny. And you're wildly possessive. I like it." Allegra took a sip of water. "You have homework?"

"Yep." Lauren tapped the book. "Probably an hour's worth."

"Why don't you come and sit in my office?" Allegra suggested. "I'd been planning to catch up on some reading tonight anyway."

"Sure." Lauren gathered up her things and took them into Allegra's office. The room that had caused palpitations in the past was now a relaxing safe haven away from the rest of the house. It overlooked a quiet part of the garden, and even the decor was soothing. Lauren felt strangely at home there, probably because it was so utterly Allegra in every way.

She set herself up at Allegra's desk and opened her books again to start working. It wasn't easy, but she saw the improvement in her skills and knew it would all be worthwhile in the end.

Allegra entered the room and picked up a book from a side table. She passed behind Lauren and paused to lean down and kiss her cheek. "I love you," she whispered.

"I love you, too," Lauren replied. She said the words with ease and so very frequently these days.

Allegra sat on the sofa, curled her feet up beneath her, and started to read. Lauren knew that she'd soon pluck the meticulously folded blanket from the back of the sofa and place it over her lap. She knew that Hugo would come in from the garage in around an hour and talk about his day before heading up to the shower.

The predictability of things warmed Lauren's heart. She'd always found comfort in repetition, whether it was her work schedule, her training, or even the pace she set herself on the rowing machine. The same warm familiarity came from living with Allegra and Hugo in a place she now called home. When she remembered.

While she sometimes forgot to call the Gables home, there was something she never forgot. She was finally a part of something she had thought would never be possible—a family.

About the Author

Amanda Radley had no desire to be a writer but accidentally turned into an award-winning, best-selling author. Residing in the UK with her wife and pets, she loves to travel. She gave up her marketing career in order to make stuff up for a living instead. She claims the similarities are startling.

Books Available From Bold Strokes Books

Deadly Secrets by VK Powell. Corporate criminals want whistleblower Jana Elliott permanently silenced, but Rafe Silva will risk everything to keep the woman she loves safe. (978-1-63679-087-9)

Enchanted Autumn by Ursula Klein. When Elizabeth comes to Salem, Massachusetts, to study the witch trials, she never expects to find love—or an actual witch...and Hazel might just turn out to be both. (978-1-63679-104-3)

Escorted by Renee Roman. When fantasy meets reality, will escort Ryan Lewis be able to walk away from a chance at forever with her new client Dani? (978-1-63679-039-8)

Her Heart's Desire by Anne Shade. Two women. One choice. Will Eve and Lynette be able to overcome their doubts and fears to embrace their deepest desire? (978-1-63679-102-9)

My Secret Valentine by Julie Cannon, Erin Dutton & Anne Shade. Winning the heart of your secret Valentine? These award-winning authors agree, there is no better way to fall in love. (978-1-63679-071-8)

Perilous Obsession by Carsen Taite. When reporter Macy Moran becomes consumed with solving a cold case, will her quest for the truth bring her closer to Detective Beck Ramsey or will her obsession with finding a murderer rob her of a chance at true love? (978-1-63679-009-1)

Reading Her by Amanda Radley. Lauren and Allegra learn love and happiness are right where they least expect it. There's just one problem: Lauren has a secret she cannot tell anyone, and Allegra knows she's hiding something. (978-1-63679-075-6)

The Willing by Lyn Hemphill. Kitty Wilson doesn't know how, but she can bring people back from the dead as long as someone is willing to take their place and keep the universe in balance. (978-1-63679-083-1)

Watching Over Her by Ronica Black. As they face the snowstorm of the century, and the looming threat of a stalker, Riley and Zoey just might find love in the most unexpected of places. (978-1-63679-100-5)

Always by Kris Bryant. When a pushy American private investigator shows up demanding to meet the woman in Camila's artwork, instead of introducing her to her great-grandmother, Camila decides to lead her on a wild goose chase all over Italy. (978-1-63679-027-5)

Exes and O's by Joy Argento. Ali and Madison really only have one thing in common. The girl who broke their heart may be the only one who can put it back together. (978-1-63679-017-6)

Paris Rules by Jaime Maddox. Carly Becker has been searching for the perfect woman all her life, but no one ever seems to be just right until Paige Waterford checks all her boxes, except the most important one—she's married. (978-1-63679-077-0)

Shadow Dancers by Suzie Clarke. In this third and final book in the Moon Shadow series, Rachel must find a way to become the hunter and not the hunted, and this time she will meet Eshee Yumiko head-on. (978-1-63555-829-6)

The Kiss by C.A. Popovich. When her wife refuses their divorce and begins to stalk her, threatening her life, Kate realizes to protect her new love, Leslie, she has to let her go, even if it breaks her heart. (978-1-63679-079-4)

The Wedding Setup by Charlotte Greene. When Ryann, a big-time New York executive, goes to Colorado to help out with her best friend's wedding, she never expects to fall for the maid of honor. (978-1-63679-033-6)

Velocity by Gun Brooke. Holly and Claire work toward an uncertain future preparing for an alien space mission, and only one thing is certain—they will have to risk their lives, and their hearts, to discover the truth. (978-1-63555-983-5)

Wildflower Words by Sam Ledel. Lida Jones treks west with her father in search of a better life on the rapidly developing American frontier, but finds home when she meets Hazel Thompson. (978-1-63679-055-8)

A Fairer Tomorrow by Kathleen Knowles. For Maddie Weeks and Gerry Stern, the Second World War brought them together, but the end of the war might rip them apart. (978-1-63555-874-6)

Changing Majors by Ana Hartnett Reichardt. Beyond a love, beyond a coming-out, Bailey Sullivan discovers what lies beyond the shame and self-doubt imposed on her by traditional Southern ideals. (978-1-63679-081-7)

Highland Whirl by Anna Larner. Opposites attract in the Scottish Highlands, when feisty Alice Campbell falls for city girl about town Roxanne Barns. (978-1-63555-892-0)

Holiday Hearts by Diana Day-Admire and Lyn Cole. Opposites attract during Christmastime chaos in Kansas City. (978-1-63679-128-9)

Humbug by Amanda Radley. With the corporate Christmas party in jeopardy, CEO Rosalind Caldwell hires Christmas Girl Ellie Pearce as her personal assistant. The only problem is, Ellie isn't a PA, has never planned a party, and develops a ridiculous crush on her totally intimidating new boss. (978-1-63555-965-1)

On the Rocks by Georgia Beers. Schoolteacher Vanessa Martini makes no apologies for her dating checklist, and newly single mom Grace Chapman ticks all Vanessa's Do Not Date boxes. Of course, they're never going to fall in love. (978-1-63555-989-7)

Song of Serenity by Brey Willows. Arguing with the Muse of music and justice is complicated, falling in love with her even more so. (978-1-63679-015-2)

The Christmas Proposal by Lisa Moreau. Stranded together in a Christmas village on a snowy mountain, Grace and Bridget face their past and question their dreams for the future. (978-1-63555-648-3)

The Infinite Summer by Morgan Lee Miller. While spending the summer with her dad in a small beach town, Remi Brenner falls for Harper Hebert and accidentally finds herself tangled up in an intense restaurant rivalry between her famous stepmom and her first love. (978-1-63555-969-9)

Wisdom by Jesse J. Thoma. When Sophia and Reggie are chosen for the governor's new community design team and tasked with tackling substance abuse and mental health issues, battle lines are drawn even as sparks fly. (978-1-63555-886-9)

A Convenient Arrangement by Aurora Rey and Jaime Clevenger. Cuffing season has come for lesbians, and for Jess Archer and Cody Dawson, their convenient arrangement becomes anything but. (978-1-63555-818-0)

An Alaskan Wedding by Nance Sparks. The last thing either Andrea or Riley expects is to bump into the one who broke her heart fifteen years ago, but when they meet at the welcome party, their feelings come rushing back. (978-1-63679-053-4)

Beulah Lodge by Cathy Dunnell. It's 1874, and newly betrothed Ruth Mallowes is set on marriage and life as a missionary...until she falls in love with the housemaid at Beulah Lodge. (978-1-63679-007-7)

Gia's Gems by Toni Logan. When Lindsey Speyer discovers that popular travel columnist Gia Williams is a complete fake and threatens to expose her, blackmail has never been so sexy. (978-1-63555-917-0)

Holiday Wishes & Mistletoe Kisses by M. Ullrich. Four holidays, four couples, four chances to make their wishes come true. (978-1-63555-760-2)

Love By Proxy by Dena Blake. Tess has a secret crush on her best friend, Sophie, so the last thing she wants is to help Sophie fall in love with someone else, but how can she stand in the way of her happiness? (978-1-63555-973-6)

Marry Me by Melissa Brayden. Allison Hale attempts to plan the wedding of the century to a man who could save her family's business, if only she wasn't falling for her wedding planner, Megan Kinkaid. (978-1-63555-932-3)

Pathway to Love by Radclyffe. Courtney Valentine is looking for a woman exactly like Ben—smart, sexy, and not in the market for anything serious. All she has to do is convince Ben that sex-without-strings is the perfect pathway to pleasure. (978-1-63679-110-4)